Black Girl / White Girl

Other Ecco Books by
Joyce Carol Oates

NOVELS
Blonde
Middle Age: A Romance
I'll Take You There
The Tattooed Girl
The Falls
Missing Mom

SHORT STORY COLLECTIONS
The Assignation
Where Is Here?
Faithless: Tales of Transgression
I Am No One You Know

NOVELLA
I Lock My Door Upon Myself

NONFICTION
George Bellows: American Artist
On Boxing

PLAYS
The Perfectionist and Other Plays

MEMOIR/ESSAY
The Faith of a Writer
Uncensored: Views & (Re)views

CHILDREN'S BOOKS
Come Meet Muffin!
Where Is Little Reynard?

Black Girl / White Girl

A NOVEL

Joyce Carol Oates

HarperCollins books may be purchased for educational, business,
or sales promotional use. For information, please write:
Special Markets Department, HarperCollins Publishers, Inc.,
10 East 53rd Street, New York, NY 10022.

FIRST EDITION

Designed by Kate Nichols

Library of Congress Cataloging-in-Publication Data

Oates, Joyce Carol
Black girl/White girl: a novel / Joyce Carol Oates.—1st ed.
p.   cm.
ISBN-10: 0-06-112564-4 (alk. paper)
ISBN-13: 978-0-06-112564-5
1. Race relations—Fiction. 2. African American women—Pennsylvania—Fiction.
3. Women college students—Fiction. I. Title.

PS3565.A8B46 2006
813'.54—dc22
2006048306

06   07   08   09   10   BVG/RRD   10   9   8   7   6   5   4   3   2   1

in memoriam, "Minette"

Black Girl / White Girl

I have decided to begin a text without a title. It will be an exploration, I think. An inquiry into the death of my college roommate Minette Swift who died fifteen years ago this week: on the eve of her nineteenth birthday which was April 11, 1975.

Minette did not die a natural death nor did Minette die an easy death. Every day of my life since Minette's death I have thought of Minette in the anguish of her final minutes for I was the one to have saved her, yet I did not. And no one has known this.

The coroner for Montgomery County, Pennsylvania, declared with no ambiguity the precise medical reasons for Minette's death and who the agent of her death was, such "facts" are not the object of my inquiry.

For "facts" can be made to distort, to lie. The most insidious of lies is through omission.

Many facts were omitted, and other facts obscured, at the time of Minette's death. I was one of those who obscured facts for there was the wish to protect my name and there was the wish to protect Minette after her death.

There was the unvoiced wish to protect Minette's family, and there was the unvoiced wish to protect Schuyler College. There was the wish—unvoiced, desperate—to protect the white faces surrounding Minette.

Fifteen years! All this time, I have been alive. I have been living, I have even acquired a professional reputation in my field, and Minette Swift has been dead. I have been aging, and Minette Swift has remained nineteen. I am a woman of middle age, Minette is still a girl.

I wonder at the strangeness of this! Who deserves to live, and who deserves to die. I wonder at the justice.

Some truths are lies *my father Maximilian Meade has said. My father was a man who acquired fame and notoriety for such inflammatory statements, that fill some of us with rage.* No truths can be lies *is my preferred belief.*

And so I begin, my text without a title in the service of justice.

Part / I

Crack

Ohhh God.

I was wakened by this cry. I was wakened instantly.

It must have been Minette, my roommate. On the other side of my bedroom door. Minette Swift, in the outer room. This wasn't the first time I'd been abruptly wakened by Minette talking to herself, sometimes scolding herself, or praying. *Ohhh God* was one of her half-grunts/half-moans.

Immediately I was out of bed, and opening my door.

"Minette—?"

My roommate was standing with her back to me, oblivious of me. She was standing very still, as if paralyzed. Her head was tilted back at an awkward angle and she was staring at the window above her desk, where a crack had appeared in the upper half of the pane. Minette turned vaguely toward me, without seeming to have heard me. Her eyes were widened in wordless panic behind her childish pink plastic glasses and her lips moved soundlessly.

"Minette? What's wrong?"

I had to suppose it was the window. There was a shock in seeing it, a visceral reaction: where no crack had been, now there was an elaborate spiderweb crack that looked as if the slightest touch would cause it to shatter and fall in pieces on your head.

The previous night, we'd had a "severe thunderstorm watch" for most of Montgomery County, Pennsylvania, which had included the 1,200 acres of land on the banks of the Schuylkill belonging to Schuyler College where Minette and I were freshmen. Local news bulletins had reiterated the warnings for hours and when Minette and I had finally turned out our lights, the worst of the storm appeared to have passed.

Each of us had a small bedroom that opened out onto our sparely furnished study room. Each of us had a college-issued desk and each desk was positioned precisely beneath a window built into perpendicular walls. It was the larger of the two windows, Minette's window, that had been damaged in the night by the fierce gusting wind.

At least, I assumed that the damage had been done by the wind.

But Minette seemed frightened, wary. She must have heard my question and must have noticed me standing only a few feet away but she ignored me, staring and blinking up at the window in the way of a stubborn child. Minette was one whom emotion gripped powerfully, and even as emotion faded, as adrenaline fades, still Minette seemed to wish to cling to her state of arousal. Coming upon her at such a moment was to feel not only unwanted but also invisible.

I thought *She has forgotten she isn't alone.* I should have turned tactfully aside as I'd learned as a young child to turn aside wishing not to see the eccentric behavior of adults, sparing both them and me.

I'd been born in 1956. My mother had liked to speak of me as a love child of the 1960s, the decade that had defined my parents' generation.

Minette spoke softly at last. It was like her to reply in a near-inaudible murmur to a question after so long a pause you'd forgotten what you had asked.

". . . got eyes, you c'n *see*."

Meaning, I could see perfectly well what was wrong: Minette's window was cracked.

I said, "It must have been the storm, Minette. Don't get too close, the glass might shatter . . ."

I hadn't meant to sound bossy. It was my mother's eager blundering way.

Minette sucked in her breath. Gave the belt of her bathrobe a tug, to make sure it was tight enough. (It was. It was very tight. Minette's belts and sashes were always as tight as she could bear them.) She said, again softly, but laughing, as if the fearful humor of the situation had to be acknowledged, "I wasn't going to, thanks! I'm not some damn old fool." Behind the lenses of her pink plastic glasses Minette's eyes shone beautifully vexed, as if I'd suggested she might perform an act not only dangerous but demeaning.

Minette had to be upset, she'd said *damn*. Minette Swift was a minister's daughter and a devout Christian who never swore and was offended by what she called "swear words" in the mouths of others.

In Haven House, as at Schuyler College generally, in the fall of 1974, Minette Swift was often offended.

I told Minette that I would report the cracked window to our resident advisor Dana Johnson. Wiping at her eyes, Minette murmured a near-inaudible "Thanks." Her nappy hair gleamed like wires in the sunshine pouring through the window moist from the previous night's rain, and the smooth eggplant-dark skin of her face was minutely furrowed at her hairline. I would have liked to touch her arm, to assure her that there was no danger from the cracked window, but I dared not approach her, I knew it wasn't a good time.

We were suite mates but not yet friends.

While Minette was using the bathroom in the hall, I dragged my desk chair to her window to examine the crack. It did resemble a cobweb, intricate in its design, lace-like, beautifully splotched with jewel-like drops of moisture and illuminated by the stark sunshine. I felt the temptation to touch it, to see if it might break.

I pressed the flat of my hand against the crack. Stretching my fingers wide.

Still, the glass didn't break.

Several feet beyond the window was an old oak tree with thick gnarled limbs. One of these had split in the storm and hung down broken, its pale raw wood like bone piercing flesh. I was reminded uneasily of one of my father's photographs, on a wall of his study in our home in Chadds Ford: a framed glossy photo of a young black man who'd been beaten by heavily armed Los Angeles riot police in April 1968 following the assassination of the Reverend Martin Luther King, Jr. The young black man lay on filthy pavement streaming blood from head wounds, writhing in agony, the stark white bone of his right arm grotesquely piercing his flesh at the elbow. Whenever I entered my father's study in his absence it was this photograph that immediately drew my eye though I would instruct myself each time *No! Don't look.*

It seemed clear that the broken oak limb had been blown against Minette's window in the night. We'd been lucky, the glass had not shattered and been blown into the room.

Minette's desktop was wonderfully neat. There was a geometrical precision to its appearance, like a Mondrian painting. Her textbooks were arranged sensibly upright so that you could see their spines, not haphazardly tossed down amid papers or strewn-about articles of clothing as in most college residences. Minette's newly purchased Smith Corona electric typewriter was kept closed—"to guard against dust"—when Minette wasn't using it. Her family photographs were arranged in an embracing arc: Minette and parents, Minette and younger sister, Minette smiling gattoothed and radiant in high school cap and billowing gown so white as to appear blinding. I was astonished that Minette could smile so happily, so unguardedly, for smiles from my roommate had been rare in my presence.

Smile! Just bare your teeth, it's easy. Like me.

My mother's advice. If you didn't know Veronica, you'd think she was joking.

Standing on my chair above Minette's desk, I turned to survey our study room. This was a new perspective. My desk, bookshelves, furnishings were in the less attractive part of the room, my window was conspicuously smaller than Minette's window, emitting less light. Earlier this month when freshmen arrived on the Schuyler campus, I had been the first to occupy the suite and it seemed natural to me, to claim the less attractive part of the room for my own. At our home in Chadds Ford, Pennsylvania, in our famously run-down "French manor" house on sixty acres, I lived in a large room with twelve-foot ceilings and six tall windows, a carpetless hardwood floor as badly scarified as an ice rink, clattering radiators in cold weather and curlicues of frost on my windowpanes, a room of funky mismatched furniture and shelves, stacks, piles of books, a way of life as spartan as the lives of my parents Veronica and Max. At boarding school in Massachusetts I'd taken pride living in small cramped spaces without complaint, and in Haven Hall with its Merit Scholars and work-scholarship residents I was eager to fit myself into such a space for I hated the possibility of being perceived as a spoiled, privileged white girl of my class.

Veronica had helped me move into Haven House, she'd approved of the choices I'd made. We both knew that my roommate was a Merit Scholar from Washington, D.C., daughter of a black minister, though we hadn't yet met Minette Swift and her family. I wanted to think that Veronica would report on my selflessness to my father (who was in federal court in Los Angeles at that time, arguing a civil rights case). It was a matter of shame and chagrin with my parents, that my older brother Rickie had broken away from the ideals of the Meades to take an undergraduate major in finance at the University of Pennsylvania; that Rickie was indifferent to "social justice"—"revolution"—"bearing witness for the oppressed"—and had tormented my father by seeming to support the Vietnam War ("making the world safe for democracy and capitalism") though, of course, Rickie hadn't enlisted in any branch of the armed services. Veronica and Max had more reason to be hopeful of me and wished to take pride in me though I knew that I was not an altogether reliable vessel for such hopes. (I was impulsive, but shy. I was well meaning, but clumsy. I wanted to do the right thing, but wasn't always sure how.) Still I imagined Veronica saying to Max on the phone that evening *Our daughter is one of us, instinctively generous. Oh Max, Genna is the real thing!*

And Max would say *Why are you surprised? Genna is our gem.*

The window above my desk overlooked a crumbling brick wall of the residence next door. Minette's window, resplendent in morning sunshine, had an aerial view of the "historic" Schuyler campus: a corner of the quadrangle of tall, sculpted-looking plane trees and carefully tended grass; the dazzlingly white eighteenth-century bell tower of Schuyler Chapel; the aged-brick facade of the Federalist mansion once owned by the college founder, the President's House, sometimes called Elias Meade House.

Last name Meade? A coincidence?

It was rare that anyone asked. Usually I murmured yes. I could not bear to be revealed as a descendant of the college founder.

Minette had never asked. For a while, I don't think she'd even remembered my name, for the names of most people seemed to drift past her unnoted, of not much significance. In our early days as roommates I'd been embarrassed several times to realize that Minette so little observed me, she'd mistaken another red-haired girl in Haven House for me and sat with her in the dining hall. When we'd first met, as Minette was moving into our room, she'd been distracted by the presence of her parents in the crowded space and hadn't taken any notice of which side of the room I had left for her. Her first remarks about the room, and about Haven House, were breathless and vehement: "S'posed to be some 'landmark' but ohhhh my goodness looks like it's falling down on our heads." The steep, narrow stairs to the third floor had "just about wore out" her parents and her and the "weird slant" of her bedroom ceiling was "like something in a ghost movie." The elder Swifts fretted that their daughter had to live on the topmost floor of an old wood-frame house, what if there was a fire?—the fire escape outside the window was rusted and looked as if it would collapse if you dared step out on it.

"See, I got to live in 'Haven House.' It's my schol'rship."

Even Minette Swift's scholarship, which enabled her to attend a prestigious liberal arts college with a tuition as high as tuitions at Ivy League universities, seemed to be a vexation!

Seeing the startled look on my face, Minette relented, with a short little laugh: " 'Course, I am grateful. My, *yes*."

Almost, Minette winked. Yet in the same moment looked away, before I could react.

Minette Swift! Her face fascinated me, it was the most striking face I'd ever seen close up, on one so young: fierce, sharp-boned, round, rather flat, with dark skin that looked stretched tight to bursting. You felt that, if you dared to touch that skin, your fingers would dart away, burnt. Her hair was wedge-shaped, stiff and jutting like wires, smelling of natural oils. Her eyes were small and deep-set and evasive and yet beautiful, thick-lashed. Her shell-pink plastic glasses gave her a look of prim grade-school innocence.

The first time I'd seen Minette Swift, on Orientation Day, before I'd known that we were to be roommates, Minette had been wearing one of her starched, dazzling-white, long-sleeved cotton blouses with a gold cross at her throat; her skirt was the gray of metal filings, and flared unstylishly at the hips; her waist, fleshy, thick, was yet tightly belted in a black patent-leather belt that looked as if it might hamper her breathing. Except for her wide hips and sloping breasts Minette might have been a precocious twelve-year-old schoolgirl dressed by her mother for a special occasion. She looked nothing like the several stylish black girls who'd been my classmates at the Cornwall Academy, daughters of lawyers, doctors, politicians, and well-to-do businessmen.

From the start, Minette was an enigma to me. A riddle, and a dazzlement. I felt clumsy in her presence not knowing when she was being serious or not-so-serious. Minette made droll remarks, but without smiling; it was her way to frown, if I laughed, as if in rebuke of my response, but perhaps it was a playful sort of rebuke, which I could not decode. As if we were playing basketball, and Minette was dribbling the ball away from me, and I was following eagerly in her wake, and Minette paused suddenly to turn, and to toss the ball at me, or to feign tossing it at me, so that I stumbled over my own feet. At other times, when I tried to talk to Minette, she seemed uncomfortable, and answered in monosyllables. I had to wonder if she'd have been happier with another roommate, a dark-skinned girl, instead of me.

I thought *I will make her like me. I will!*

Eventually Minette told me that, except for summer Bible camp, she'd never had to share a room with anyone before. "Had to share" was uttered in a tone meant to be neutral but Minette's lips curled in disdain. (Still less had she "had to share" a room with a white girl, I supposed.) She'd graduated "with honors" from Booker T. Washington High School of Arts, Sciences, and Music—"About the best there is, of the public schools"—in Washington, D.C., and she'd always lived at home. At Schuyler College, Haven Hall was one of the older residences, known as the "most integrated" in bringing together "young women of diverse races, religions, ethnic and cultural backgrounds"; Haven Hall was billed as a "haven" for the most serious, brainy students. Yet Minette didn't appear especially impressed, as, in her droll, frequently sarcastic way, she wasn't especially impressed with Schuyler College traditions and rituals. "Know what my daddy calls this kind of thing?—'white Mickey Mouse.' " Minette snorted with laughter, I tried to join her, not knowing if this was the right response. For wasn't I *white*, and part of the joke? Or, since Minette was confiding in me, which Minette rarely did, maybe for the occasion I wasn't somehow *white*, and therefore privileged? I said, "At the prep school I went to, there was all this 'tradition,' too, some of it was okay but some of it . . ." my voice trailed off, I heard myself sounding clumsily eager, ". . . was just, what the girls called it, bullshit."

The girls. As if, even in this moment of awkward camaraderie, I couldn't bring myself to say *we*.

Minette laughed: "Yah. White bullshit."

I laughed with Minette, I think I laughed. I wasn't sure what I was laughing at, but I laughed.

In fact, I'd always felt privileged to be a student at my prep school and I certainly felt privileged to be a student at Schuyler. Max and Veronica had drilled it into my head since I'd been capable of comprehending words that I'd damn better be grateful for whatever I had in the world of "tragic inequities compounded by human greed" (as Max would say) as I'd been trained to finish every meal I began and, if possible, to clean up neatly after myself in whatever kitchen in which the meal was prepared. Though Max allowed Veronica to wait on him, and to keep his things relatively in order, Max believed on principle that it was immoral, it was obscene, to allow anyone to wait on him. The Meade family property at Chadds Ford included a baronial old house of at least twenty rooms and a former stable converted into a guest house, yet my parents were reluctant to hire and "exploit" local help to keep these properties maintained; the grounds were overgrown; fallen tree limbs, sometimes fallen trees lay haphazard and scattered where they'd fallen, for months. The ideal was to avoid "unnecessary consumption of resources or labor" by living frugally and fending for ourselves when we could.

Unlike Minette Swift, I wasn't attending Schuyler on a scholarship. My tuition was being paid in full. (By my parents? Or by a Meade relative? This wasn't clear.)

I took care to carry my chair back to my desk and to replace it exactly as it had been. If Minette suspected that I'd been looming over her desk, she'd have been offended. Though often in her absence I drifted into her side of the room not to touch anything but simply to stand in Minette's space as if somehow, by magic, I might know what it was like to be Minette Swift, for whom a likeness of Jesus Christ was framed like her family photographs and arranged on her desk in an orderly row.

Minette's Jesus Christ was, so strangely, a very pale-skinned Caucasian man with long wavy dark hair, smoldering dark eyes, and reddened lips. He wore what appeared to be a purple satin robe and his right hand was uplifted in a blessing like a greeting.

Sometimes at her desk Minette whispered or murmured beneath her breath. I knew that I wasn't supposed to hear, these were private utterances, possibly prayers. Minette's prayer to herself before eating was a simple murmured *Thank you, Jesus!* with downcast eyes.

Daydreaming at my desk, glancing up from my work I would find myself mesmerized by a poster on the wall beside my roommate's desk: at least four feet long, two feet wide, a beautiful gilt cross on a luminescent background, with, in the foreground, blood-red letters:

I AM THE WAY THE TRUTH AND THE LIFE

CHRISTIAN YOUTH FELLOWSHIP

June 6, 1974
Washington, D.C.

Max, who detested Christianity, believed it was "tragic farce" that, through a cruel accident of history, black Africans seized and brought to America as chattel, forcibly "converted" to the white slavers' hypocritical pseudo-religion, had not repudiated the religion when they'd been freed.

It was utterly confounding, perplexing! It was a God-damned riddle! One of the ironies of Christianity was, of course, that it had been in its earliest, most vigorous phase, a slave religion; a "revolutionary" religion; but had quickly become a religion of rapacious white masters lacking all Christian charity, especially for those whose skins were darker than theirs. Especially, Max was upset by the willingness, the childlike eagerness, of so many American blacks to align themselves with a religion that preached pacifism (while waging war), heaven-after-death (while seizing and exploiting the world's resources), hellfire for the damned (while imagining themselves "saved"): exactly as Marx named it, the opiate of the people.

I understood that Max was probably right. Still, I hoped that Minette would wish to convert me. When I saw her frowning over her Bible before bed, when I heard her ardent whispered praying, fragments of gospel songs and hymns she sung under her breath with such pleasure, I felt a pang of envy, and anticipation. Clearly, there had to be more here than Max knew.

"Minette? Are you—"

But by the time I returned from reporting the cracked window to our RA, Minette was nowhere in sight. I'd had the impression that Minette was going to wait for me in the front parlor, but she was gone.

I ran to the dining hall, two blocks away. How bright and beautiful everything was, after the storm of the previous night. The very air looked washed clean. Droplets of moisture shone on leaves, pavement. Everywhere was storm debris I leapt over on the sidewalk. My heart beat in my chest with a strange enchantment. *The way. The truth. The life.* Though I could not believe in Minette Swift's savior yet I might believe in another kind of salvation. I thought *I can be a good person. I can be a way of happiness to others.* Minette and I had shared the waning edge of Hurricane Audrey, that had, at its worst, along the coast of North Carolina, blown 115 miles an hour. We hadn't been in any actual danger (had we?) and we'd been in separate rooms through most of the night, but still we'd been together, one day we might look back upon the experience . . .

I was an ardent impetuous girl with eager eyes and a frizzy mane of burnt-apricot hair like dandelion seed. Lean, lanky, supple as a whippet, Max observed. Whoever smiled at me, I smiled back at.

Love me! Trust me! I am so lonely!

At first, in the dining hall, I couldn't find Minette. And then I found her, trying not to be disappointed that Minette was sitting at a remote table, her back to the room. *She wants to be alone* I thought. Yet, I carried my breakfast tray to her.

Girls from Haven Hall often sat together. Yet not Minette, who kept herself detached from our neighbors. It had been commented upon, that Minette Swift made no special effort to befriend other black girls. Once, in the dining hall, I'd seen her stare coldly at one of the popular black girls on campus, who'd dared to approach Minette Swift as if she knew her: Minette disliked what she called "familiarity"—"pushiness."

When I sat across from Minette at the table, Minette glanced up at me with a faint twist of her lips and a mumbled *H'lo.* As she might have greeted a sister, with no display of enthusiasm yet without disdain. Minette's analytic geometry text was open beside her breakfast tray, she was frowning as she underlined equations.

Minette identified herself with some pride as a "math major, pre-law." She'd told me that her father intended for her to become a tax lawyer so that she could assist him with the finances of his church, the Temple Vale of the World Tabernacle of Jesus Christ. This church, Minette had told me, was "every year growing bigger." It was crucial for Minette to excel in math, but to her shock, she'd received only a C- on the first test in Introductory Geometry and Calculus, her "lowest math grade ever."

Impulsively I'd told Minette that math wasn't a strong subject of mine. I had managed to get A's in prep school but hadn't any natural gift. If I did, I'd have tried to help her.

Minette stared at me in genuine surprise. As if my offer, that wasn't really an offer, had touched her, deeply. Almost inaudibly she'd murmured, "Thank you." Some time later when I'd thought the subject had been dropped she added, in a prim voice, not meeting my eye, that Jesus was "all the help" she needed, with anything in her life.

Now, when I told Minette that I'd reported the cracked window to our resident advisor, she frowned, and shivered, and looked away. Almost inaudibly she murmured what sounded like *Thankyou.*

I recalled Max warning me, when we'd first learned that I would be rooming with a black girl from Washington, D.C., that there were areas in my roommate's life, her "family-background" life, that I must not pry into, for I would likely discover something that would upset me.

What Max meant, he hadn't said. It was Max's way to hint of menace and unease, without explaining. As if the world, so seemingly clear and guileless in its appearances, yet held secret crevices, cracks, unimaginable interiors, opaque to our knowledge.

I thought A *cracked window. A broken window. Glass breaking.*

I thought *She's frightened. I must help her.*

Sitting with Minette in the dining hall, I felt both protective and awkward. Though I could see that she probably wanted to concentrate on her math text, yet I felt the need to make conversation with her. I asked if she'd been able to sleep much the night before, with "all the wind howling," and Minette swung her head in a way to suggest maybe yes, maybe no. I felt foolish talking of weather like someone for whom words had only literal meanings, in conversation with one for whom words had deeper and more secret meanings, yet could not bear to simply sit in silence with Minette, as if there were a rift between us. When she was agitated, Minette ate compulsively: she'd soaked several pieces of pulpy French bread in maple syrup and butter, and with this she would drink a full glass of whole milk and two or three cups of coffee whitened with cream and sugar. Her jaws worked rapaciously even as she hunched over her textbook and a piece of notebook paper folded lengthwise, covered in equations.

Another time I wished that I knew more about math, that Minette and I were taking the same course and might commiserate with each other.

Just then, two girls from Haven House with whom I was friendly (oh, I was friendly with anyone and everyone, who encouraged me with a smile!) came to sit at our table. These were white girls who, like me, were somewhat in awe of Minette Swift, whose efforts to befriend her had been met with a coolness that was sometimes polite and sometimes not so polite. This morning, Minette barely acknowledged them and took no part in our conversation about Hurricane Audrey. I told them about the cracked window, where a broken tree limb had been blown. Minette hadn't appeared to be listening but a moment later she shut her book, pushed back her chair and carried away her tray without a word. Her face was shut like a fist, she seemed furious. Left behind, the three of us looked after her bewildered.

Three white girls. Looking after a black girl, bewildered.

"Is something wrong with Minette this morning?"

" 'This morning'! Any morning."

Quickly I said, "The storm kept her awake. She's afraid of hurricanes. Her family is from South Carolina . . ."

Girls in Haven Hall sometimes asked me about my roommate: what was she like, when you got to know her? I was evasive in answering. I did not want to confess that I had not yet gotten to know my roommate and felt at times that, as the weeks passed, I was coming to know her less and less.

In the freshman class at Schuyler, Minette Swift was emerging as something of an enigma: a black girl who didn't act "black." A girl with a strong personality who was generally admired and respected but not, so far, much liked.

I was upset, seeing that Minette was upset. I left my hardly touched breakfast and hurried after her. At a table near the door where trays were piled, she was wrapping what remained of her syrupy French toast in paper napkins, to take back to the room. Seeing me, she grimaced and shoved her pink plastic glasses against the bridge of her nose. Her voice trembled. "Ohhh why'd you tell them. Give them the satisfaction!"

Minette sounded hurt, vexed. I had no idea what she was talking about.

" 'Satisfaction'? Why?"

" 'Scuse me, you know why."

Minette turned from me, as if trying not to cry. I had never seen her so shaken and would recall, afterward, that this was the last time I would see my roommate in so unguarded and vulnerable a state. I would recall this exchange, and think *She trusted me, and I let her down. Out of ignorance, stupidity.*

I left the dining hall hurriedly, with Minette. I wanted to apologize but wasn't sure what I had done wrong. Minette hated the possibility of being talked about, maybe that was it. She had a younger sister named Jewel who was "always into my business" and I felt at such times that Minette thought of me as a kind of Jewel, with exasperation yet not without affection. Or so I wished to think.

We walked in silence back to the residence. I was astonished at the storm damage, which was worse than I'd seemed to notice on the way to the dining hall. Several of the stately old plane trees had been split, destroyed. A beautiful juniper pine lay fallen ignominiously in a heap. A tree service crew had set up barriers in a street where a gigantic oak had fallen. Everywhere were broken-off parts of trees, wet leaves blown into gutters, crevices and corners. And wet leaves stuck to our shoes like tongues.

Minette walked head-on, eyes straight forward, unwavering. She seemed scarcely to be taking notice of the storm damage. Her forehead furrowed cruelly, she was lost in her own thoughts. I felt a prick of alarm, I seemed to be losing my roommate. I was determined to be cheerful: through my years at boarding school I'd combated homesickness, loneliness and sorrow and a general fear of all-that's-to-come by being cheerful, which means mainly talking, smiling and talking and drawing out others, in an effort to make them cheerful, too.

Another time, I told Minette that her window would be repaired good as new, probably that afternoon.

Minette stared at me. Her fleshy lips trembled.

"You say so! And what good'll that do, they will only break it again."

When will we meet your roommate, Genna? At Thanksgiving? Christmas? It would be wonderful if Minette's parents can visit, too. We have plenty of room, we would love to meet the Swifts, I hope you've made Minette understand how welcome she would be at Chadds Ford?

Shame

In the stupor of late summer 1974. In the mostly empty house at Chadds Ford. My father's hoarse broken voice pitched up the stairs commanding me, his daughter, to get downstairs immediately *This is an historic occasion*.

In even his fever state of anticipation Maximilian Elliott Meade could not fail to observe the propriety of correct speech: *an* historic occasion.

In the popular press Maximilian Meade had been long ridiculed as a radical-hippie-lawyer-druggie who'd smoked so much dope with his scruffy clients in the 1960s, his brains had turned to vapor. You would be inclined to forget that Max had graduated summa cum laude from Harvard, class of '41, and that he'd served "with distinction" in U.S. Army Intelligence as a decoder during World War II. You would be inclined to forget that his first published book was his Harvard Ph.D. dissertation, *Identity in Democracy: Freedom in Peril*, and that he'd once lectured on the "radical political consciousness" of Hegel, Feuerbach, Marx, Engels and Nietzsche in enormous teach-ins at Columbia University in the old bad days when he'd been on the faculty there and by his admission cravenly hoping to be a "card-carrying academic" in political science and not a "crusading activist" in law.

Now it was the evening of August 8, 1974. Max stood at the foot of the stairs calling *Get your sweet ass down here, girl, it's almost begun*.

You were meant to note with what virtuoso agility Max Meade descended from British propriety to American vernacular: *get your sweet ass down here*.

I wanted to resist! I'd have liked to climb out one of my screen-less windows onto the crumbling slate roof of the old ruin of a house and crawl on hands and knees to the highest pitch of the roof to press my hands against my ears to tune out Daddy. *Why* I wanted to cry *why must I come running, I don't care for your history or for you.*

None of this was true. Not in the slightest true. I could not have believed it myself for the most fleeting of moments.

Of course I knew: this evening was a long-awaited hour in the house at Chadds Ford as in countless other households in America. It was to be a sacred time. It was to be a shared memory of surpassing significance. Whatever I was pretending to be doing in my room behind my closed door (my journal in a water-stained old ledger I'd found in the attic, paperback books strewn across my bed in the margins of which I wrote schoolgirl annotations to be one day discovered by someone duly impressed) were weak defenses against Max Meade's summons. For this historic occasion Max had, he wanted us to know, cut short his travels and returned home. Wherever Max Meade had been, which of his confidential/"classified" locations, Max had left abruptly to return home.

Generva he was calling now. *Generva* when he demanded unhesitating daughter-obedience.

Genna-girl! he was teasing. *Genna* meant good-natured funnily weird slaphappy-Daddy of whom it was absurd to be frightened.

Within a few minutes of meeting you, Max Meade would explain in his sandpaper voice: he was the survivor of a bloody beating at the age of twenty-six in East Brunswick, New Jersey, on the night of October 16, 1949. An assistant professor of political science at Columbia, he'd come with a dozen others to protest a Ku Klux Klan march and he'd been attacked, knocked down, kicked-and-stomped in the windpipe by Klansmen while uniformed police officers kept their distance and so his voice afterward was not a human voice exactly but a whispery pleading grating noise like sheets of sandpiper being rubbed together.

This sandpaper-noise I would hear all my life. If not in the presence of Max Meade, in his absence.

Gen-na! Gennnn-na! Last call.

I threw down my ledger journal. I kicked aside my paperback books. Though my father scared the hell out of me when he was Mad Max on the rampage you can be sure that I came down those stairs flying.

Ohhhh yes! When Mad Max summoned them, the girls came flying.

Historic occasion.

Remember all your life, Genna.

To share. Just us. The triumph of justice.

August 8, 1974. The thirty-seventh president of the United States was resigning his office on network TV. Conceding his shame on network TV. Unprecedented! Unparalleled! Nothing like this before in our beleaguered American history! For years the dream of Max Meade and his comrades that the criminal president would go down in disgrace and now the miracle was imminent!

I was not a child. I was eighteen years old. In seven weeks, five days (I was crossing off days, on my calendar) I would depart for Schuyler College, which was one of the most exclusive and academically demanding women's colleges in North America, except of course I was also a daughter. I was Maximilian Meade's daughter and when Daddy gripped my hand so hard the bones felt as if they'd cracked my only perceptible response was a wincing laugh—"Dad-*dy.*"

In the TV room, as it was sometimes called, amid a mess of newspapers, discarded mail, manila envelopes and files and dirtied glasses, plates, cutlery and ashtrays, in a confusion of mismatched furniture and careworn carpets and small convoys of drifting mosquitoes and gnats (no air-conditioning in the old house in Chadds Ford, windows lacking screens were carelessly shoved up) we gathered to watch the ceremony of shame.

At last! Justice.

Except, Veronica was having trouble adjusting the set. Kneeling on her bare knees on the bare hardwood floor. Awkward agitated Veronica muttering Oh! Oh God where is that channel! Isn't it the Wilmington channel . . . Veronica Hewett-Meade's beauty-in-ruins face and fresh-dyed black hair in a cascade of erotic abandon down her back. On what was, despite the president's public shame, an ordinary and very warm summer evening in rural Chadds Ford, Veronica was wearing one of her East Indian caftans, shimmering fabric gaily spangled with gold and glass and mirror-moons through which you could see, if you didn't avert your eyes quickly enough, her small tremulous pointed breasts (from the front) and (from the rear) the small tremulous waxy-white vertebrae of her spine. On her lower body Veronica wore zebra-stripe bikini panties. (These had come in a boxed set from a Parisian lingerie store, a gift from a man friend. Veronica had passed a pair on to me, who'd thrown them away in disgust.)

Since my parents scorned television as they scorned most products of capitalist-consumer America, we owned only a small unreliable set predating color. For who would wish for the vulgarity of color TV in this debased culture? Max Meade had believed that the only value of color TV would have been, in the days of the Vietnam War, to have seen the actual color of blood in news footage if you wished to see the war brought home, and if you could trust U.S. reportage. (Some reporters you could trust, if most reporters you could not.) Yet now like an agitated ten-year-old, Max was pleading with Veronica to get the picture clearer, get the damned thing tuned, hurry!—running his hands rapidly over his hairless head in the way of a man trying desperately to appear calm.

Mad Max's hairless head. It was something to behold. Where in the 1960s Max had worn his thick burnt-apricot hair Viking-style to his shoulders, now out of vanity he shaved his head: though not carefully, and not at regular intervals. He was fifty-three, with a face like a much-kicked football. His style was haphazard, careening. His style was to reach into a closet and grab what was nearest. Pushing his feet into what was nearest. It was a vanity you might mistake for indifference to the world's vision of him.

I knelt beside Veronica to help with the TV. I took care not to offend my sensitive mother who was easily hurt if you "took over" one of her household tasks. Close up, I smelled whiskey on her breath. It was a sweet familiar smell I preferred to the sour-rank smell of her breath after a sweaty barbiturate sleep of twelve hours. Scotch whiskey meant celebration, an historic and not a merely private occasion.

In fact, there were glasses on the floor. Max and Veronica had begun their celebrating of the president's shame before their daughter had entered the scene.

As I turned dials, there appeared on the zigzagging screen the distorted figure of the president. He seemed to be peering through reading glasses into a void. As in a Pop Art collage with comical intent the president was replicated in triple: his shaky image jerked upward, another shaky image appeared and jerked upward, and yet another out of the mysterious deranged soul of the machine. I managed to steady and clarify the picture. The president was an aging, haggard-faced man, you felt a stab of pity for him. You saw a human soul dragged inside-out like a soiled sock.

Veronica laughed, wiping at her eyes. Oh how silly she was being, she knew!

Quickly saying it was Pat Nixon she grieved for. Those tragic Nixon women, look at their faces.

Why is it we so much more vividly recall shame, than pride? Our own shame more than the shame of others.

My memories of my parents were confused with dreams. My dreams of my parents were confused with memories.

It happened, they've gone my brother had said.

Unless my brother had said *Don't know what the fuck happened, where they've gone.*

This was long ago. Seven years before. Already I had known what shame was. What shame is. My mother had been Mommy then. It was later she became Veronica. Went away and when she returned she was not Mommy and became upset if she was called Mommy and did not wish to be touched for she did not wish to "contaminate" me for she loved me so much *You know that, Genna! Say you do.*

"Sickness" was a term of that era. If you had a "sickness" there would be a prescription for it. If society was "sick" there was certainly a prescription. Only a matter of finding the right one and enforcing it.

Ten years old, and then I was eleven. At Chadds Ford Day School where I was in sixth grade. Tall for my age, you might believe that I was mature for my age, too. That I was not a bed wetter! Not a frantic nose picker! Not a girl who could recite multiplication tables in a bright parrot voice but had no idea where Mommy had gone. No idea where Daddy had gone. When gone, and when-to-return.

Don't know how the fuck should I know. I don't!

You could not tell: if Rickie was angry, or laughing.

Rickie was waiting for me on the crumbling front steps. Waiting slouched and glassy-red-eyed smoking what he called a joint. The front door was wide open. The front door of the old manor house that was never used, as the front steps were never used and surrounded by thistles and tall grasses gone to seed. I saw the shame in Rickie's eyes. Saw his mouth move before I heard his words as you might see through the wrong end of a telescope a vision sharpened but in miniature. *Don't know where the fuck they are, and I'm going, too. And don't follow me.*

And there was Max talking of shame with one of the old-young men who used to come to stay with us in the house at Chadds Ford for a day, a night, a week, six weeks until abruptly one morning he'd have disappeared. Except Ansel had reappeared. Ansel with his face so narrow, so pained-seeming, it looked like it had been squeezed in a vise. Ansel with bristly black spider-hair and a ragged wisp of a beard. And there was my father saying that Ansel had done the right thing. Ansel, and his comrades. My father saying in his hoarse voice if he had the guts himself the bombs he would detonate! If he had the guts to assassinate Nixon, Kissinger, Mitchell. Just to make the attempt. To declare open war. Then he'd know, Daddy said, he had done some permanent good for the country of his birth and for humankind and he would go into the underground and wage guerrilla warfare and what remained of his life would be redeemed.

Not this life of shame. Privileged shame in a white man's skin.

The president's face! It was shocking to see, for it was not a TV face. It was haggard, old. The nose was bulbous at the tip, the nostrils were black and nasty. Bruised dents beneath the eyes and quivering jowls of the kind you never see on TV. And the prune-mouth from which hollow words issued slowly and with effort.

A man, Max said in disgust, who shits with his mouth.

The president was speaking. The president was frowning over his old-man glasses. In angry fervor declaring *I am not a quitter* and Max chortled in derision Ohhhh yes you are! Yes you are you utter bastard! and the president was saying *Mistakes yes but for personal gain never* and Max began to howl Liar! Fucking li-ar! you made yourself and your fucking criminal associates rich and you know it! and the president was saying in dogged determination *For the good of the country resigning my office* and Max howled To avoid impeachment you bastard! To avoid a trial! and the president was saying in righteous dogged determination glaring through his prim-old-man glasses *Ahead of my personal fight for vindication the good of the country resigning my office* and Max howled To avoid prison you bastard you lying bastard I could tear out your lying throat with my teeth, staring at the screen as it began again to quiver as if in mockery of Max Meade's frustration.

Max had ceased rocking on his heels. His near-empty whiskey glass he'd have dropped except Veronica took it from his fingers with shaky fingers of her own. Max was moaning Oh God oh God can you believe it.

The president had concluded his speech. The president was visibly perspiring. The president looked like a man who has soiled his underwear and is sitting in excrement but wishes to believe that no one has noticed for if no one has noticed—has it happened? It has not! The president will retreat with a smile. Brave smile of the wounded leader. Man of dignity. Man of courage. Hounded into resigning his office by political adversaries merely. Not a man of shame. The president turns to wave to TV America, breaking now into a true smile. It is a death's head smile and yet it is a true smile. It is a smile of triumph. It is a smile of victory. Both arms lift sudden and loose as puppet arms. Both hands flash V-for-Victory in the way of a naughty boy flashing obscenities.

And here was the shocking thing: Max leaned forward suddenly and spat at the TV screen.

The nape of Max's neck was creased livid in rage. His vein-riddled bald head was flushed and mottled in rage. I was backing away from the spectacle. I had too often witnessed my parents in states of emotional detonation. I was not certain what I'd actually seen on TV. I was not certain whose shame I had witnessed. As Max raged, Veronica fumbled to switch the set off. For, somehow, Veronica was becoming the brunt of Max's rage. Veronica swiping at her runny mascara eyes, *Forgive me, darling! I can't help it, you know how ridiculous I am. It isn't him my heart is broken for it's the wife and daughter—* as Max in his fury and frustration nudged Veronica's back, caused her to topple over in a childish spill of bare legs, not-clean bare feet, a tangle of shiny black hair and a pathos of see-through muslin.

I made my escape. Long I would recall my father's spittle trickling downward making a rivulet through the film of dust on the television screen like tears.

Next day, Max sought me out. Not red-eyed Mad Max raging like Wotan but the other Max. This Max's breath wasn't fiery with liquor but smelled primly of Listerine. His massive bald head no longer pulsed and pounded like an upright blood-engorged penis.

Genna! Sweetheart.

Yes?

Coolly I smiled. I knew, to win Maximilian Elliott Meade's heart, even the very prettiest girls (I was not one of these) had to speak with poise, candor.

For here was the man who'd written so eloquently and persuasively on the "inextricably ethical component of all political acts"—the "search for the Archimedean principle, *what is the truth for which I am willing to die?*" He had taught his young adoring disciples of the 1960s the Kierkegaardian principle "the individual is the highest truth" and he had been daunting in his courage to oppose the U.S. federal government in the courts. I could not bear it that the naughty-boy president in the very act of becoming the ex-president had kicked my father in the belly, and a terrible vomit had spilled from his mouth.

In Max's eyes was the acknowledgment of shame, he could not bear it, either.

Saying calmly, "Nixon will be pardoned as he would not have pardoned others. He will be pardoned by his lackey vice president, of course. It's enough for us, the criminal has resigned in shame."

Max delivered these words as one might speak into a tape recorder. For here was his Brunhilde, avid to listen and record.

The broken throaty voice, calm: "You are too young to be touched by the shame of my generation, Genna. But you can share in our regeneration."

Max touched my shoulder, hesitantly. Happily I smiled. As if I understood. So badly I wanted to believe.

Secret Passageway

The first time I saw Minette Swift I didn't yet know her name. I didn't yet know that we were to be roommates. The bell of Schuyler Chapel was ringing its heart out overhead.

Half-consciously I'd been staring at her. A dark impassive face, a black girl my age. She was several yards ahead of me exiting the Schuyler College Chapel with her family, her parents and younger sister. I wanted to think that I could see the family resemblance among them, but it had to be that they were blacks amid a crowd of mostly whites and I was white, and felt keenly how it might be, how it must be, so conspicuous in one's skin, in this public place.

Amid so much that was white. Glaring-white like the interior of the formerly Quaker chapel with its spartan white walls and plain hardwood floors and pews and tall narrow windows whose aged glass panes emitted a curiously wavering light as if underwater. The bell was so clamorous overhead, my heart began to pound with its accelerated beat.

The president of Schuyler College had just delivered a spirited welcome to the class of 1979. We'd been told that the generation of women to which she belonged, as a 1952 graduate of Radcliffe College, had had to be feminists "exploring" the wilderness. The class of 1979 would be "settlers and harvesters."

It had been a rousing address. Numerous times we'd interrupted this wonderful woman who looked no older than most of our mothers, to applaud. Though the prospect of graduating from Schuyler College, from the perspective of my first day at the college, seemed remote and improbable as science fiction.

I felt quite safe! Four years were a lifetime.

I was watching Minette Swift in profile. Minette Swift beside a blunt-browed black man, his skin even darker than hers, stocky in build, not handsome but imposing, a man of vigorous middle age with a broad nose that looked as if it had been flattened by force. Here was an individual who carried himself with dignity. If in the predominantly white chapel this black man had been made to feel acutely conscious of his skin it was not an uneasy sort of self-consciousness but one that suggested pride. I understood that this was a public man of some kind, for he reminded me of Max: a politician? preacher? ex-athlete? entertainer? If a businessman, he was successful. He was accustomed to courtesy from others, even deference. No one was going to intimidate him. If he smiled, it was a smile that had to be earned, for it would not be lightly cast out. On this humid September day he wore a stylish tailored navy pinstripe suit that fitted his muscular upper body like a glove. The cuffs of his starched white shirt flashed gold. His necktie flashed bronze. There was a hint of gold in his teeth. His eyeglasses rode the bridge of his wide blunt nose as if embedded in his flesh: perfectly round, rimmed in gold, with lenses that magnified the calm dark assessing stare of his eyes. Once outside the chapel he paused to remove his coat with a kind of ceremonial slowness and wiped his face with a white handkerchief, decorously. There was no haste in any of his motions, no suggestion of discomfort or annoyance. I saw how his wife took the coat from him like a servant, unasked; how carefully she folded it over her arm.

By this time I was staring so hard the thought came to me in warning *Now he will see you, he will look right at you!*

I prepared to look quickly away and felt a mild pang of disappointment, when the dignified black man took not the slightest notice of me.

His wife was less striking. Lighter-skinned, with an attractive powdered face and shiny dark lipstick. Her hair had been partially straightened. Her large sloping breasts and wide hips strained at her lavender knit suit, the skirt was bunched and wrinkled where she'd been sitting in the cramped pew. She was very warm, there were damp half-moons beneath her arms. Naturally she was wearing stockings, and high-heeled black patent leather

pumps. On her head, a wide-brimmed black straw hat that looked lacquered. She was dressed as if for church, for a festive occasion that
nonetheless brought with it some strain, for her manner was preoccupied.
In the chapel and now outside she was engaged in a mother's tug-of-war
of wills with the restless younger daughter, a lanky girl of about thirteen
with stiff plaited hair and a mocking mouth, white anklet socks and shiny
black patent leather shoes. And there was the self-possessed older daughter whose name I did not yet know though I determined I would know her,
she would be my classmate and perhaps my friend. Minette who wasn't
softly plump like her mother but compact and durable like her father. Like
a schoolgirl uniform she wore a long-sleeved white blouse covered in eye-
let ornamentation, and a wide black leather belt so tight it made her waist
crease. She wore stockings and high-heeled shoes, the only girl in the class
of '79. And those shell-pink plastic glasses that looked as if they must be
pinching her face. *Her!*

Always there was this curious aloofness to Minette Swift, a maddening
quality of abstraction, disengagement. As if she were indifferent to the
eyes of others. Only the father was real to her, the mother had been outgrown. But the father would not be outgrown and his power would not be
bypassed.

At first I thought *She has a father, he loves her.*

And then I thought *She is the daughter. She is his.*

I saw that Veronica was watching the black family, too. Their dress and
manner marked them as distinctive. Unlike other blacks at the Orientation
Day events they might have been of the 1950s or earlier, a tableau by
Norman Rockwell for the old *Saturday Evening Post*. They were of the era
of Martin Luther King, Jr. They were not of the era of King's assassination,
of Malcolm X, Elijah Muhammad, Muhammad Ali, Angela Davis. They
were of an era when *family* still prevailed.

I was in dread of what my mother might do. My middle-aged-hippie
mother. It was like her to approach strangers like a welcoming committee,
smile her dazzling-seductive smile and introduce herself and me: "We're
the Hewett-Meades." In theory, Veronica would be asked if we were somehow related to the Meade family, to the founder of Schuyler College

and/or the controversial activist Maximilian Meade, and Veronica would hesitate before admitting, yes. *By marriage, me. By blood, my daughter.* Most of the time, fortunately, this question was never asked.

As Veronica was poised on the brink of impulse, staring at the blunt-faced black father who was now conferring with his elder daughter about the Orientation Day schedule, I warned her: "Veronica, no." I could not bear my sensitive mother making a fool of herself and being rebuffed, I'd witnessed such episodes in the past.

Some of them in our very house at Chadds Ford.

"No what!" Veronica laughed at me, annoyed.

"Don't speak to them. Please just *don't.*"

The black family was moving away. Headed across the green. I had dared to take Veronica's wrist.

A thin wrist, a prominent bone. I knew that, on the underside of the wrist, a swollen blue vein pulsed.

"You"—Veronica pulled away from me, looking wounded—"are ridiculous. You are paranoid"—fingering her very black very shiny hair twisted into a glamorous if untidy topknot at the crown of her Nefertiti head—"as a damned Seeing Eye dog that won't let his master walk six feet for fear of *stumbling.*"

It was a classic Veronica outburst. Extravagant, inspired-deranged. Dropping acid in the 1960s had rewired my mother's brain in ways that were sometimes startling and original, if most of the time not.

I told Veronica, Seeing Eye dogs are noble dogs. And paranoia in the service of common sense is a good thing.

"Paranoia! As if you know! You sound like your father. The one that is now, not the original."

Veronica spoke with the sort of vehement protest that asks not to be taken too seriously. Even her anger had a hurt-child air of wanting to be forgiven.

The one that is now meant Max Meade in the 1970s. *The original* was Max Meade in the 1960s. There did not seem to me such a difference between them as Veronica believed, but then I was only Max's daughter.

The black family had disappeared. We were surrounded by mostly white faces. Girls my age in the company of parents, siblings, relatives. I felt involuntary pangs of envy seeing my future classmates with families, fathers. I could not help myself glancing about to see how many were in the company of *just mothers*.

Though no mothers were like Veronica Hewett-Meade.

For Orientation Day at Schuyler College, Veronica wore: an ankle-length crimson dress that looked disconcertingly like a nightgown, with a dramatic V-neck that showed the tops of her pale pear-sized breasts, the thin muslin fabric threaded with silver like exposed nerves; silver jewelry, that clattered; extravagant makeup, including turquoise-lidded Cleopatra eyes; thonged sandals on her bare, very pale feet. There was the glamor topknot from which tendrils and wisps of black-shiny hair escaped, there were nails and toenails flashing crimson lacquer. A talcumy-perfumy-anxious odor wafting in the woman's wake.

When she'd been Mommy, she had loved me, I think. I know that I loved her.

Later, as Veronica, she'd confided in me with the air of one imparting wisdom, that "love" is an illusion of the ego, no more substantial than vapor.

If I disappear your feeling for me will disappear. Because there is no source for it. If I die, you should not grieve. If you die, I will not grieve. I promise!

Veronica was shading her eyes, peering at the clock tower of Schuyler Hall as we passed below. Vaguely, we were moving in the direction of the president's private residence where, at noon, we'd been expected for lunch. Veronica checked her watch against the clock above: "If it's twelve-ten P.M. here, it's nine-ten A.M. in Los Angeles. Max should be awake by now."

. . . something strange and wondrous about the family. Something monstrous about the family. The family is a many-headed creature like the Hydra. The family is the locus of obsession. The family is about possessing and being possessed. The family is the transferral of genes from one genera-

*tion to the next. The family is pure self. The family is a freak. The family is
extinct. The family is private life and there is no value in private life. There
is no value in any life but the life of the People. The life of the Revolution.
In a time of Revolution like our time the private life has ceased to exist as the
private life ceases to exist in a time of war.*

These impassioned words Maximilian Meade wrote in the mid-1960s.
I discovered them in an anthology of essays titled *World on Fire: Essays of
Our Time* taught in my prep school in Massachusetts, in 1972.

I hadn't realized that I had memorized Max's words. My father's voice
in my head like a sledgehammer-incantation.

No one at the Cornwall Academy had needed to ask if Maximilian
Meade was my father, somehow this was known. Facts are known of us
over which we have no control. No one asked what I thought of Max's
words. Though there were cruel girls at my school no one wished to be
that cruel.

Until the end of the Vietnam War, and the collapse of opposition to
the war, Max had believed that the private life was essentially irrelevant.
By 1974 he'd modified certain of his beliefs, he was living again with us in
Chadds Ford, or what remained of us. (Rickie was gone, of course. Rickie
had moved out when he was sixteen.) By 1974 Max had become disillu-
sioned with "revolution" and never uttered the word except as if set off by
quotation marks as you might utter the name of an old love who has betrayed you, lacerated your heart and proved herself worthless yet whose
name has the power still to make your voice falter.

"Should we? We can pretend it's all new to us."

Veronica was in a mood, one of her elated moods. Her clammy-pale-
powdered skin glowed. Her bruised-violet eyes were dewy. Her fingers
could not seem to stop twining themselves in the loosening topknot. She'd
bypassed the president's private luncheon—"She only wants us because
we're Meades. Fucking don-ors." She'd bypassed other events on the
Orientation Day schedule saying she couldn't stand any more confine-
ment, being talked-at and made-welcome—"Max says the people who

want to meet you are the people you sure as hell don't want to meet." Instead she was leading me across the quadrangle to Elias Meade House where, if we hurried, we could join a group of about twelve visitors to be taken on a guided tour.

"... *there?* Oh but why?"

No good my resisting. Veronica Hewett-Meade was in one of her moods.

As a child I'd been taken through Elias Meade House more than once. My brother and I had been taken through a number of Philadelphia/ Wilmington-area properties once belonging to my wealthy Quaker ancestors that were now national landmarks open to the public; we'd been made to know how distinguished our family was, or had been. The austere old faded-brick Federal house on the Schuyler campus was now a museum maintained by the college and the National Historic Society featuring period furniture, portraits of the Meade family, publications and artifacts having to do with the anti-slavery movement and the Underground Railroad. My memory of the house was vague. I could not even recall who'd taken me through it, an older Meade relative, I think, one of my father's elder aunts and not my hot-skinned mother.

Though now Veronica was saying, laughing and tugging at my arm, "As if for the first time, Genna! As if we're strangers to the Meade kingdom."

It was so: Veronica and I were Hewett-Meade. This may have been our sole mother-daughter bond.

By this time, 2 P.M., I was wishing that my mother might leave me. It was true, I'd been hurt and disappointed that my father had not accompanied us but I had not been much surprised, to be Max Meade's daughter is to lack a capacity for surprise though not for disappointment. Now I was wishing I might be alone if only to feel lonely. I had had enough of Orientation Day. I had had enough of being greeted by exuberantly smiling strangers and my hand shaken and *Where are you from?* shouted into my face. I had had enough of Veronica hoping to seduce with her bleating "Hewett-Meade" and the crimson-glinting fingernails primping her ridiculous dyed-black hair.

Then, outside Elias Meade House, I saw the black girl whose name I did not yet know was Minette Swift. I saw her father looming beside her, still dabbing at his forehead with a handkerchief. The mother in the black straw hat and wrinkled knit suit and the lanky-limbed younger sister had just entered the Elias Meade House. The tour guide stood in the doorway, holding the door open waiting for stragglers as Veronica called out, "Wait for us! Please."

I gave in, suddenly. For where else other than Elias Meade House would I have liked to be, at this moment?

The interior of the quaint old house was dimly lighted with low-wattage electricity to suggest candle flames. Even sunlight slanting through the narrow-paned wavy-glass windows looked sallow. The tour group was mostly adults, attentive and curious. I was hoping that Veronica wouldn't strike up a conversation with the tour guide, ply her with questions. The woman was about Veronica's age, in her late forties with a helmet of coppery hair and a professional smile. Though she must have uttered her bright brisk words countless times welcoming us to "the noble-minded past of the remarkable Meades" yet she spoke with an air of spontaneity, pleasure. She wore a dark green linen blazer with gold piping and a pleated skirt to match, the Schuyler College colors.

Led in a slow shuffle along a corridor, peering into the first of the cordoned-off rooms, I found myself glancing sidelong at the black girl in the starched white blouse. I could almost make out what she wore glinting at her throat: a gold cross. In profile, she might have been mistaken for a boy. Her nose was blunt and snubbed, her chin was somewhat heavy. Her lips were parted as if her teeth were overlarge. Among even her family the girl held herself apart, aloof, and detached. At the time it did not occur to me that the girl might have been anxious about college, being left here alone. So self-possessed she appeared, it could not have occurred to me *She is anticipating loneliness among strangers. People like me.*

I tried to catch her eye, I smiled, for obviously we were both freshmen, class of '79. If the girl noticed me, if her gaze behind the prim-pink glasses took me in, in that same instant she ceased to see me. And when we met again only a few hours later in our suite on the third floor of Haven House, she would not recognize me.

Here was the paradox of the Meades: they were one of Philadelphia's wealthy families, yet as Quakers they led spartan lives. Even as a younger man Elias Meade was giving away his money in the belief that *Money is a blessing that becomes a curse in rapid time*. Furnishings in the Elias Meade House were not lavish as in other landmark homes in the region but rather minimal, functional. The old house itself, Federalist in design, had been expanded several times with no apparent eye for maintaining the original structure and was therefore, as the tour guide conceded, "rambling, haphazard." Except for a showily beautiful German-made pianoforte allegedly played by Elias Meade's first wife, the sofas, settees, tables and chairs displayed in the somber low-wattage rooms had a Shaker-style simplicity. The carpets were threadbare, the hardwood floors uneven. "These were not 'conspicuous consumers' of material goods like their wealthy contemporaries, these were deeply idealistic, spiritual people! These were people who believed in the Quaker principle of the equality of all souls before God—the 'guiding light within.'"

I felt a childish thrill of pride. I was embarrassed at being a Meade in this place and yet, invisible and anonymous, I loved hearing such words. I glanced over at the black family to see how they were reacting: the father was listening attentively and with respect, I thought; the mother was smiling politely; the younger sister, running an illicit finger along the yellow pianoforte keys, not exerting quite enough pressure to make any sound, wasn't listening; the older sister who would be my classmate was staring at the tour guide, brooding and somber.

Equality of all souls. Guiding light within. Max said there were things you wished to believe but could not, and there were things you wished not to believe but did. I wished to believe in the Quaker ideals though I was not a Quaker and though I could not believe.

"Oh yes! Yes it is ironic. Many commentators have noted how ironic, and yet how wonderful—" The tour guide was breathless responding to a query from one of the visitors, speaking of the paradox that Elias Meade who'd made his fortune as a dry goods manufacturer and eventual founder of Philadelphia's major department store, had cared so little himself for material possessions, even for food and drink. (As an elderly, ill man he simply ceased eating and "passed away" like a wraith.) The passion of Meade's life had been the anti-slavery movement: beginning in 1845, he'd hidden countless runaway slaves in this house and in other properties of his elsewhere, he'd defied authorities and paid thousands of dollars in fines for violating the fugitive slave law of 1850, he had even risked imprisonment. His original dry goods store on Chestnut Street, Philadelphia, had been set on fire by arsonists in 1851, yet the following year, he became the principal financial backer of the Philadelphia Vigilance Committee, that systematically coordinated the maneuvers of the Underground Railroad. Slaves fleeing the South were routed through the Philadelphia area and north to Boston or upstate New York; eventually, many made their way to Canada. Elias Meade's first wife Lucinda had helped to establish the Philadelphia Association for the Moral and Mental Improvement of the People of Color, and after the Civil War, and the death of this wife, Meade married a young woman named Generva, a former servant who would become a crusading feminist and educator of "people of color . . ."

We were in a gallery now of portraits in heavy gilt frames. Several portraits of Elias Meade at different stages in his life, portraits of the first wife Lucinda alone and with children. As the guide uttered the words *people of color* I could not avoid seeing how the black family reacted, self-conscious and displeased. The younger sister who'd been larking about in the other rooms now poked her face daringly close to a portrait of my great-grandfather Elias Meade as a saintly old gentleman with white side whiskers, a boiled-pink skin and too-blue eyes, looking as if she were about to spit on him. *White folks! Ain't white folks hot shit, now!*

Quickly I looked away blushing.

Wanting to protest, *But these were good people!* By the standards of 1974 they sound condescending but they were good generous self-sacrificing people and Negroes in America had no friends otherwise.

Adjoining the gallery was a room devoted entirely to Generva Meade, Crusader Feminist and Educator. It was illuminated in a way to suggest votive candles, like a saint's shrine. My great-grandmother's most famous pronouncement was *In God's Eyes All Equal* which was the title of one of her pious-militant poems. In the room were a number of portraits of my notorious great-grandmother that bore little resemblance to one another except that in each she was fierce-eyed and unsmiling. On display also were daguerreotypes, photographs, and drawings of Generva Meade in youth, middle age, and eventually as the wild-white-haired old woman on crutches and in a wheelchair the world came to know. There were even caricatures of Generva Meade as a deranged female, a witch in outlandish costumes (bloomers, men's trousers, stovepipe hats, hip boots) cavorting with ape-like Negroes around a fire. There was a cruelly comic likeness of Generva Meade in 1913 as a hunchback crone on crutches brandishing a picket sign GIVE WOMEN THE VOTE SO THEY WILL TURN INTO ME.

In glass display cases were copies of the many journals and newspapers in which Generva Meade had published her "crusader" verse and essays that had met with ridicule in some quarters, admiration and adulation in others. There were handwritten manuscripts of her many speeches and her biography of the radical feminist Victoria Woodhull, *Sister Victoria* (1901). There were scattered first-draft pages and a first edition of her autobiography *A Day in the Evening of My Life* which was published after her death in 1927 and was now a classic feminist text. (I'd seen *A Day in the Evening of My Life* in the Schuyler College bookstore, required reading for at least three courses.) There were quaint hand-tinted studio photographs of Generva's children, including my grandfather Alden Meade, my father's father; there was a front-page *Philadelphia Inquirer* photograph of Generva Meade, Charlotte Perkins Gilman, and Harriot Stanton Blatch on the brink of being admitted to a Philadelphia polling station, in 1912. (The women were allowed to vote, but arrested twelve days later on a charge of "voting fraud.") There was the famous, much-reproduced photograph of black historian and activist W. E. B. DuBois standing beside a frail but indomitable Generva Meade on crutches, taken in 1919 on the auditorium stage of the Free Library of Philadelphia. By this time the tour guide was speaking with breathless enthusiasm and familiarity of "Generva" who'd been a friend and ally of Susan B. Anthony and other prominent feminists and reformers, and a "financial supporter and respected associate" of DuBois. Generva had helped provide funds for *Crisis*, the official publication of the National Association for the Advancement of Colored People, and as Elias Meade's wife, she'd had a good deal to do with the early decades of Schuyler College. Here was an illiterate servant girl who'd virtually educated herself, married her widowed employer and became famous in her own right, fearless in the controversial causes of feminism and Negro rights who'd lived to see women's suffrage become law in 1920. The tour guide spoke of Generva as a "raw-boned young beauty" when young but there was little evidence of conventional beauty in these likenesses. She seemed to have had an angular and somewhat asymmetrical face, not very delicate features, heavy eyebrows that nearly grew together at the bridge of her nose. Her dark hair grew thick and rather low on her forehead. There was an intolerant glisten to her eyes, which were deep-set and fixed, that reminded me of Maximilian Meade, but I couldn't imagine this stiff-backed woman capable of relaxing into a playful mood as Max frequently did, willing to laugh at himself, swooping to hug, tickle, kiss a child.

My great-grandmother! The woman's fierce staring eyes took me in and dismissed me for I was but one individual, and a crusader like Generva Meade must concern herself with multitudes.

The tour guide was answering questions. Generva was far more popular than Elias Meade. One of the questioners was Veronica, who wanted to know why no birth date was ever given for Generva Meade, only just a death date, 1927. And was it true, as some of the caricatures suggested, that Generva had "mixed" blood?

I gave my mother a sidelong look of disgust. Why was she asking such a question, as if she didn't know the answer!

The guide said, "Generva Meade had many enemies. They spread all sorts of rumors about her. The most persistent was that she was part Delaware Indian. Her birthplace isn't known, or her exact birth date. Near the end of her life she acknowledged she was seventy-nine and if so, she'd have been born in 1848. But that was never verified."

Veronica said, with seeming naïveté, "A 'mixed-breed servant-girl' marrying her wealthy Quaker master—that must've been a scandal, a hundred years ago! That's the real reason they hated her."

We were too many crowded in the room, the air had become warm and stale and smelling of bodies. My mother's remarks were annoying to me, I could not understand her motivation. And why she'd insisted upon revisiting Elias Meade House on a day that should have had nothing to do with my father's family history.

The guide was concluding her remarks on Generva Meade, crusader feminist and educator. The woman spoke with such breathless enthusiasm, you might think she meant to ridicule her subject: "And these are Generva's authentic hickory carved crutches, feel how *heavy*."

Several visitors lifted the crutches, exclaiming and laughing. The younger black girl insisted upon trying to walk with them, lurching and stumbling across the floor, until her parents expressed displeasure and she let them fall with a clatter to the floor.

The father would blame the mother for the girl's misbehaving. The mother loudly whispered, "You, Jewel! Pick those crutches up."

I had to laugh. I liked Jewel's spirit. There was too much sobriety here in Elias Meade House. Too much white-skinned heroism, martyrdom.

As the group shuffled from the room, Veronica leaned to whisper in my ear, teasing, " 'The family is extinct'—or is it?"

My mother had a way of reading my mind. I was made to feel weak, childish at such times. As if my private thoughts, in Veronica's words, were being mocked.

As if Max's words about the family, we'd heard somberly uttered numerous times, were being mocked.

At the rear of Elias Meade House, in the low-ceilinged nether region of the servants' quarters, the guide was asking with schoolteacher enthusiasm if we all knew what the Underground Railroad was. At first, no one answered. Not the black girl in the starched white blouse, who surely knew; and not me. Then someone volunteered: Negro slaves who escaped from the south made their way north on trains? hiding in boxcars? and were hidden by white sympathizers along the route until they were safe in the North?

The guide expanded upon this answer, speaking of the Abolitionist movement in the Philadelphia area, the American Antislavery Society and the Philadelphia Vigilance Committee, the many fleeing, destitute and desperate Negroes whom Elias Meade had personally helped on their way to freedom, had in fact hidden in this house. He'd arranged for them to be brought by night across the Schuylkill. He'd arranged for them to move on to "safe houses" in Wilkes-Barre and Scranton. The guide recited names, dates, statistics. In her brisk blithe way she spoke of "fugitive Negroes"—"runaway slaves"—"men, women, children of color." Though she was certainly aware of the black family staring at her she seemed oblivious of their unease for this was a bright spirited recitation she'd given many times in the past and the words had become worn smooth in her ears, unabrasive. As she spoke of Elias Meade's alliance with William Lloyd Garrison, the heroic editor of *The Liberator*, and how much these courageous men had done for the Abolitionist cause, the black man I would later know to be Reverend Virgil Swift interrupted impatiently: "Yes, ma'am! Maybe so, ma'am! But it was not just white folks who saw to the 'railroad.' It was Negroes helping Negroes, too. Tell me there was anybody like Harriet Tubman amongst the whites! Or William Still! Ma'am, if you speak of the 'railroad' you need to speak of these folks, too."

The black man might have been speaking from a pulpit, his voice was so deep, reverberating, quivering with indignation. The gold-rimmed lenses of his glasses shone. There was a glint of gold in his upper teeth. The guide stared at him blinking in surprise. A shiny-coppery-haired middle-aged Caucasian woman in a school blazer and pleated skirt, suddenly humbled as if stripped naked. You could see that she'd never before been challenged in Elias Meade House. The black man had addressed her with the air of one accustomed to authority, deference; the woman instinctively knew to defer to him, but her memorized words were of no help to her. I had some knowledge of Harriet Tubman, an escaped slave from Maryland who had become a legend in her time helping hundreds of slaves to freedom at great risk to her life, but I knew nothing of William Still. I wanted to say something in support of the offended black man and his family but I seemed to know that any interference on my part would be resented by them; and I felt sorry for the white woman whose discreetly rouged cheeks were now flushed dull-red, and who smiled at her challenger like one whose coquetry has been flung back into her face.

"Harriet Tubman—oh yes! And—William Still. These are—there were—many Negroes active in the Underground Railroad of course—some of them were friends and allies of Elias Meade. In Mr. Meade's *Abolitionist Record* he wrote of them and kept accounts of their lives. If anyone is interested, copies of Mr. Meade's *Record* are for sale in the college bookstore . . ."

The black man seemed to accept this weak response to his remarks as the apology it was. Like a distended wheel the clumsy moment passed.

The tour was concluding in the airless low-ceilinged kitchen of Elias Meade House where the guide stooped to open a small pantry door in a brick wall beside a crumbling fireplace and invited us to peer inside: "Firewood was stored here, to throw slave catchers off the trail if they searched the house. After the hateful fugitive slave law, slave catchers had the legal right to search private homes. Elias Meade had a secret passageway built behind the fireplace here, if you crouch down you can see stairs leading up into the attic. There was a secret partition in the attic also, where as many as twelve runaway slaves could hide in a windowless space . . . Would anyone like to crawl inside, and investigate the secret passageway? I have a flashlight."

It was a playful question of course. A shudder of revulsion rippled through the group. For who would wish to voluntarily crawl into such a place!

But here was prankish Jewel: "Meeee!"

And quick-echoing Genna: "Me, too."

It was a quicksilver alliance. Naughty young girls defying disapproving/astonished elders.

Before her parents could stop her, Jewel grabbed the flashlight from the startled guide's fingers. In her black patent-leather Mary Janes she squatted on her heels and shuffled into the passageway that seemed hardly larger than a rabbit's burrow, shining the flashlight up the steps. Nimble and brash as a monkey! I pushed away Veronica's hand and followed Jewel into the passageway behind the fireplace. I was taller than Jewel but not much heavier. I was nimble and brash as a monkey, too. It was rare for me to instigate risky adventures but I was readily drawn into the risky adventures of others.

"Oh *man.*"

Jewel shone the flashlight up into the darkness. She whistled, the prospect was so daunting. The steps were nearly steep as a ladder, and looked rotted. The width of the passageway could not have been more than fifteen inches. Everywhere were cobwebs brushing against our faces. A strong odor of mouse droppings and dirt. The adults behind us were exclaiming in alarm, indignation. We only just laughed, climbing the steps. I thought that I could smell the pungent scent of Jewel's stiff-plaited hair. I wanted badly to touch her, I knew that her skin would be hot and oily-damp to the touch as my own was hot and dry.

The steps creaked. The steps sagged beneath our weight. We were in danger of plunging through. We laughed together wildly as the adults pleaded with us *Come back! come back it isn't safe.*

It must have been the tour guide calling *Girls! Oh please girls it isn't safe!*

Yet it was safe. We made it to the top of the steps. Jewel was able to stand upright, brushing cobwebs from her face. "Damn nasty spiders, look at 'em." I stood beside her. We were panting, excited. Everywhere the flashlight beam moved, the cave-like space was festooned with cobwebs. Pale light shone through chinks in the aged brick. The smell of dirt and time was stronger here. We began to cough, and then to choke. We were laughing, and choking. I managed to say, "My n-name is Genna." But Jewel resisted: "Ain't gonna say my name, I'm a FUGE-Y-TIVE." She spoke in a mock-Negro drawl, a caricature of black speech. I did not want to think it was speech in contempt of my white skin but only just playful and spirited. "Like that white lady been sayin I be a 'SCAPED SLAVE OF COL-LOR."

"And me, too."

"You!" Jewel snorted in derision.

I tried to imagine twelve adults crowded into this space, in terror of being discovered and captured like beasts and hauled back into slavery. My imagination weakly fluttered like a trapped butterfly. Jewel was lunging about with the flashlight, her laughter was high pitched, wild. "Lookit here! Lookit here!" I saw nothing but cobwebs, shadows. I was worried that

Jewel was stomping about so heavily on the old floorboards. The thought came to me that someone had died in this place, it was the smell of death we were inhaling. I was desperate to leave. I plucked at Jewel's arm and she threw me off, quick as a snake.

When we returned down the steep creaking steps, subdued now, covered in cobwebs, the sallow light in the kitchen seemed to have brightened. Jewel's scolding mother hauled her out of the passageway by her arm, and Jewel did not resist. And there was Veronica waiting for me. She'd been upset, for impulsive behavior not her own invariably upset Veronica Hewett-Meade, no matter how innocuous. She was trying to laugh, scolding me for behaving like a headstrong child, look at me covered in *cobwebs*. For us, the tour was over. She couldn't wait to escape Elias Meade House.

We left by a rear door with a warning sign NO EXIT. But Veronica pushed the door open, and pushed me through. In the grassy alleyway behind the house Veronica pushed me again, a little harder with the heel of her hand. She would have liked to slap me, hit me with her fist. But pushing me would have to do. We were both breathing quickly, panting. Veronica clawed for a cigarette out of her black net bag, lit it and exhaled luxuriantly. The shiny black topknot had loosened into cascading strands of hair, tendrils and wisps. The Cleopatra eyes appeared bloodshot.

"Fresh air! I hate history."

Schuyler College. It's austere, very demanding, for serious students.

Our daughter loves it.

It's wonderful, her roommate has become her closest friend. A black minister's daughter from Washington, D.C.

What Good

What good'll that do. They will only break it again.

These words! Soaked in sarcasm as the slices of cold French toast Minette brought back to the room were soaked in maple syrup, to attract small black glistening ants.

These words in fact I had not heard clearly. Or, if I'd heard, I had not understood. Yet they would echo in my ears with a throbbing tenacity for days afterward.

I would not forget the hurt sullen look in Minette's eyes magnified by the lenses of her pink-plastic glasses. Her exasperation with me, as if I'd betrayed her.

Did she think that I talked about her to the other residents of Haven Hall? I never did!

I was hurt, humbled. I had only meant well. I saw Minette turning to walk swiftly away from me that morning, without a backward glance. If there were fallen tree branches on the sidewalk before her, Minette kicked through them.

For days afterward Minette seemed anxious, distracted. When we met on the stairs or on the sidewalk outside she murmured hello only if I spoke first. She left for the dining hall early, without waiting for me; if I called after her, and ran to catch up with her, she relented, and tried to smile, but clearly she was thinking of other things. I said, "Minette, is something wrong? I hope you will tell me," and Minette said, not meeting my eye, "Ohhh *no*. Don't mind *me*. My momma says, I am susceptible to moods, what I need is somebody right close behind me to give me a swift kick in the rear." Minette spoke of herself with such sharp vehemence, I was reminded of my mother's violent self-loathing when she was in one of her "bummer" moods.

Minette began to take food back with her to the residence, to eat in her bedroom with the door closed. Each week, a bulky package arrived for Minette from her mother and in these packages were tins containing baked goods which Minette devoured in private, in her bedroom.

Sometimes I saw Minette glancing at me sidelong. That look like a clenched fist. In her eyes a glisten of distrust. I wondered if she'd been betrayed in the past by girls who'd befriended her, then turned against her. I thought *I won't give up so easily!*

The cracked window had been repaired. The new pane perfectly matched the old except the new pane was much clearer than the old and sunlight poured through it more intensely on our bright-blinding October mornings.

The damaged oak outside the window had been severely pruned, all the broken and dying limbs removed. The gale-force winds seemed to have traumatized the tree, its leaves fell early and so our room was brighter than ever. Sometimes, I had to shade my eyes, glancing toward Minette's side of the room. I was struck by the glittering gold of the cross on Minette's poster and those garish red words like a prophecy: "I AM THE WAY THE TRUTH AND THE LIFE."

Here was the riddle of the Sphinx. Minette had told me proudly that her father, "the Reverend Virgil Swift," had hosted the Christian Youth Fellowship Conference that summer in Washington, to which "many thousands" of young Christians from all over North America had come. "For prayer and thanksgiving and to renew their pledge to Jesus" in the Temple Vale of the World Tabernacle of Jesus Christ.

All this was a riddle to me. Yet I believed that one day Minette would take pity on me and explain. When we spoke more easily together. When (somehow, I had no idea how) I had proved myself to Minette, that I might be trusted.

How happy I was, alone in our room on the third floor of Haven Hall!

Alone in our room and Minette away at class and I could examine the photographs arranged in a perfect arc on her desk. Never did I touch these photographs. I leaned close, my breath left a faint film on the glass, but I never touched. It made me smile to see mischievous little Jewel as a child of nine or ten, belling out her cheeks in a sassy grin, captive in frilly white in the company of stout black women in gaily colored dresses and remarkable flower-laden hats. Like upended upholstered chairs the women were, opulent in their flesh, richly made-up, while Jewel, renegade Jewel with whom I'd climbed the cobwebby staircase of the Underground Railroad, was wiry and restless as a monkey.

When I asked Minette about her sister she only just shrugged and made a face. "Ohhhh is that one *spoil*-ed!"

I stared at a photograph of the Swift family taken outdoors amid gorgeous red peonies. Minette and Jewel, Mr. and Mrs. Swift in Sunday clothes, beaming with pride. How strange it was to me, to see my roommate who so rarely smiled in my presence, smiling so happily! Minette was wearing the silky white graduation cap and gown and had removed her glasses for the picture. Her eyes were widened, myopic and beautiful. The black vertical gap between her two front teeth gave her a look of childlike innocence.

I had yet to meet that Minette. I had to wonder if I ever would.

The largest photograph on Minette's desk was of Reverend Virgil Swift in his preacher's robe that was shiny-black with brandy-colored stripes and what looked like a velvet hood, loose on his shoulders. Reverend Swift stood beside a pulpit, his massive head covered in graying nappy hair like wires. He exuded an air of both humility and strength. He reminded me of the carved prow of a Viking ship I'd once seen in a museum. His dark face was a beacon of light. His gold-rimmed glasses glittered in righteousness and his big-boned hands were uplifted in a gesture of welcome. Such a man would address you deep in your soul.

From such a man, you could not hide.

I wondered: if one day, Max Meade and Virgil Swift would meet and shake hands with each other. I wondered what they would say to each other. I wondered if they would include me in their conversation. I wondered if I would be there, to be included.

"Ohhh *damn*."

Minette muttered beneath her breath. Seems like, every time she tried to type now, her fingers made mistakes! She'd learned "perfect" touch-typing back in ninth grade. Now, she was forgetting where the keys were. She thought it had to do with her desk, where it was "situated."

When I offered to switch desks with her, Minette quickly agreed.

But as we began to switch our things, however, Minette suddenly changed her mind. " 'Scuse me? I'm thinking maybe *not*. If, maybe, it's meant for me to . . ." She swiped at her nose in a brusque, pained gesture.

I laughed at Minette's seriousness. I said it couldn't possibly matter which desk was hers, or mine.

I had been noticing Minette hunched at her desk, shoulders rounded and tense. The way, since the cracked window, she would glance up worriedly as if expecting an object to be hurtled through the glass onto her.

Minette shivered, and snuffled, and tugged at her tight-notched belt, and tried to laugh with me, not very convincingly.

She said, "Never mind. I better stay in one place."

I said, "But not because it's 'meant,' Minette. You can have my desk, we can trade anytime. You can just sit at my desk to study, if you want to, and I can study somewhere else. You can have my bedroom, we can switch if you want to." I heard myself becoming fanciful, I knew Minette had no interest in my bedroom. But I felt that pinprick of opposition in my room-mate, the obduracy of a child, that roused me to a kind of combat, for Minette's own good.

But no. Minette couldn't be reasoned with. Minette knew that things were "meant to be" and some things were a "test" of how you could take them.

There was weakness, and there was strength. Oh, in the smallest things!

"Do you believe that every day is a 'test,' Minette?"

Minette sniffed, fixing me a look confident as Reverend Virgil Swift's at the pulpit. "Every *day*? Every *minute*. Why'd you think, we are here on earth in *clock-time*?"

I asked Minette how else could we be here, except *clock-time*, and Minette said briskly, " 'That which hath been is now; and that which is to be hath already been.' " This was a reply I could not challenge for I had no idea what it meant.

It was clear, Minette felt uneasy in the study room. She began to suggest in her oblique, roundabout way that we study in the library after supper, but once we arrived there, Minette drifted off to sit alone at another table, as if we hadn't come together. She prowled the library stacks and disappeared into the downstairs lounge where vending machines sold soft drinks, potato chips, candy bars. I was hurt and annoyed that Minette ignored me in the library though she seemed grateful for my company on the way over, and especially when we returned to Haven Hall at about 10:30 P.M. The darkened and mostly deserted campus, the avenue of tall leafless plane trees, the over-bright bell tower of Schuyler Chapel that was illuminated through the night seemed to subdue and depress her. I wanted so badly to speak with Minette at such times when we were alone together yet not obliged to look at each other, when we were neither in one place nor in another, shivering with cold, I wanted to ask Minette about her life, her family, her Christian beliefs, what it might mean that a Jewish prophet of ancient times might "dwell" in your heart and might "save" you from "damnation"—but I dared not for I knew that I would blunder, and Minette would be offended. Though once, crossing the quadrangle with me, Minette pointed to a glaring-white full moon overhead, where shreds of cloud were being blown in fretful gusts, and said, "Used to be, I was a little girl I believed that was the eye of God, watching." She laughed, and shuddered. "The moon is a pagan idol, see. It's only pagan people believe in the moon." I thought of how Veronica would protest: we are born pagans! we are born without sin! Uneasily I said the moon was beautiful, no matter what it was or wasn't, and Minette drew away from me primly: " 'Scuse *me*. 'Beauty is the eye of the beholder.' "

Soon after, Minette ceased going to the library in the evening. She began to retreat to her bedroom shortly after dinner, changing into pajamas and her tightly belted navy blue wool flannel robe and bedroom slippers, as early as 9 P.M. Sometimes she left her door ajar as if to invite me to witness her hunched over books and papers spread across her bed, a look of fierce and pained concentration on her face, though if I called to her, tried to speak with her, she was likely to shrug without replying. If she shut her door I was given to understand that Minette didn't want me to intrude upon her privacy even to call out good night.

One morning when I was alone in our study room and sunlight flooded through the window above Minette's desk I saw a trail of small black ants making their way across the floor. From out of a crack beneath the radiator they appeared. In the old house in Chadds Ford it often happened that ants "appeared" in similar marching formations out of cracks between floorboards or lighting fixtures. I watched as the ants made their way up a leg of Minette's desk. Into one of the drawers. I hesitated not knowing if I should open the drawer. Minette would be upset if I touched anything of hers as I'd learned the first week of school when I'd brought her mail upstairs for her. Another girl on our floor had brought one of Mrs. Swift's packages upstairs to Minette, and Minette had not liked such "familiarity."

Yet Minette hated insects. She would be horrified to discover ants in her desk drawer drawn by her hoarded food, which was itself meant to be secret.

I approached Minette's desk slowly and with misgivings. Cautiously I opened the drawer steeling myself for what was inside: something wrapped in paper napkins from the dining hall, swarming with ants. There were small scattered packets of ketchup, sugar. There was a tin that probably contained baked goods, sent by Minette's mother, but the ants didn't seem to have gotten inside this, only a few trailed across the cover.

Ugh! I came close to gagging. I wanted to shut the drawer, pretend I had not seen. If I left the room, Minette would return at noon and discover the ants for herself.

Quickly I put on leather gloves and removed the offensive object, that damned French toast, tossed it into my paper bag–lined wastebasket, managed to kill every ant in sight (so many!) by squashing them in tissues and dropping the tissues into the wastebasket, carried the wastebasket down two flights of stairs to toss into the Dumpster behind Haven House.

On my way back upstairs, a friendly girl on the second floor asked, "Is something wrong, Genna? You're looking *stark*."

I laughed. *Stark* was how you feel interrupted in the midst of William Blake's *Songs of Innocence and Experience* by a sudden need to kill ants.

I would not tell Minette, I thought. Unless she asked me about having gone into her desk drawer. Unless she confronted me, intruding into her privacy.

I would spare my roommate embarrassment and I would spare myself.

Yet Minette's words continued to haunt me like a riddle of long-ago that has never been explained.

What good. They will only. Again.

What is it like to be a descendant of heroic individuals? Do you share in their stature, or are you diminished by it? Do you share in their idealism? their courage? their faith? Do you imagine that you can know them? Do you measure your life against theirs? Have you become a better person because of them?

The Norton Anthology of American Literature

" 'Scuse*me?*"

Tremulous and indignant Minette Swift stood in the doorway of my bedroom. She was holding the heavy paperback anthology with the tissue-thin pages that was required for our American literature course, which looked as if it had been dropped in mud and kicked about.

It was a rainy evening in October. It was several weeks after the incident of the cracked window.

I asked Minette what had happened to her book and she said that was what she wanted to know: "What's *goin on here.*"

When she was excited, Minette spoke with an accent. She spoke with childish urgency and not in her normally poised and somewhat disdainful manner.

Only rarely did Minette call me "Genna." Though I called her "Minette" often for it was a melodic name in my ears. If she required my attention she would clear her throat and murmur " 'Scuse*me?*" sometimes politely, sometimes not.

I had no idea what Minette meant. I could see that she was upset, her textbook had been damaged. I stared at the torn pages smeared with mud.

"Oh, Minette. What happened?"

" 'What happened'? Maybe you know?"

"I . . . I don't know."

" 'Scuse me then, who would know?"

Was Minette accusing me of damaging her textbook? I was shocked, my voice faltered. I could not follow Minette's words that were rapid and incoherent but there was no mistaking the fury in her eyes. I was made to recall those times I'd unwisely caught a basketball tossed to me in gym class, immediately an aggressive guard rushed at me hoping to throw me off balance.

The previous day, Minette had been upset to discover that her copy of the *Norton Anthology of American Literature* was missing. She had not known if she'd left it in a classroom or in the library or in the dining hall, for Minette often misplaced things; or if someone had taken it. She'd been frantic with worry, as I had never seen her before. Saying her parents would be "furious" with her, they had not believed how expensive college text-books were, she'd had to explain on the telephone and finally mail copies of receipts from the bookstore. . . . I'd gone out with Minette to look for the book, but without luck. I'd told her that she was welcome to use my copy, for we were enrolled in the same course, but now Minette was telling me she'd found it after all, in the alley behind our residence—"Just layin' there in the damn mud. Like, you know what?—somebody tossed it out a window. For meanness."

Which window? My window? (My bedroom window, a small squat window about the size of a porthole, overlooked this alley. I saw Minette staring at it.)

I was hurt, incredulous. "Minette, it wasn't me! How can you think it might be me!"

"Nobody sayin *you*, is there? Did I say *you*?"

Minette laughed, unexpectedly. When she had me cowed, she took mercy on me.

A week after the cracked window, Minette finally thanked me for re-porting it. For several days after the ants she'd said nothing until suddenly she abruptly thanked me for "cleaning out some mess" in her desk drawer she'd "totally forgotten." (There was no mention of ants. But I know Minette discovered a few, and deduced what had happened.)

Still my voice was faint, faltering. Minette had the power to make me feel guilty, no matter how unjustly. Not since grade school in Chadds Ford had I been so aggressively confronted by someone my own age. "I'm so sorry, Minette. I can't imagine who might have—"

"Can't, huh? You sayin you *can't*?"

"But why on earth would—"

"You tell me 'why.' Seems you know so much, you tell *me*."

In fact I could imagine: Minette had made herself generally disliked in Haven House and elsewhere on campus, for her fiercely outspoken and independent ways. She'd snubbed friendly overtures and spoken out bluntly in situations where others spoke more diplomatically or evasively. She had stomped on the floor of our study room, to protest loud music in the room below; her sharp ears could detect noise in the most remote room in the house. Reverend Virgil Swift was obviously her model: I could hear the cadences of the man's deep-booming voice in Minette's voice, and I could see the furrow of his brow in Minette's way of frowning when others spoke. I guessed that Reverend Swift valued truth-telling above the genial hypocrisies of ordinary conversation, like Minette, and that he, too, in the way of his model Jesus Christ, did not suffer fools gladly. Minette had a way of vehemently agreeing with you—"Yes! That is so!"—that sounded mocking, though it was sincere, like her way of demanding, "*Is* it so?" Minette had been on her award-winning high school debate team and had learned to deliver her opinions in a forceful manner intended to intimidate. At the start of the semester Minette had so impressed most of us in Haven House that we'd elected her as our representative to student government, an impulsive act some of us later regretted. Since then, Minette had had disagreements with a number of girls in Haven Hall and had resigned her position. Especially, several black girls in the residence were ambivalent about Minette Swift who astonished them with her arrogance.

It was possible that, if Minette had left her textbook somewhere, one of these girls might have hidden it, as a prank. There were sixteen girls in the residence beside Minette and me and some of them weren't above practical jokes.

Yet I tried to defend them to Minette. It was a hapless role I'd found myself in at the Cornwall Academy, trying to mediate between feuding girls. Minette laughed sharply: "Girl, you don't know the devil's ways. The 'worm of iniquity' in the heart. Recall how the devil tempted Eve, and Eve succumbed to evil, and paradise was lost, out of ignorance. Shhhh!" Minette shook her head, my naiveté was laughable.

In that instant, of bemused contempt for me, I heard my father's voice. It was the most subtle intonation, yet unmistakable. For this was the preacher's manner and you had no way to refute it. You were naive, ignorant, a child. In those days in the house in Chadds Ford, there was a shifting population of strangers who'd lived with us, for varying periods of time. Mattresses on bare floorboards on the third floor, sleeping bags scattered through the rooms. Like black-bristly-haired Ansel the strangers had been mostly young though they had not always looked young. Some were distraught, physically ravaged and ill. Some dared to question Max Meade's authority and had to be refuted.

Minette lost patience with me. Taunting, "*Is* that so! Think I'm some kind of *fool!*" She stalked off into her room and slammed the door behind her.

I was shaken. I could not believe this encounter. There had never been any hostility between Minette and me in the past for I was eager to placate my roommate and circumnavigated any possibility of a confrontation. Yet now she'd glared at me with a look of contempt.

I had not become accustomed to emotional outbursts in the house in Chadds Ford, though I'd frequently witnessed them. *Is this real, or is this make-believe? Should I run away and hide, should I be frightened? Should I laugh?*

The torn and mud-splotched *Norton Anthology of American Literature* lay on our study room floor where Minette had thrown it. I picked it up to examine the damage. Of the nearly three thousand small-print pages probably less than fifty were mutilated beyond repair. I carried the book into the bathroom out in the hall and cleaned away the worst of the mud with wetted toilet paper. Those pages that weren't too badly ripped, I mended with Scotch tape. The cover was luridly water stained so I fashioned a new, sturdier cover out of stiff paper. I was proud of my handiwork, that reminded me of an elementary school project, and left it on Minette's desk where, when she emerged sullen and glowering from her bedroom later that evening, she would discover it.

" 'Scuseme, what's *this?*"

I was hunched over my desk trying to write a five-page report for Sociology 101. Our text was the hardcover *Social Basis of Individual Behavior*. The platitudes of sociology seemed to me neither true nor false though I understood that, to get a high grade in the course, I had to seem to agree with the professor whose criticism of "bourgeois twentieth-century culture" was a restrained echo of Maximilian Meade's more extreme criticism. Through a headache-haze I saw Minette standing in front of her desk, staring at the mended textbook, hands on her hips, head flung back, frowning.

"Like this makes some diff'rence! Like this means nobody stole my property and vandalized it out of meanness! *That's what you're trying to tell me?*"

I did not know what to say. I tried to imagine what I would feel if something of mine had been so damaged. *But I am white, it could not be the same thing.*

I told Minette she could use my anthology whenever she wanted to. Or, we could trade books. Minette snorted in derision: "Could be they will mess up your book, too, Genna. Then what?"

Genna! The name, unexpected in Minette Swift's husky alto voice that quavered with indignation, thrilled me like a caress.

Safe House

Is our house a *safe house*? I asked Daddy.

Oh, I wasn't really that young any longer to ask such a question of Daddy! I was ten, at least.

Asking my father in a little-girl pretense of not knowing he would be upset by it. A pretense of not knowing he would blame my mother.

Already I knew: there were *safe houses* you could drive to from our house in Chadds Ford if you were very careful. There was a *safe house* that was a farm somewhere called Altoona and there was a *safe house* that was a farm somewhere called Port Alleghany. Our house in Chadds Ford was not a *safe house* because it was under surveillance (by the enemy) and had been raided more than once.

I had not been in the house at that time. Rickie either. Daddy had taken us to stay with relatives in Rittenhouse Square.

Still I asked, Is it, Daddy? Is our house a *safe house*?

A look in Daddy's face wanting to grab, shake, shout.

But Daddy said, Yes of course our house is safe, Genna. What a silly question, aren't you a silly little girl.

And Daddy said, You know that your daddy will keep you safe in this house or any other house. You know that sweetie, don't you?

Not a little girl really. A shrewd fifth-grader who'd learned the mean trick of making Daddy shout at Mommy to punish Mommy who was bad.

Yes-sss, Daddy, I said. I think so.

Daddy stooped to kiss me. His jaw was scratchy where he had not shaved and his breath smelled like a heated oven where something has burnt. Almost, as Daddy kissed me, Daddy was walking out of the room and his footsteps were heavy on the stairs. And overhead in the hall seeking out the bathroom where Mommy lay dozing in tepid bathwater her head fallen forward like a doll with a broke neck.

When Max Meade spoke in righteous anger his voice was hoarse, harsh. His voice was furious like dried reeds whipped in the wind.

What the fuck have you been telling her, are you crazy what have you been saying she has overheard, you and your junkie boyfriend, and Veronica was wakened protesting, Nothing! Not a fucking thing, what would I know of your fucking life, I'm not the woman to ask am I?

Safe house. Saying the words to myself in secret. For *safe house* made me smile. *Safe house* made me feel warm. *Safe house* was something small you could hide in, I thought. Like a dollhouse where if you were small enough to fit inside you would be so small nobody would come looking for you.

Suspicion

Now through Haven House there was *suspicion*.

And where there is suspicion, there must be *suspects*.

"Minette has not suggested that she thinks you had anything to do with her textbook being 'vandalized' but Minette has suggested that you might know something about who did it, and why."

These words. I stared in dismay at our resident advisor Dana Johnson who'd summoned me downstairs to speak with her. Ms. Johnson was a big-boned woman in her early thirties with hair clipped so short her head was made to appear disproportionately small on her elongated body like a Henry Moore sculpture. She had a blunt beige face and ice pick eyes. She was an assistant professor of anthropology as well as our RA and her field was, rumor had it, aboriginal cannibal tribes of the African Congo.

"But I explained to Minette . . . I don't know."

"Yes, Genna. But Minette has told me adamantly that she believes you do know, you're 'protecting' one or more of the others."

Dana Johnson paused, delicately. *Genna* was gently yet firmly uttered in the way of a patient elder addressing a recalcitrant child.

Ms. Johnson was Caucasian, and edgy-apologetic; she chose her words with care, as if they were being taped; she had to know that she herself was under scrutiny, if not exactly suspicion, since Minette had reported her to the dean of students in early October as "wishy-washy"—"irresponsible"—after Minette had complained to Dana Johnson several times of noise in the residence and our third-floor bathroom "like a pigsty" some days.

I told the woman *no*. I was not protecting anyone.

"Well, Genna. I know. I mean, I know what you have told me. But, you see, Minette strongly believes . . ."

Here was an adult woman, an instructor at Schuyler College, intimidated by my eighteen-year-old freshman roommate. I listened to her not knowing how to reply. To protest *I am not a liar* in the shabby-comic way of our disgraced ex-president protesting *I am not a crook*? Ms. Johnson had assured me that this was to be a conversation, not an interrogation, but it had the feel of an interrogation, passing in a haze of anxiety, confusion. I could only repeat stubbornly that I did not know anything about Minette's damaged textbook except what Minette had told me, and Ms. Johnson could only repeat in her careful way that Minette seemed to have "reason to believe" that I did know. Minutes passed excruciatingly as hours, the two of us locked together as in a very small cell.

Dana Johnson was liked if not loved in Haven House. Respected if not admired. It was speculated that she was a lesbian (of course) and yet, she did not "behave" like a lesbian; in her classes, she did not emphasize gender, and was said to be as "objectively critical" of matriarchical societies as patriarchical. Her usual clothes were khaki trousers, fresh-pressed shirts beneath pullover sweaters, square-toed boots. Her hands and feet were unusually elongated. Her voice, in times of stress, sounded like a scratched record.

Ms. Johnson was new at Schuyler, and uncertain. Of the eighteen girls in Haven House she had cultivated no favorites. Out of a kind of adult shyness she had cultivated no friends. She would have no strong supporters if Minette Swift made trouble for her. Yet, if she sided too emphatically with Minette, she would alienate the rest of us. In the past I had been on good terms with Dana Johnson, who was clearly most comfortable with girls of my type: quiet easy-smiling good-natured girls with no evident urges to break rules, behave rebelliously. Because Dana Johnson was new at Schuyler, I had good reason to think she knew nothing of my Meade family background.

Now I was beginning to distrust her, and fear her. I resented it that she chose to take Minette Swift's word over mine even as I understood why she might make such a choice. Not once had Ms. Johnson said *Your roommate is black. Of course she feels vulnerable. We, in our white skins, what can we possibly know . . . !*

There was logic in this. Maximilian Meade had written in the 1960s of the distortions of "skin-consciousness": how what we see is largely determined by who we are as what we know of the world is largely determined by the linguistic structures into which we are born. I knew, I understood! If you believe *Some truths are lies* you must believe *Some lies are truths*. Yet I could not tell Dana Johnson what she was pushing me to admit. She was asking me to "suggest" the names of the girls who might have wished to hurt my roommate and I could not oblige her.

Our conversation, that was not an interrogation, lurched and skidded to a halt. We were in the RA's sitting room, a quaintly furnished parlor of bygone years. It was late afternoon, Haven House was near-deserted. Dana Johnson had prepared coffee and set out a plate of Pepperidge Farm cookies in the elaborately fussy way of one unaccustomed to "entertaining" but the coffee and cookies remained untouched. My tongue felt too big for my mouth, numbed as if with Novocain.

Of course there were girls in Haven House more likely than others to have taken Minette's textbook but I wasn't about to name them. Singling out any individual—Diane, Trudi, Crystal, Lisette—would be cruel, unjust. Unethical. Illogical. For even if I spoke sincerely, I might be mistaken. Once a name was uttered, once Dana Johnson wrote it down and passed it on to the dean of students . . . From my parents I knew of the "campaign of terror" of Senator Joseph McCarthy in the 1950s, and I knew of FBI "infiltrations" and "investigations" into the civil rights and anti-Vietnam War movements of the 1960s, I knew what a mistake it was to cooperate, and how seductive.

As I was leaving, Dana Johnson touched my shoulder: her large long ungainly hand light as air. In a lowered voice she said, "You don't think that your roommate has imagined any of this, do you, Genna?"

Genna. It was a caress of a name.

"You can tell me, Genna. This is a confidential matter, I promise."

Confidential! Of course it wasn't.

I did not think that Minette had consciously imagined anything, yet I was not convinced that anyone had deliberately taken her book and "vandalized" it. Vaguely I shook my head *no*. Politely easing my way past Dana Johnson, avoiding the woman's anxious eyes. Allowing her to interpret *no* any damned way she wished.

Suspects

There came to be in Haven House a smell as of subtly polluted air: *suspicion.*

Quickly word spread through the residence that something belonging to one of us had been "vandalized" and that there was a "racial element" involved. One by one the residents of Haven House were summoned to the RA's sitting room to be quizzed.

Not an interrogation only just a conversation.

Confidential! I promise.

In the flurry of rumor and speculation, in the wake of Minette Swift's refusal to speak of what had happened, details about the incident varied. The "missing"—"stolen"—"vandalized"—textbook was variously a math text, a sociology text, a lab book, an anthology of black poetry. The book had been dropped in mud, its pages had been torn and mutilated and defaced with racial slurs.

There was initial shock, there was sympathy for Minette, but there came to be doubt, disbelief. The most vocal residents were those who roomed on the third floor of Haven House and were well acquainted with Minette Swift.

"Are we 'suspects'? I can't believe this!"

"Nobody has said we're 'suspects.' Not exactly."

"But it's so petty! Someone loses a textbook, it winds up in the mud! I lose things all the time, I don't make a big deal of it."

"Well, this isn't you. It's Minette Swift."

Minette's most severe critic was a light-skinned black girl named Crystal Odom. The two had clashed several times, for Crystal had a personality as brash and unyielding as Minette, though Crystal was far warmer, funnier, more playful. Wickedly Crystal made her circle of admirers laugh with her imitations of Minette's dour frown, her haughty posture and way of walking heavily on her heels. Wickedly Crystal described Minette Swift as a minister's daughter—"A Ne-gro-minister-thinks-he's-Rev'nd-Martin-Luther-King, Jr.'s daughter oh *yessss*."

Crystal Odom had been valedictorian of her class at Stuyvesant High School in New York City. She was the only freshman on the Schuyler field hockey team. She was a chemistry major/theater minor. Her astonishing smoky penumbra of hair seemed to explode from her beautifully shaped head. Her eyes were wide-set, thickly lashed and mischievous. Often she was the only "minority person" in a group and played her role with zest. She had little patience for clichéd racial pieties. White-girl discomfort made her laugh as if she were being tickled. One of the tales she told of Minette Swift was of Minette's behavior in the campus singing group Bob-o-links, to which both Crystal and Minette belonged: "Oh my! Bragging she's been singing in this 'international tabernacle choir' since practically in diapers and never been 'critiqued.' Now, Minette has a nice-enough voice, not Marian Anderson but nice, which is to say about average for Bob-o-links, still that girl can't take the least bit of a suggestion from our director, flares up and gets all moody like all her life she's been told by Jesus Her Savior she's *perfect*."

We'd gathered in the first-floor lounge, one early evening before dinner. The mood of the house was scintillant, rowdy and aroused. If this mood had been a gas, the striking of a minuscule spark would have caused a violent explosion. By this time everyone in Haven House had been summoned to speak with Dana Johnson, served coffee and Pepperidge Farm cookies and assured that this was conversation, not an interrogation; nearly a week had passed since Minette had gone frantically searching for her *Norton Anthology of American Literature*. Yet nothing seemed to have been resolved, and Minette was scarcely speaking with anyone, including me. When I was asked what it was like to room with Minette Swift, I felt the collective wish of the group that I would expose her to their scorn, ridicule and mock her, but I said only that Minette was one of the most serious and hardworking people I knew and that she had been "very hurt" by what had happened.

It was a pious principle of my own at that time in my life. That I never utter any words about anyone in any circumstances that I would not utter in the presence of that person. And no exceptions even to make my friends laugh!

Crystal Odom, quick as on the hockey field wielding a stick, challenged me: "Exactly what did happen?"

I knew that Crystal would ask this. Or Trudi, or Diane. There was Lisette, and there was Midge, and there was Lisane staring at me. I said, "I don't know what 'happened' exactly but I saw the look on Minette's face when she showed me her book, the genuine hurt and anger. It was like Minette's soul had been mutilated, she was that upset."

(But was this so? Or was I inventing, improvising? I had not had the thought until this moment yet it seemed to me, as I uttered these dramatic words, that it was true, Minette was behaving as if her soul had been mutilated. Whether other people "liked" her was not important.)

"Someone might have taken Minette's book in the dining hall. Maybe." Lisane Kendall spoke doubtfully in the way of one trying to be fair-minded.

Sharply Crystal said, "Somebody from Haven House? One of *us*?"

"Well, not deliberately. By accident . . ."

" 'By accident' somebody picked up that heavy old book and carried it out not noticing it and when they did, instead of seeing whose book it was they trotted out behind the house here and dropped it in the mud and kind of *kicked it*? That's what you're saying?"

Crystal was a girl to arouse others to laughter. She was so funny in her scorn, rapid-fire and indignant in her delivery, you wanted badly to give in to her. But I said, "Crystal, it doesn't matter how it happened only that it did happen. I helped Minette look for that book, we went back to her classrooms and over to the dining hall, we looked around here, it was really missing! And she doesn't have much money—"

"So who does? This is Haven House not Shangri-la."

"—so it was cruel, whoever did it. I'm not saying it was one of us. But it was cruel, if it was meant as a joke it wasn't funny."

"*She's* the joke! Dropped and lost her own damn book, and wants to blame *us*."

"No. I don't think so."

I was stubborn. My voice was quavering. Now all the girls turned on me, protesting.

"Don't think what, Genna? Your roommate is imagining it all, or your roommate is plain-out lying?"

"Minette is *not lying*. She is *not*."

I had to leave, I was becoming upset. Childish tears sprang into my eyes. There was such a powerful yearning in me, to side with them, against Minette! You are made to understand the terrible yearning of the lynch mob at such a moment. You are made to understand your terrible weakness. How in the smallest matters, you can betray another's trust.

Blindly I left the room. On the stairs I overheard one of them say in a lowered voice, "Max'milian Meade's daughter, what can you expect?"

The others laughed. Crystal Odom's high-sparkling laughter rose distinctive as a fountain.

The wish to know another person fully is a way of appropriation, exploitation. It is a way of shame that must be repudiated.

Weeping

Those days. Nights. Like a moon battered by clouds my brain raced with unwanted thoughts.

If I have no soul! A soul even to be mutilated . . .

The wish to know another is a way of shame Max believed. For Max did not wish us to know him. Not even his children who were flesh of his flesh and spirit of his spirit not even us!

Yet I felt: if I could know a single other person, in a way that I had come to understand I could never know my father, my mother, my brother Rickie from whom we were estranged . . . If I could know Minette Swift.

Such thoughts we have on the brink of sleep. Drifting into sleep unaware. A thin frothy agitated sleep like surf breaking on a littered beach, and at once withdrawing back into the ocean. And in my sleep the slightest sounds were jarring. An airplane high overhead passing with excruciating slowness, mysterious vibrations and creakings in the old house. Through the makeshift plasterboard walls between our crypt-sized bedrooms the sounds of another girl's sibilant breathing, her unconscious mutterings and moans, snoring, an occasional startled-sounding snort that must have wakened her momentarily. And sometimes a sound of Minette praying. *Our Father who art in Heaven hallowéd be . . . Thy kingdom come thy will be . . .* Intimately I would come to know the very cadences and rhythms of my invisible roommate's praying voice, and this an unexpected voice of childlike yearning, a voice you would not identify as the assured public voice of Minette Swift.

Our Father, hal-low-éd, thy kingdom were stressed as in a poem, always in the same way.

Sometimes I heard a less definable sound. Initially I was not certain it could be Minette, I thought it might be a rattling of the steam radiator or a sound of plumbing, pipes. Then, pressing my ear against the plasterboard wall, I knew: Minette grinding her teeth, in her sleep.

A curious sound as of small pebbles being tossed together, grating. This was a nervous habit I'd been told as a child that I had myself, Veronica would wake me softly calling *Genna! You will wear out your teeth, baby.*

Those lost nights in the house in Chadds Ford when Veronica had been Mommy, concerned for her daughter's well-being.

Tonight in the third-floor room in Haven House after I'd run from the girls' laughter. Not even that their laughter was jeering or scornful but rather indulgent, amused. *Max'milian Meade's daughter what can you expect.* Sleepless listening to the sound of my roommate's bedsprings creaking a few feet away on the other side of the plasterboard wall knowing that Minette too was sleepless in the aftermath of crueller laughter. Then I realized that I was hearing another, more muffled sound: weeping.

I sat up in bed. I switched on my bedside lamp. It was only just 2 A.M., much earlier than I'd thought. Minette had disappeared into her bedroom sometime in the late evening while I'd been at a Film Society screening, when I'd returned to the room at midnight the light beneath her door was out.

Quietly I opened my bedroom door. It was very dark in our study room at the rear of Haven House. Minette's window looked out toward the sky but the sky was dense with clouds no moonlight could penetrate. There was no light beneath Minette's door and I could hear now more distinctly the sound of weeping, muffled against a pillow. I hesitated before knocking at the door.

"Minette . . . ?"

No answer. But the sound of weeping ceased.

Emergency?

Days shortened abruptly. The sky was visibly shrinking. Mornings were brittle cold. The Schuylkill which bounded the eastern edge of our sprawling hilly campus reflected leaden clouds. One November afternoon disintegrating like wet tissue to dusk by 4:30 P.M. there was a pink slip in my mailbox at Haven House. *Gena please call Verronica! Urgent!* Our names misspelled by whoever had taken the call in haste yet in the confusion of the moment I had the vague idea that my mother had misspelled our names herself in a Veronica-gesture of "anarchic playfulness."

My fingers shook as I dialed the old-fashioned rotary phone. I stood with my back to the doorway, that no one could observe my face. I shut my eyes as the phone rang in the house in Chadds Ford and continued to ring as in a coolly elegant European film of desolation in which the restless camera-eye moves through high-ceilinged sparely furnished rooms of a stately old mansion/mausoleum from which all life has departed yet still a telephone rings.

Mother damn you! Please answer.

Mother are you my mother please please answer.

It had to be an emergency and if an emergency, it had to be my father Maximilian Meade.

Max was dead, or dying. Heart attack, plane crash, murder.

Mad Max's life had been threatened many times. He'd been physically accosted, beaten. In the streets of Chicago during the Democratic National Convention of 1968, by Chicago police. Outside courtrooms. In hotel lobbies. In the street. His daughter was not supposed to know of such things and, if knowing, was forbidden to speak of them.

Max had a "tricky" heart, too. I did not know details. Health matters were private matters.

Intermittently for hours I would call home. I would listen to the phone ringing with stoic calm. Telling myself that so long as I did not know what the emergency was, what *urgent* meant, I had no reason to be frightened. I had no reason to think *That part of my life is ending: daughter*.

I had no idea where my father was. I had not spoken with Max for three weeks, two days. And then he'd been "away"—"traveling on business"— "meeting with a client in Montreal." (Among Max's scattered clients were U.S. draft dodgers, as they'd been called. Permanent exiles in Canada who would be arrested by federal agents if they returned to the United States.) At least once a week I spoke with Veronica on the phone and our exchanges were friendly, casual. Often, we laughed. In this new post-hippie/radical phase of my mother's life she'd begun to cultivate a Lucille Ball–style of droll delivery, 1950s sitcom where 1960s opera/tragedy had failed her. Our conversations evoked no emotion on either side. Our conversations were very different from, for instance, Minette Swift's conversations with her mother which were, on Minette's side at least, extremely subdued. *Uh-huh* Minette would murmur gripping the phone receiver tight against her ear her eyes heavy-lidded sighing and nodding *Yesss ma'am!* and rarely any laughter, that I overheard.

"If Max is Dad. I mean, if Max is dead. If . . ."

For *daughter* is a leash around the neck. *Daughter* is a thorn in the heart. *Daughter* is acid-anguish shaken in a bottle to foam and froth and spill over scalding your hand.

Now you are eighteen: no need to love them in such desperation.

That evening I did not go with the others to the dining hall. I moved upstairs to monitor the third-floor phone. When the phone rang, I answered it: numbly, I took messages: the calls were never for me. In Haven House residents did not have private phones, each floor shared a single phone. Haven House was the cheapest residence at Schuyler College and so we did not have private phones in our rooms. I approved of this, my parents approved of this. I would not know if my parents had bribed the college to admit me but I did know that they approved of Haven House for its frugality. There is spiritual merit in frugality, non-luxury. As my Quaker ancestors knew. There is merit only in character, integrity. There is merit in self-sacrifice. Most of the girls in Haven House, so far as I could determine, were Merit Scholars. Which meant girls from "disadvantaged" economic/academic backgrounds. I was eager to believe that I had come to seem one of them. My clothes, my demeanor, my behavior did not suggest entitlement, privilege. Set me beside Crystal Odom and you would unhesitatingly choose Crystal as the rich girl, Genna as the poor girl. I was liked by most of the girls in my residence, I think. By some, I was very well-liked. I was grateful to be liked, and I believe that I was a good friend. No one had ever said to me in bemused scorn *But you are Max'milian Meade's daughter, we know who you are!*

I was a friend to Minette Swift as well though Minette continued to hold herself at a guarded distance from me as from others in Haven House like a martyr who has forgiven her oppressors as a Christian principle if not in her heart. You wanted to protest *But I didn't do anything to hurt you, what is it I have done?*

We were made to feel guilty in Minette's sight. No explanation had ever been found for the missing/mutilated textbook but the wound was still raw. At our last house meeting Dana Johnson announced that Minette had resigned as Haven House rep to student government, Minette herself had stayed away. Even Crystal Odom shrank from confronting Minette, in person.

At about 9 P.M. when I was trying to call home another time, Minette passed by. I'd heard her ascending the steep stairs with a kind of angry dignity. Since September, Minette had gained weight: eight pounds, ten? There were new, raw-looking notches made with a scissors in Minette's shiny black leather belt. The waist band of her good gray flannel skirt no longer fit, I'd had a glimpse of her ingenuity in fastening it shut with linked safety pins hidden by a loose-fitting pullover sweater. Minette would have been stung with embarrassment if she'd known that I had seen but I was a sly one long practiced in not-seeing as I was practiced in not-hearing what was not meant for me to overhear.

Seeing me there, hunched over the phone like something broken, Minette paused. She was breathing hard from the stairs. Since the textbook incident, Minette carried a selection of her more expensive books with her in a backpack as if—I suppose this had to be the reason—for safekeeping. It was not like Minette to pause like this. It was not like Minette to acknowledge me outside our room. Yet now seeing in my pinched face a prospect of bad news, Minette paused waiting for me to glance up at her but I did not, I would not, like one trapped in quicksand I could not move my head, I was in thrall to the phone ringing unanswered in the house in Chadds Ford. Thinking *Please answer! Why are you punishing me!*

When finally I looked up, Minette was gone.

At least, after 11 P.M., the phone rang, and it was Veronica calling me.

By this time a desperate plan had shaped itself in my head: I would borrow money from Dana Johnson, I would take a taxi to Chadds Ford fifty miles away. The very place I'd been eager to escape, now I was desperate to return to. It did not seem to occur to me, or if it did I repelled it as unconsciously you repel a buzzing insect, that if Veronica wasn't answering the phone very likely Veronica wasn't home.

I was standing in the corridor outside Dana Johnson's door summoning the courage to knock. A wan light shone beneath the door, I could hear typing from an inner room. Since our awkward conversation (that had not been an interrogation) I had avoided Dana Johnson as others avoided her, out of resentment, or guilt. Yet I would have to borrow money from Ms. Johnson for the taxi ride, I had less than ten dollars in my wallet, and no credit card. (My parents did not approve of credit cards, seeing them as capitalist scams.) So I would have to humble myself to borrow money from a stranger. I would stammer, "My mother called with an 'urgent' message, now I can't reach her. I think something happened to my father . . ." It was my wish to believe that Dana Johnson had no idea who my family was in the way that, I was certain, Minette Swift had no idea.

Then, the telephone rang at the front desk a few feet away. The friendly proctor called over: " 'Generva Meade'? For you."

It was Veronica, agitated.

". . . Genna? Thank God! Tell me you didn't hear anything about your father . . ."

No, I said. I had not.

". . . because I think, Genna, I have reason to think, it will be all right, it won't be released, it will be kept out of the, what is the word, the media, Genna. I mean, I think so. I haven't spoken with Max directly. I didn't want you to hear about this from other sources, I didn't want you to be frightened, Genna, or anxious, because I think, I mean I hope, it will be all right. The latest I've heard it will be kept out of the media at least."

I asked Veronica what would be kept out of the media.

"Genna, that's it: I don't know. I mean, I don't know specifically, you know Max, Max communicates through intermediaries, you know what things are like." Veronica was speaking rapidly, her voice was excited, slurred, she sounded like a giddy drunken woman on a suddenly tilting platform trying to keep her balance. "No one can talk over any phone, our phones are 'bugged' Max says, that thin whistling sound, d'you hear it?— that's FBI 'surveillance.' I think I hear it, I mean I'm sure that I hear it. Though this should be a safe phone, though my God"—Veronica laughed, just having thought of it—"of course they'd 'bug' your residence, too: of course. Anyway Max wants you to know, he's anxious for you to"—but here a stranger's voice intruded, a man's voice, words not quite audible, and Veronica laughed nervously, there was an exchange between her and this intruding stranger, I saw Veronica fingering her tumbling-down hair glossy-black as the proverbial raven's wing, I saw Veronica's dilated eyes shining, and the flush in her face—"Max wants you to know *he is not arrested*, anyway not yet and possibly he won't be, if we are very lucky he won't be, he is in federal custody I think in Buffalo, stopped at the border, I'd thought he was in"—but again the voice intruded, perhaps it was more than one voice, there was another exchange, I heard muffled words that made no sense, and there came Veronica back on the line excited, breathless—"it wasn't at the border, he'd gotten back and they came for him in court, in federal court but he isn't 'arrested,' honey. The term for what he is, is, it's, what is it: 'material witness.' I think that's it. And I think that is all it is, Genna. If luck is on our side."

I asked Veronica what Max was a material witness to.

". . . I said, didn't I explain, honey, we can't talk about these matters on the phone. Because the fucking-fascist-FBI is wiretapping us! Illegally! Because—" There was a scuffling sound as if an unknown party was trying to take the receiver from Veronica, Veronica repelled him, her voice shrill in my ears like a rain of needles. "—my life is being ruined, my son has been taken from me, Gestapo persecuting us, Max Meade is an officer of the court and has never violated any law in his life and Veronica Hewett-Meade is totally out of the loop, never was in the loop, I have a new consciousness now, I believe that the revelation must come from within, I mean the revolution must come from within. There is no salvation in the masses. Believe me, I know, for I am of the 'masses' and I know. Only in the soul. So please I beg you *leave us alone*. Fucking Gestapo *leave us alone*."

Abruptly the line was disconnected. Veronica had begun to cry. Someone might have taken the receiver from her and slammed it down. When I called back immediately, the phone rang unanswered. And I thought I *don't know where she is. Where either of them are. Only where she says she is. And I don't know that, either.*

Blueberry

In the room on the third floor of Haven House with its faint smell exacerbated by damp of something rancid. In the twilight of a November afternoon. All day it had been raining. Not a glimmer of sun had appeared. I had not gone to my classes. I had not left the room. I had not washed my face, combed my hair out of my face, changed from my sour-smelling flannel nightgown. Minette came thumping into the room smelling of rain. Smelling of rain-sodden sneakers, grease-stiffened hair. " 'Scuse me?" Seeing me, startled. Minette had perhaps seen me in more or less the same position, the same posture, when she'd left for classes that morning. It was not like Minette to take such note of me. She switched on the overhead light and stared. I winced and hid my face. I told her I was all right, I was tired and didn't want to talk. Minette made a *tsk*ing sound with her lips. Minette was a medley of irksome sounds: mutterings, mumbles, exaggerated sighs, humming, singing, and of course praying, grinding-teeth, occasional weeping. Minette switched off the overhead light. Minette padded into her bedroom and switched on the light there, which gave to our shared room a wan ghostly comforting light. The other day, Minette had carried upstairs cradled and half-hidden against her breasts one of her mother's zealously wrapped packages. It was Minette's custom to open these packages from home inside her bedroom with the door shut. I knew that scissors were required, I knew it could not be an easy task, to open Mrs. Swift's packages that were crisscrossed with adhesive and masking tape. I had smelled something yeasty, sugary: baked goods. But I had not been allowed to see what was inside the package of course. But now, sighing and muttering to herself, Minette emerged from her bedroom carrying a tin of about eight inches in diameter, held it out to reveal to me a half-dozen muffins inside, in neat fluted waxed paper.

The smell was overwhelming. I thanked Minette and told her I was not hungry.

"Hell girl you are *not*."

It was more a grunt than a command. We sat in the twilight of our shared study and ate. The muffins were blueberry, and the blueberries were still moist. The muffins were delicious. We sat close together, we ate blueberry muffins and listened to the rain.

Part / II

. . . so good for Genna to have such a friend, to be exposed to unique individuals not racial stereotypes.

Black Girl/White Girl

Minette Swift born April 11, 1956/
Generva Meade born April 13, 1956

Minette Swift born in Washington, D.C./
Generva Meade born in Chadds Ford, PA.

Minette Swift: five feet five inches/
Generva Meade: five feet six and a half inches

Minette Swift: (approximately) 140 pounds/
Generva Meade: (approximately) 105 pounds

Minette Swift's parents: Virgil Duncan Swift and Lorett
    Sweet Swift/
Generva Meade's parents: Maximilian Elliott Meade and
    Veronica Hewett-Meade

Minette Swift: one sister, Jewel, born 1961
Generva Meade: one brother, Richard ("Rickie"), born
    1951

Minette Swift's religion: Christian
Generva Meade's religion:——

Minette Swift's church: Temple Vale of the World
    Tabernacle of Jesus Christ, Washington, D.C.
Generva Meade's church:——

Minette's Bible. A large Bible, and heavy. Bound in soft white simulated leather stamped with gold-gilt, pages edged in gilt. A "special Bible" printed to be sold in Reverend Swift's Tabernacle containing sixteen full-color illustrations, maps of the Holy Land in the Time of Jesus ("Canaan, as Divided Among the Twelve Tribes," "The Dominions of David & Solomon," "The Kingdoms of Judah & Israel," "Palestine in the Time of Christ," "Babylonia, Assyria: Countries of the Jewish Captivities," "The Journeys of St. Paul in the region of the Great Sea, or the Mediterranean"), and a three-page large-print appendix describing the history of the Temple Vale of the World Tabernacle of Jesus Christ, founded in 1958 in Washington, D.C., by the Reverend Virgil Duncan Swift.

This Bible! The Holy Word of God! Covertly and with a pang of envy I observed Minette reading it several times a day and always before going to bed; reading with scrupulous attention, head bowed, forehead furrowed, her lips shaping silent words. Why doesn't Minette read the Bible to me? I wondered. Don't Christians wish to convert heathens?

Minette's Bible whose gilt-edged pages spilled in a dazzling waterfall when riffled.

Minette's Bible that slipped through my stealthy fingers as I lifted it from her desk one day when I was alone in the room, and unobserved; slipped from my fingers and fell, hard, as if in rebuke, striking a sharp corner against my foot.

Whoso eateth my flesh, and drinketh my blood, hath eternal life: and I will raise him up at the last day. A cannibal religion, Max believed it. And the Holy Word of God, the so-called Hebrew Bible clumsily conjoined with the so-called New Testament, an anthology of lunatic scribblings of no more scientific, historic, moral or spiritual significance than a slew of comic books.

Yet I was mistaken to think that Minette Swift was "merely" Christian.

Our first Sunday at Schuyler College, several girls in the residence invited Minette to join them for chapel, and when Minette returned to our room afterward she was incensed: "That 'chaplain'! Some messy-gray-haired woman! Homely old horse like something left out in a field, who'd take her word for anything even the good news of the Lord!" Minette puffed out her cheeks making a snorting-derisive noise.

Ever after when Minette was invited to chapel she shook her head vehemently as if insulted. "Why'd I want to do *that*."

Minette was homesick for her father's church. She was homesick for the Temple Vale Choir in which in "gleaming-white robes" she'd been singing since the age of ten.

"A church like ours, there is a purpose to it. You feel that purpose when just you step inside. Jesus is waiting!"

I never attended services in the Schuyler Chapel but sometimes in one of my undefined moods (melancholy? wistful? yearning? in dread of the future?) I entered quietly to sit alone in one of the hardwood pews; in a place of austere white walls and windows of plain glass brooding in that Quaker region of the soul that is wordless silence, wonderment.

No one was waiting for me in the Schuyler Chapel and yet I was happy there, so long as I remained silent, wordless and unthinking I was happy. *I am not homesick. I am free of home!*

Most Sunday mornings Minette dressed eagerly for church and was gone before 9 A.M. She hummed to herself, primping her stiff helmet of hair, tugging at her panty hose. Sometimes I watched for my roommate from the window above her desk, seeing her burly figure two storeys below; always she was alone, walking swiftly away, down-looking, aloof and indifferent to her surroundings. I took some small satisfaction in assuming that Minette would have no companion. Schuyler College was just outside the small town of Schuylersville, there were several churches there but when I asked Minette which was the one she attended her gaze became evasive behind the lenses of her glasses and she mumbled something not-quite-audible that might have been *This church I found*.

"Is it anything like your father's church?"

Now Minette looked at me frankly, laughing: "Like my daddy's Tabernacle? Nooo, ma'am!"

Yet if I asked Minette about the Tabernacle, or the Temple Vale as she sometimes called it, her answers were vague and brief. Not that she was embarrassed or annoyed but simply uninterested in explanations.

Because I am white? I wondered. *A white girl?*

Maximilian Meade had written in the 1960s that "skin-consciousness" determines vision. Virtually all Caucasians are born blind, even those who are victims of capitalism, we must be educated to *see*.

I envied Minette Swift her Christian faith for it was a special faith. Her God was a special God whose omnipotence she did not care to dilute by sharing it with just anyone.

Naively I asked, "But is there heaven, Minette?" and Minette replied with a prim downturn of her mouth, as if such a silly question must have an ulterior, occluded meaning, "Why sure there's heaven! Only not for *everybody*."

As Minette rarely called me "Genna" so Minette never asked about my family. And this not out of discretion like others at Schuyler College but out of indifference. I was embarrassed to recall how, at the start of the semester, I'd worried that my roommate might be suspicious of the name "Generva Meade." The Swifts' guided tour through Elias Meade House had passed in a haze of boredom for Minette, I now realized.

Yet, perversely, I often tried to speak to Minette about my family. I heard myself confide in her that the Meades had once been Quakers but that was decades ago, before I was born; now, even those relatives who were Christians (most of them older, female relatives of my father's) belonged only nominally to congregations but rarely went to church: "I mean, an actual church. A building."

Minette puckered her forehead, trying to envision this. For how'd you go to any church that wasn't a building?

I said, "Mostly they believe in the here-and-now, and 'humankind.' Not any God outside of time but 'the betterment of mankind' by social and political means."

Minette smiled but did not laugh. A certain wistfulness in my voice seemed to have stirred her sympathy, or pity. She said, "Y'mean like the United Nations, I guess? That kind of speeches, talking . . ."

Max Meade despised the United Nations as a capitalist/bourgeois front but it was fair to suggest that my less radical/liberal-Democrat relatives "believed in" the United Nations in the vague way in which most Americans "believe in" the United Nations without knowing or wishing to know more about it.

"Yes," I said. "Like the United Nations. Speeches and talking but sometimes sanctions, too. Sometimes military actions."

"Well," Minette said, in a way of offering me solace even as she closed the subject, "the United Nations *is* a building. In New York City."

Minette Swift called home often, Generva Meade called home rarely.

It was at about 8 P.M. on Sundays and Wednesdays that Minette called home, as well as at other, unscheduled times through the week. There was no customary time for me to call home.

When Minette called home, someone answered. Often when I called home, no one answered.

On the phone, Minette was surprisingly childlike. She was subdued, docile. She had an air of one being instructed. She nodded vehemently, her responses were mumbled *Uh-huh, uhhh-huh.* If you passed by Minette at the telephone table on the third-floor landing she would take no notice of you, frowning and staring at the floor, in rapt obedience to the parental voice in her ear. After the Norton anthology was taken from her and vandalized, and after midterms, Minette was on the phone as frequently as twice a day, speaking with her mother. (I think it was Mrs. Swift with whom Minette spoke, in her distress. Truly, I tried not to eavesdrop!) During these conversations with her mother Minette sounded like a hurt little girl; she was whiny, sarcastic, sullen; resentful, defiant; she'd received low exam grades in English, math, and biology, and only just C's in her other courses; yes, she'd gone to speak with her instructors; no, they refused to raise her grades . . . Minette half-sobbed in anger, frustration. And then she was silent for a long time, listening to her mother.

After the ordeal of calling the house in Chadds Ford so many times in a single evening, dialing the number another time would have made me physically ill and so I did not dial it again for weeks. Veronica had given me a "tentative number" for Max with a 716 area code meaning Buffalo, New York, but when I dialed this number a smug recorded voice informed me *The number you have dialed is not currently in service will you please check your information and dial again.* Veronica tried to call me several times since that night, pink slips were left in my mailbox but the pink slips were not marked *Urgent!* and so I did not call Veronica back.

I wondered if my parents were separated. If "separated" was a word in the vocabulary of their marriage.

For days I awaited news of Maximilian Meade's arrest. I awaited headlines RADICAL LAWYER "MAD MAX" MEADE TAKEN INTO CUSTODY BY FBI. In a trance of dread I attended classed faithfully, I wrote my midterm papers and studied for exams. Since elementary school Generva Meade had been a "good" student and such zombie-goodness did not fail me now. I did not seek out news of course, I avoided TV and newspapers. It seemed to me that people were observing me in Haven House and on campus but I smiled at them as if nothing were wrong of course. For years I had known or half-known that my father Maximilian Meade was a target of FBI harassment for his pro bono defense of Vietnam War conscientious objectors and so-called draft dodgers and his involvement with such high-profile radicals as the Berrigan brothers, the Roman Catholic priests who'd been arrested numerous times in the 1960s for sabotaging draft offices, destroying draft files. Max was one of a cadre of lawyers who'd defended antiwar protestors indicted on felony charges after the "Days of Rage" in Chicago, October 1969. And there were outstanding warrants against Ansel Trimmer and others personally associated with Max, who'd stayed in the house at Chadds Ford. But I'd thought, or wanted to think, that since the end of the Vietnam War and the reaction of American public opinion against the war, the harassment of people like my father had ended. . . . Though as Max had said in one of his gloomy/defiant moods *It will never end, they will hunt me for my hide and eat my heart if they can.*

In my fantasy of dread there came Dana Johnson to summon me to her sitting room where mugs of steaming coffee and a platter of now-stale Pepperidge Farm cookies would be set out. So many times I'd rehearsed Ms. Johnson's somber words *Genna I'm afraid I have bad news for you* it seemed to me that this had already happened.

But no news came of Maximilian Meade. Not from Dana Johnson or any other source.

Minette Swift was a Merit Scholar at Schuyler College, her parents would pay less than $500 for her academic year. Generva Meade had no scholarship, her parents would pay $4,000.

Minette Swift confessed she'd never heard of Schuyler College before her high school guidance counsellor encouraged her to apply, Generva Meade had been hearing of Schuyler College all her life.

Minette confided in me proudly that her father had graduated with "top honors" at the Towson Bible Institute in Towson, Maryland. Her mother had been a registered nurse before getting married. Her favorite uncle had been a U.S. Army major wounded in Vietnam, he'd been "decorated" with several medals. Of her numerous cousins, aunts and uncles, Minette was the first to graduate from high school with a "real" diploma. Of course she was the first to attend college. There was jealousy of her among the relatives, you had to expect: "The wise man builds his house upon the rock, the foolish man builds his house upon the sand. But see, the foolish man has got to blame somebody else for his folly."

Minette laughed, a rare raucous belly laugh that made me want to laugh, too.

Wise man. Foolish man. Rock, sand.

So simple! So clear.

Minette was proud of having received a "half dozen" scholarship offers from various colleges and universities she'd applied to, including Howard University, the "famous Negro school." It was Reverend Swift's decision that she come to Schuyler College which had such a "special reputation" it would be easier for her to be admitted to Georgetown Law School afterward.

I congratulated Minette on the scholarship offers. I told her I was happy she'd decided to come to Schuyler instead of Howard, and Minette shrugged. "Ohhh well, Howard, the money was itty-bitty. Here, it's more'n three times that. And the people here, that dean of admissions lady, she talks to you like you are *special*."

As a child I'd been taught to say "black"—"Afro-American"—"African-American"—but never "Negro." (And never "colored"!) Yet here was dark-skinned Minette Swift uttering "Ne-gro" with casual dignity as one might utter the name of an exotic foreign country: Nigeria, Ethiopia, Zaire.

In fact everything that Minette took the trouble to name in her throaty alto voice was exotic to my ears while my own voice seemed to me ever more hesitant, papery-thin.

Bob-o-link! Bob-o-link!
Roused by dawn's first gold!

Of Schuyler's several singing groups, Bob-o-links was the oldest (founded 1898) and the most exclusive (never more than twenty girls). They sang a cappella. They sang with the zest of girl marchers. They sang five-part harmony like marchers on five levels of stairs simultaneously. They sang with expression and they sang with "spirit." They sang at holiday concerts and at college fund-raisers where guests were wealthy alumnae and potential donors. By tradition, the head of the Music School directed Bob-o-links. The boast was that competition was cutthroat to be admitted but once you were in, you were a Bob-o-link for life. The group's repertory was varied: unabashedly sentimental songs by Stephen Foster, Irving Berlin, and Cole Porter, traditional ballads and blues numbers, protest and folk songs. Their delicately phrased signature song had been composed by a Schuyler College music student in 1911:

Bob-o-link! Bob-o-link!
Roused by dawn's first gold!
Sing of spirit mysteries yet untold!

Embrace Schuyler's sisters in thy fold!
Bob-o-link! Bob-o-link!

This song, cloying-sweet and numbingly repetitive, was a personal favorite of Minette's which she sang often in the room as if oblivious of my presence.

It isn't as if she doesn't see me. But for Minette, I don't exist.

I wondered what Max would make of my roommate: a black girl who doesn't much care that she's black, and doesn't care at all for your caring.

Minette's voice was a husky, rich alto with a tendency to go sharp when she sang loudly or aggressively. In an edgy mood Minette was physically restless; pushed and shoved things about; slammed drawers shut, dropped books, yanked and thudded and grunted and all the while sang, or loudly hummed. Fresh from a Bob-o-links rehearsal, Minette would sing one of their songs; after a while lapsing into one of her more familiar tabernacle choir hymns like "The Old Rugged Cross" and "Faith of Our Fathers." Minette sang without listening to herself, perhaps to comfort herself. At my desk, trying to work, I had trouble concentrating, yet I hesitated to leave the room, not wanting Minette to think I was annoyed by her for in fact I wasn't annoyed, only distracted. It seemed to me a kind of privilege, to be in Minette's presence and yet invisible to her, as if I were a family member of hers, taken utterly for granted. I loved music, I would have loved to be able to sing like Minette, yet my love did not translate into musical ability.

Vaguely I planned: Max would visit me sometime, and his visit would coincide with a Bob-o-links performance. He would meet Minette Swift my roommate and closest friend. . . .

My father's favorite music was American jazz, his favorite musicians were exclusively black. I had grown up listening to Louie Armstrong, Count Basie, Duke Ellington, Thelonious Monk, Charlie Mingus (whose piano pieces were haunting to me); there was an old, scratchy record of Billie Holiday's "Strange Fruit" that Max played obsessively when he was in a somber mood in retreat as he called it from the world of time, heartbreak, betrayal. The voice of Billie Holiday singing this song was haunting to me, riveting. Like Max, I listened to it many times. But I did not understand it: *Southern trees bear a strange fruit* . . . Until one day Max led me into his study, a large, high-ceilinged room sparely furnished but cluttered with books and papers, off-limits to Rickie and me, and Veronica as well, and there Max showed me, on the wall, framed, a hideous photograph: a bonfire, a crowd surrounding the fire, a tree with a broad trunk whose leaves were ablaze, and hanging from the tree, an object, a human figure, at which I stared perplexed as a child might stare at a visual puzzle and when at least I realized what it was, I hid my eyes and turned away.

Max said, in a teacherly voice, " 'Strange fruit.' The body of the black man, lynched by a Southern white mob. This is the record of one such lynching. How many hundreds, in the twentieth century alone, never prosecuted! You see, Genna, our race is the slaver-race, the darker-skinned races have been enslaved by us. We protest—'Oh! *We* are innocent! *We* would never do such a thing!' But we are all incriminated, the blood is on our hands, we are of the privileged white race, it's our curse. People who feel as I do are reviled as 'nigger lovers'—'bleeding hearts.' Because we are not fearful of loving, and we are not fearful of bleeding."

Yet my father spoke wistfully, not as grandiloquent Mad Max. I shrank from such words as I would have been dazzled and entertained by Mad Max.

Ever afterward, I could not bear to listen to the Billie Holiday song.

Proudly Minette claimed never to have heard Billie Holiday sing. She disdained jazz as "low-life." Blues was "moping and whining"—"dope fiends." Ella Fitzgerald, Lena Horne, Bessie Smith. These were women very different from the choristers of the Temple Vale of the World Tabernacle of Jesus Christ and women of whom Reverend Swift strongly disapproved.

When I told Minette that I'd heard recordings by these singers many times at home, that both my parents admired them very much, she looked at me sharply as if she thought I must be teasing her. When I told her that their voices were beautiful, the songs they'd recorded were not only haunting but were historically important, she laughed in disbelief. When I asked if she'd listen to some of my jazz records, I could bring them from home, she scowled as if the joke had gone far enough: "Now why'd I want to do *that*."

Minette was yet more contemptuous of rock and roll: "The devil's music, you bet."

It was a matter of extreme pride to Minette, she'd been accepted into Bob-o-links. It was a matter of extreme annoyance to Minette, the only other freshman who'd been accepted this year was Crystal Odom.

"People act like that girl and I should be friends, and we are not! That's an insult to me, we are *so different*."

Minette was incensed by Crystal Odom who was all "personality"— "pushy"—"show-offy." She complained (to me, privately) that Crystal was "the worst kind of New York type." At Bob-o-links, Crystal had a "phony" soprano voice like "somebody on TV." Minette was stiffly polite when she encountered Crystal publicly; she seemed to have no idea how Crystal mocked her behind her back, how brilliantly Crystal mimed Minette's voice and mannerisms. In fact, Crystal was like someone on TV. I had to concede that Crystal was funny, if cruel; cruel, if funny.

One evening in November when Minette was at a Bob-o-links rehearsal, I dropped by the Music Building and listened unnoticed at the rear of the auditorium. It was certainly true, the girls of Bob-o-links were talented. I was proud that my roommate was one of them. As it happened, that evening the group was rehearsing an insufferably energetic pseudo-African song ("The Lion Hunts Tonight") and Crystal Odom sang solo; the others were reduced to chanting and humming. It was a hive-sound, ferocious. As Crystal was coached by the director Miss Bidelman who was clearly enamoured of her and did nothing to tamp down her exaggerated facial mannerisms, Minette and the others provided choral backup, swaying their heads like demented cobras. I saw the wrath in Minette's strong-boned dark face.

"Girls! Please."

The chorus hushed. Crystal Odom broke off in the midst of an animated musical phrase.

The ruddy-faced middle-aged director, head of Schuyler's Music School, chided the chorus: "You don't want to drown out your soprano solo, girls. You are backing her up, you are enhancing her."

Enhancing! I felt the sting of the word, as Minette must have felt it. I slipped away from the auditorium hoping that Minette had not seen me.

" 'Scus*eme*? Is 'Bidelman' a Jew—Jewish—name?"

I was surprised by the vehemence in Minette's voice.

I told her I didn't know. Possibly.

"You're not Jewish, are you?"

For the first time, Minette stared at me assessingly. I felt my face burn. Guardedly I said, "Maybe. Partly."

Veronica claimed Jewish blood. Her more exotic ancestors, she said, had been Portuguese Jews who'd fled Portugal at the time of the Inquisition and had made their way eventually to England.

Maybe this was so. Or maybe it was my mother's mythopoeic construction of herself, who had once declared in my presence that she believed in reincarnation, she'd been a black woman in a previous lifetime.

Minette said, frowning, with the air of one wishing to be absolutely accurate, "But if you were a Jew—Jewish—would you say so? I mean, just to anyone? A Jew doesn't have to say he's a Jew, like a Christian has to say he's a Christian. Like, say, a Christian knows that he will be martyred for his Savior if he identifies himself but a Jew if he knows he will be martyred for his religion, it's allowable for him to lie and pretend he's a Christian."

Minette spoke earnestly, in the way she spoke sometimes of the academic subjects that were giving her difficulty, as if they were riddles, snarls to be unraveled that might be dealt with just in words. I could not determine if she thought the Jewish strategy was a good idea, or not.

"And so—?"

"So. What?"

"Is that good, that a Jew might 'lie' to a Christian, to save his life? Or not?"

Minette lifted her pink-plastic glasses, to rub at her eyes. She had a sty on her left eyelid and she'd been coughing irritably, clearing her throat. It was the day following the Bob-o-links rehearsal.

Minette shrugged. With the air of one delivering a matter-of-fact judgment she said: "Good or not-good's got nothing to do with it, if you're a born Jew and going to be killed for being so and there's no salvation for you anyway 'cause you are a Jew you might's well live or try to, long as you can. It's only *smart*."

> **I prefer to room with an individual or individuals of a race
> or races other than my own.**

Of course I had checked YES before this statement on my application for a freshman residence at Schuyler, in spring 1974. It was natural to assume that my roommate Minette Swift had checked YES, too.

Now I was coming to doubt this assumption. Each time there were forms in our mailboxes, or passed out to us at Haven House meetings, Minette sputtered and sneered at "pushy"—"prying"—questions. She was roused to indignation by "nosy" questions pertaining to race or ethnic background. In any case her scholarship, endowed by a grant of $20 million to Schuyler College in 1959, by my father's father Alden Meade, would have cast her into Haven House, and a roommate like me.

In mid-November there was the annual much-anticipated "Fall Mixer" with young men from Haverford College to which residents of Haven House were invited.

Everyone in Haven House attended this mixer except Minette Swift who said she had "better things to do than *mix*" and Minette's roommate Generva Meade who stayed away upstairs, with Minette.

My roommate was a virgin, I was sure. Of Generva, I was less sure.

"Shhhh!"

Minette came stomping into the room. The pink plastic glasses were steamed up. She was muttering to herself angrily, crumpling a paper to throw into the wastebasket. I asked what was wrong and, in a startling gesture, as her playful younger sister might have done, she tossed the balled paper at me: "So smart, girl, you tell *me*."

I knew that Minette had toiled for days over the assignment, a "close analysis" of T. S. Eliot's "The Love Song of J. Alfred Prufrock." She had typed and retyped seven pages sighing and moaning and complaining of the poem that didn't rhyme right and the silly poet who if he had something to say should "come out and say it." Minette had not wished me to read her paper before she'd handed it in to our professor, as she had no wish to read my paper. Now as I began to read what she'd written, Minette changed her mind and snatched it back.

" 'Scuse *me*."

"Minette—?"

"No never mind."

Tears flashed in her eyes. But she was laughing, so indignant. I was reminded of her sister Jewel. The tossed-out *So smart* would echo in my head for days.

Later, when Minette was out, I searched for the crumpled paper in her wastebasket. She'd made no serious attempt to hide it or destroy it. However our professor had graded it, what comments she'd made, Minette had haughtily rejected.

Here was a surprise: so many red marks and queries riddling the neatly typed pages like bloodstains. Yet more of a surprise, Minette's spelling and grammatical errors. Her sentences were predominantly primer sentences, simple in declaration, suggesting an utterly literal mind. Minette had labored to explain the poem line by line as if the poet's language was a barrier to its meaning; she seemed to have no grasp of metaphor, symbolism, ambiguity, irony, though these had been discussed frequently in class. Passages that read as if they'd been taken from reference books, listing biographical facts about Eliot, our professor had outlined in red ink with the query: *Source?* It was a paper that might have been written by a diligent but unimaginative ninth grader yet the grade was C– and the professor had written on the last page *Promising! Recast & revise & hand back & schedule for conference next week?*

I felt a sting of envy. I would have liked to be given the option of recasting and revising my paper for the professor, too. My grade had been A–, a disappointment; the – a small whiplash of rebuke to one so obsessed with performing well in school. But I had to realize: I was not Minette Swift, I was not attending Schuyler College as a Merit Scholar. I had not graduated from a large public high school in Washington, D.C., but from the prestigious-preppy Cornwall Academy in Massachusetts. I did not wish to be known as a descendant of the college founder and so I was not. I did not deserve special attention from my professors. As Maximilian Meade would have said, I've been born to unearned privilege, in my white skin.

More and more it seemed that Minette was unhappy, short-tempered. She sighed heavily to herself. She grumbled, fussed, hummed loudly and leafed through her Bible muttering to herself, as if seeking random solace. To keep her scholarship she was required to maintain an average of C+ but she had long been accustomed to being an honors student: hadn't she graduated in the "top ten" of her high school class?

Minette had complained dryly to me, she'd have been salutatorian of her class except for this "crippled-up little guy like a monkey, in a wheelchair" who'd had special tutoring through high school and took his exams with a "special proctor" so naturally he had breezed through his exams while the rest of his classmates, like Minette, had had to *work.*

Since midterms, Minette prayed more frequently. Through the partition-wall separating our bedrooms her prayers had taken on an element of impatience, coercion. *Our Father who art! in Heaven! Hallow-éd be thy name!* Minette's bedsprings creaked. In my stuporous half-sleep I imagined my roommate gripping the very shoulders of God and giving the old guy a good hard shake.

Though Minette had never shown much interest in my courses in the past, as she'd never shown much interest in me, now she began to inquire, in her elliptical way, how I had "managed to do" on my midterm exams. I felt my face burn, all talk of grades was embarrassing to me, for nothing is more petty, nothing is more trivial, yet if you are a student, if you are a student in the grip of a fanatic wish to prove yourself worthy, nothing is more important. I was surprised and flattered that Minette should turn her attention on me, though I understood it was confirmation she sought, that I, too, had done poorly on my exams. I could not tell the truth. I lowered my eyes, I shrugged evasively. Vaguely I murmured in mimicry of certain of Minette Swift's speech-mannerisms: *Ohhhh!* (with a pained grimace, meaning *Ohhhh don't ask!*).

Minette smiled grimly, hearing this. But she smiled. We were sisters now, were we? For a brief fleeting instant as Minette resumed her breakfast of griddle cakes lavishly smeared with strawberry jam and pork sausages awash in ketchup. She would finish this plate, and return for a second. Saying, with a droll twist of her mouth, "Well! At least you don't have some old 'Merit Scholarship' to hang onto. Girl, count yourself blessed."

My heart sank as it began: the throb, the beat. Raw bawling Bob Dylan.

Through the floorboards of Minette's and my room, the opening chords of "Subterranean Homesick Blues." Again!

You had to wonder if the girls directly beneath us meant to be provoking. Meant to be cruel, malicious. Several times during the semester Minette had shouted down the stairs at them, gone to knock sharply at their door, she'd complained to Dana Johnson, and each time Ms. Johnson "spoke with" the girls the loud music subsided for a few days, then resumed. Now Minette began to rage, stomping on the floor so violently the windowpanes rattled. "Devils! Damn devils go back to hell where you belong!" I crouched at my desk pressing my hands against my ears hoping the floor wouldn't collapse beneath my roommate's weight.

I was frightened of her. This husky girl with her hard-muscled legs, a look in her face of contorted choked fury.

The girls below us were not seemingly mean girls. They were capable of being "nice"—"friendly, warm"—"funny"—when I spoke with them, baffled by their behavior. (In prep school, I'd often been baffled by the behavior of my classmates. Why some girls wished to provoke and hurt others, why feuds and hatreds flared up with the rapacity of wildfire, I could not comprehend. *Why hurt another person?* I wondered. Max Meade would have said *Why hurt another person except to educate?*) These girls below us: only Audrey was Caucasian, an ordinary-seeming girl with a fondness for rock music. Lisane was Korean-American, Traci indefinably "of color"— cocoa-skinned, dewy-dark-eyed, a beautiful exotic from Bermuda with Caucasian features and a Brit accent who presented herself as bemused by "American Negroes" as she called them. The three were close friends, conspirators. Why they disliked Minette and me and were thrilled to upset us, I could not imagine.

Minette continued to rage and stomp on the floor. Yelling of devils, damn-devils-to-hell. By this time all of Haven House must have heard her. I was astonished by her outburst, not knowing what to do. Minette slammed her chair against the floor, collided with her desk and knocked a lamp to the floor where the bulb shattered and went dark. A memory came to me, one of the ugly memories, Veronica crying, hysterical and weeping, tearing at her clothes and hair, screaming when I ran to console her. *Don't touch! Get away! I am poison.*

Maybe she'd been drinking. Maybe it was amphetamines. Alcohol plus amphetamines. That long summer when I'd been a little girl and Max was away and Veronica had "dropped" acid with a hippie-lover/disciple of Baba Ram Dass.

I couldn't bear it, I went to Minette to try to take her hands. She flailed at me, furious. "You get away! You, too! Damn devils go back to hell where you belong." I managed to clutch Minette's hands and still her and she began to cry, her mouth distorted like an infant's. But her fury was spent, she'd stopped screaming and stomping. There was a shocked silence as in the aftermath of an explosion. "Subterranean Homesick Blues" had been turned off.

I could imagine Audrey, Lisane, Traci trembling below us, staring at the ceiling above their heads. What madness they'd provoked!

Suddenly, Minette smiled. Flashed her gat-toothed smile. Her very white chunky teeth glistened.

"See, girl? Now the devils *know.*"

Dana Johnson, ashen-faced, summoned me downstairs to speak with her. Asking if I believed that, after Thanksgiving break, it might be a good idea for Minette and me to meet with Audrey, Lisane, Traci—"To work out a badly needed compromise for peace."

My heart was hardened against Ms. Johnson. She had failed to stop the girls from harassing us, now she had no right to intervene. Nor did I wish to speak of my roommate behind her back, as if Minette couldn't be trusted to have an opinion of her own. Politely I said, "This is between Minette and them, I think. It has nothing to do with me."

"But, Generva, you're living in the midst of it. You must have some opinion."

Generva. Why call me *Generva!*

The woman wanted me to think of my heroine ancestor, was that it? Wanted me to feel guilt, shame. The pettiness of my behavior.

"No. I'm living at the edge of it. I am not *involved.*"

In excitable moments my voice was taking on the southern cadences of Minette's vehement accent. *In-volved!*

The Beacon. Subtitled *The Messenger of the Christian Way.*

Like Minette's resplendent ivory-white Bible, this religious publication seemed to be on display in our room. As in a library, current and back issues lay faceup on Minette's windowsill. Though Minette had never suggested it, I assumed that she would have liked me, or anyone who visited our room, to examine the magazines which contained such articles as "My Voyage to Jesus," " 'A Joyful Noise Unto the Lord': 25 Years a Choir Master," " 'I Was

Blind But Now I Can See.' " In its bright-ink colors and crude typography, the pulp-paper magazine resembled a comic book in prose.

When Minette left early for Thanksgiving. I was resentful of her leaving, and I missed her. Standing over her desk blinking away tears. Here were Minette's neatly stacked papers, her typewriter, a row of textbooks including the mutilated/mended *Norton Anthology of American Literature*. So many times I had stared at her framed family photos, I'd almost come to think that I would find myself among them.

I would not pull open any of the desk drawers. I had no wish to see if Minette was hoarding food from the cafeteria, packets of sugar, synthetic dairy creamer, ketchup.

I was very disappointed. Minette had vaguely promised that I would be meeting her parents when they drove up to fetch her home for Thanksgiving, but when I hurried back to the room after my last Wednesday class, Minette was gone.

She'd left no note behind. It hadn't been important of course.

Minette had packed the night before, methodically. She would be taking work home with her. Eagerly she was looking forward to "getting away from this place." In her absence, her side of the room exuded an air of indefinable mystery. The door to her bedroom was closed, but not locked; but I would not open it. The door to her closet was closed. Wanly illuminated by a parallelogram of November sunshine, the CHRISTIAN YOUTH FELLOWSHIP poster was fading before my eyes.

In the days following Minette's outburst, there was respectful quiet from below. Minette gloated in her victory, she'd read in a thrilled voice to me from her Bible those starkly narrated verses from St. Luke in which Jesus drives out devils from an afflicted man, and the devils enter a herd of swine causing them to rush into a lake and drown. *Poor swine!* I'd thought. But Minette read dramatically: " 'And Jesus asked him, saying, What is thy name? And he said Legion: for many devils were entered into him.' "

I had no idea what this might mean. I smiled to think of Max Meade gnashing his teeth, confronted with such "superstition."

Oh, but I was missing Minette! The dean of students had issued a "directive" reminding us that classes before official Thanksgiving recess were not to be cut by students eager to depart. Minette had ignored the directive, with a sneer. Her parents had arrived to take her home while I'd been in my sociology class.

Often Minette spoke of how her family took in "strays" and "orphans" at holiday time. I knew it wasn't likely but I had fantasized that, if I'd met the Swifts, they might have impulsively invited me to their home for Thanksgiving.

Am I free, yes I think so. Yes.

Yes I would love to join you. Thanks!

I'd been leafing through the most recent issue of *The Beacon*. Vaguely I recalled Minette mentioning that there was a feature on Reverend Virgil Swift and his church in this issue, or in another. I replaced the magazine on Minette's windowsill in such a way that Minette might notice that I'd picked it up. She would say nothing to me about the magazine nor would I say anything to her but she would notice, I think.

Genna please! Come stay the weekend honey. I am so lonely.

An almost imperceptible pause before *lonely*. Veronica pausing to wet her lips resisting the wish to say *fucking lonely*.

It seemed that Veronica was expecting me for Thanksgiving in the house at Chadds Ford. I knew, or seemed to know, that she'd invited Rickie, too. I did not have to inquire to know that Rickie sure as hell wasn't coming.

Thanksgiving! I had come to dread it.

My father scorned American holiday rituals as smug, hypocritical, self-indulgent and self-congratulatory. As a lawyer he objected to the "state religion" of Christianity imposing Christmas on non-Christians. Thanksgiving was nearly as offensive, though secular: a gluttonous meal, obscene in the light of world famine. Max was often away at Thanksgiving, and/or the house at Chadds Ford was overwhelmed with guests, or besieged by crisis. In principle Veronica agreed with Max's disdain for holidays but often at Thanksgiving she weakened, and surrounded herself with strays and orphans of her own, of which she knew many. This year she'd begged me to come home, for Max was away and she dreaded being alone after the FBI scare, she had reason to believe that not only were the phones tapped but the house itself was under surveillance—"As if anyone 'wanted' would show up *here*."

Every holiday, my father's wealthy elderly widow-aunts in Philadelphia and Wilmington invited the remnants of their nephew's family to visit them, but we never did. For decades these very nice women had been hinting that they "would not forget" Veronica in their wills. (They believed that my mother was a faithful, loyal wife to a man who found marital fidelity difficult to sustain. They believed that Veronica had repudiated the dangerous radical politics of her husband and might be a force eventually in his return to sanity and respectability.) Veronica spoke rarely of her own scattered family and relatives who lived in upstate New York, Pennsylvania, West Virginia. She'd said she was "politically and morally" estranged from these "racist hillbilly Christians" who voted Republican though they lived barely above the poverty level, belonged to the National Rifle Association and considered Maximilian Meade a traitor to the United States for his opposition to the Vietnam War and his defense of "draft dodgers."

On the phone Veronica cajoled me as often I'd overheard her cajoling my father, or another man.

"Genna? It will be just you and me, I promise."

I hesitated. I was remembering other Thanksgivings when in a last-minute flurry of activity Veronica had invited a miscellany of individuals scarcely known to one another.

"And where is Max, exactly?"

"Max! Well. The man is"—Veronica lifted her voice in one of her extravagant flights of speech, as if taunting an invisible third-party wiretapper—" 'in the wind.' As the Feds say."

I laughed uneasily. This was a provocative remark for Veronica to make, almost boastfully. And it wasn't true, Max was not in hiding. He was certainly not underground. Very likely he'd returned to Los Angeles. Very likely he had a female associate there, one of a shifting number of admiring young women lawyers, legal investigators and interns attached to Maximilian Meade. *In the wind* had a dashing sound, though. The romance of *underground, wanted, safe house.*

"Your father will call us on Thanksgiving, Genna. He has promised."

"How can he, if our phones are bugged?"

"Don't be paranoid! You know our phones aren't bugged *now*."

"I thought you'd said they were."

"But Max has nothing to hide! God damn you know that, Genna."

I was tempted to hang up. Break the connection forever. But there was a mystery here. And always, with Max Meade, there was romance.

And if I'd remained in Haven House over Thanksgiving break I would have been the lone girl. Just Dana Johnson and me. Ms. Johnson had hinted the two of us might "have" Thanksgiving together at the Schuylersville Inn.

"Genna, I just don't know. I am so *sleepy*."

Her skin exuded a hot-acrid scent as of burnt orange peel. Her eyes, thin-lashed without mascara, a faded blue-gray, seemed to have difficulty focusing. Embracing me when I arrived, Veronica almost stumbled in my arms. Her breath smelled of fresh mint leaves she was in the habit of chewing.

Thanksgiving 1974 in the house at Chadds Ford, just Veronica and me, might have been a deeply meaningful, memorable occasion except we were not exactly alone. Much of the time Veronica was distracted, glancing out the windows, waiting for the phone to ring. There had been times in our lives when I had believed that Veronica was anxiously awaiting my father only to learn afterward that it was another man whom Veronica had been awaiting; there had been times when the reverse was so. Vaguely now Veronica was saying that possibly my brother might show up—"He has not returned my messages to say *no*."

I was resolved: not to investigate my mother's medicine cabinet to see what powerful medications she might be taking for chronic insomnia, depression, loss of appetite and libido, "suicidal thoughts"—that catalogue of woes shared by middle-aged hippie-survivors of the psychedelic revolution. I would not even ask if Veronica was seeing more than one doctor and hoarding prescriptions.

Thanksgiving morning, Veronica slept late. It was true, as she complained, she appeared to be unnaturally "sleepy." We did not get the turkey into the oven until early afternoon. This turkey Veronica had ordered from a Chadds Ford grocer, ludicrously oversized for two people at sixteen pounds. For long hours it roasted in our lopsided oven. Its clammy-pale skin did not turn crispy golden as promised but charred-black. Through the house wafted a sickish smell of scorch. Dreamily I thought of Minette Swift and her family, a large warm boisterous gathering of relatives, "strays" and "orphans." I understood that very likely there would not have been a place for me at the Swifts' dinner table, however large.

From her lover who'd been a disciple of Baba Ram Dass, Veronica had learned to meditate. *Be here now!* was the mantra. *Be here now!* was the curse. *Be here now!* was the inescapable fate of most lives. In the house at Chadds Ford on a long rain-spotted Thanksgiving Day shading into a premature dusk I felt this truth like stitches in the flesh. Waking Veronica from a sluggish late-afternoon nap long after nightfall so that the mother/daughter team could struggle to remove the roasting pan from the malfunctioning oven, and the scorch-skinned turkey from the roasting pan. "This is impossible without a man. You do need a man. Not just a penis you need, you need fucking *muscle*." Veronica laughed shrilly, bare feet slipping in grease on the floor. The worn linoleum floor of our kitchen. By this time the walnut-mushroom stuffing out of a mix was dry as wood chips. Mashed potatoes, broccoli, baby carrots out of a package had cooled. A bottle of Max's expensive French chardonnay, opened for dinner, was half depleted. Just as Veronica poked a carving knife into the turkey breast, causing watery blood to spill out, the phone rang. I was struggling to hold the doomed bird in place, to prevent it careening to the floor. Veronica cursed under her breath. "Don't answer, baby! The fucker will only break our hearts."

After Thanksgiving 1974, Minette Swift returned to Schuyler College two days late. Generva Meade returned to Schuyler College two days early.

For a very liberal college of emancipated women Schuyler was a honey-comb, you might say a hive of "traditions." One of the most absurd was triggered by the first snowfall of the season when otherwise sensible young women threw down their books, seized one another's hands and ran out-side in the cold coatless and bare-headed whooping and cavorting like drunken naiads in an impromptu procession to a Victorian gazebo/Temple of Minerva a quarter-mile away overlooking the Schuylkill. One December night Minette and I were interrupted in our studying by a sudden outbreak of shrieks, high-pitched laughter from outside, thunderous footsteps on the stairs of Haven House. The first snowfall of the winter.

Minette snorted in derision: "Some fools going to catch their death of cold."

I'd been reading and rereading the same paragraph of leaden prose in *The Social Basis of Individual Behavior*. Outside our windows was a flurry of snowflakes like tiny white butterflies. I felt a sudden wildness, a wish to run outside, shriek with laughter to no purpose other than to shriek with laughter. But I only laughed, dryly. "A 'revered old custom' dating back to ancient Greek times. Except the worshippers should really be naked, and rend and flail their flesh."

This was unfair. Worship of Minerva was worship of wisdom, not to be confused with the orgiastic worship of Dionysus. But Minette appreciated my forced irony whether it made sense or not. She squealed in mock dis-gust: "Ohhhh no. 'Scuse me but nobody better run naked here, I sure don't want to see 'em. There's a reason the good Lord gave us *clothes*."

Unknowing I called him "Daddy" when we spoke on the phone. This child's name for a father I had long outgrown as (I'd thought) I had long outgrown "Mommy."

The fucker will only break our hearts but hadn't this already happened? And many times?

How eager I was, hearing that hoarse broken voice in my ear—"Genna?

It's Max." My father's wounded-ebullient voice. When you heard Max Meade speak you were made to recall how he'd been savagely attacked by the enemy but not stopped. Not once but numerous times.

The phone ringing in the house at Chadds Ford on Thanksgiving evening had not been Max Meade after all. Only one of Veronica's strung-out friends. Max would call later, not to apologize (Max never apologized) nor even to explain (Max rarely explained) but to say how he missed us.

"Not that personal happiness can matter, much. In a time of political crisis. Sometimes I feel it's the 'personal' that is the root of all futility. If we could live in the 'impersonal,' the ideal . . ."

"Oh, Daddy! You do that all the time."

As with Minette Swift my manner was likely to be dryly ironic, to make Minette laugh, so with Maximilian Meade my manner was likely to be little-girl playful, to win Max's heart. For inside his hard bald dome of a Lenin-head Mad Max was a notorious softie.

Break my heart! Try.

Max had called to speak with both his daughter and his wife, but it seemed to me that he had more to say to his daughter, and this was flattering. He wanted to explain the crisis of a few weeks ago which Veronica had apparently misunderstood. True, Veronica had been given misinformation, and out of this she'd spun yet more misinformation—"You know your mother, darlin'. The very Mozart of misinformation."

Eagerly I laughed. Veronica was drifting in the hallway barefoot and hot-skinned smelling of burnt orange peel and her eyes welling with tears. *The very Mozart of misinformation!* It was a cruel delicious father/daughter moment, in alliance against the mother.

In fact, Max had not been arrested at the Buffalo border. He had not been arrested by FBI agents at all. A federal judge in Los Angeles had declared him in contempt of court for refusing to surrender to prosecutors several tapes of "confidential, privileged" conversations he'd had with former clients and with individuals who he insisted were his clients and therefore were protected from exposure by the law. In "contempt of court" Maximilian Meade had been taken away by bailiffs to the L.A. County House of Detention but within a few hours the ruling was rescinded and he'd been freed, and triumphant! "They should know by now that they can't harass Max Meade, as they've harassed so many others. Now the Era of Shame is over."

But Max wanted me to know, he'd been thinking of me these past few weeks and hoping that I was not anxious on his account. Because certainly he had nothing to fear. As a lawyer and an officer of the court he took care to maintain the highest "ethical/legal" standards and no legal maneuver of his, dating back to his earliest cases, could be faulted. His enemies knew this, and respected him. And I, his daughter, was to know, and must not worry.

"But, Daddy, where are you? When will we see you?"

Max laughed. It was a sound like bullrushes whipping in the wind. "Genna, I'm *out*. I'm not *in*. I can breathe. What's it matter, where?"

"In California somewhere, or back here?"

Not in a *safe house*, I knew. For Max could not telephone his family so openly, from such a place.

Max mumbled a vague evasive reply. He would tell me when he saw me, he said jovially.

"But when, Daddy?"

"Soon! I promise."

Max had called also to ask me about school, he said. How did I like Schuyler College, what were the courses I was taking, who were my instructors, what did I perceive to be the "political atmosphere" there; was I being intellectually challenged at Schuyler; was I making "interesting" friends at Schuyler; what was "your generation" thinking, post-Vietnam and post-Nixon? He had heard from Veronica that my roommate was the daughter of a "prominent" black Washington preacher.

I wasn't sure that Reverend Virgil Swift was "prominent." Though maybe. Minette would be pleased to think so. Eagerly I told my father that I hoped he would meet the Swifts soon, he and Reverend Swift would have much in common.

Max sounded doubtful. "He's political-minded? A black Christian preacher?"

"Well, Daddy! Look at the Reverend Martin Luther King, Jr. He was political."

Max laughed. He would not speak disparagingly of the Reverend Martin Luther King, Jr., though he disdained non-violence as a political strategem. Passivity, pacifism, Christian forebearance and martyrdom: these were outmoded, ineffectual. These were tattered remnants of a bygone era.

Max asked what my roommate was like, and I told him what seemed true to me: I had never met anyone like Minette Swift before.

Lawyer-like Max asked, "How so?"

I hesitated. I could not think. No words seemed quite adequate to suggest Minette Swift's vivid presence.

I stammered he'd have to meet Minette in person, and see for himself.

Max promised. Yes he would. And very soon. He would call me, and arrange to visit the college, stay a few days at the Schuylersville Inn. He had not visited Elias Meade House for at least fifteen years. . . . He would take my roommate and me out to dinner and get to know us both.

This was a joke, I think. We both laughed.

May I please speak with Minette Swift?

That rich rolling dark-baritone voice like music: Reverend Virgil Swift.

I'd answered the phone on the third-floor landing. Like one bearing good news I ran to fetch Minette in our room. When I said, "Minette, I think it's your father—" I saw a look of speechless outrage in my roommate's face, that I should presume to speak of her father whom I had never met.

Minette brushed past me to take the phone. Heavily she threw herself down in the chair beside the telephone stand, massively she sighed. It was the week following Thanksgiving and in the intervening days one or another of the elder Swifts had telephoned Minette at least once each day that I knew of. The evening before, I'd heard Minette crying. Tonight I did not remain in our room but hurried downstairs to avoid even the possibility of eavesdropping.

Break my heart, fucker! Try.

Days passed. The December sky continued to shrink. My father Max

Meade did not call. I told myself I was not surprised, wasn't I Veronica's daughter, too?

One evening Minette returned home early from her Bob-o-links rehearsal. Days in succession the singing group had been preparing for their annual Christmas concert, a candlelit ceremony held in the college chapel. I knew from the angry weight of Minette's footsteps that something was wrong. When I glanced up from my desk Minette said savagely, " 'Scuse*me!*" and slammed into her bedroom. Next day, from Crystal Odom, I would learn that Minette had quit Bob-o-links after a disagreement with the director.

I was shocked. Bob-o-links had meant so much to Minette. I asked Crystal what had happened and Crystal said airily: "Ms. Bidelman is a perfectionist, and Minette Swift thinks she's already perfect. What do you think happened?"

Loud as a hive of bees came the humming: "The Old Rugged Cross."

Immediately I recognized it. As soon as Minette began to hum.

It was an acid-bright chill morning, December 8, 1974. This date would be significant. Already by 8:30 A.M. Minette was dressed for church, primping into a mirror, wetting and smacking her lips. Minette had said nothing to me of quitting Bob-o-links and of course I could not inquire. Instead of going out to rehearsals, Minette retired early into her bedroom, in navy blue bathrobe and pajamas. Her general mood was sullen-sulky. On Sunday mornings, however, Minette appeared cheerful, defiant. This was her time to detach herself from Haven House and from Schuyler College. She wore stockings that strained against her dense, muscular calves and snub-nosed black patent leather shoes. Rarely did Minette wear makeup except on Sunday mornings and then only plum-colored lipstick of the somber shade Mrs. Swift had worn on Orientation Day. Now that it was winter, Minette wore her "good" winter coat, bulky dark red cloth with a synthetic leopard skin collar and on her hair stiff as a helmet a white angora scarf carefully knotted under her chin.

She wore black knitted gloves. She carried a sturdy black handbag with a gold buckle. Even close up, she resembled a middle-aged woman.

Minette mumbled *G'bye!* not waiting for me to ask if I would see her at dinner. On Sundays, "dinner" was in the early afternoon and was breakfast for most of us.

Since the evening when I'd called her to the phone to speak with Reverend Swift, Minette had been stiff with me. I was made to understand that I had trespassed into her private life. There seemed no graceful way of apologizing, though from past experience I knew that Minette's annoyance with me would fade after a few days: I was her only ally in Haven House. This morning, I planned to follow Minette when she left the residence, to her mysterious church which I would have supposed to be the First Baptist Church of Schuylersville. I had given up waiting for her to invite me to join her; naively I thought that I might sit at the rear of the church and when Minette noticed me she would think *That girl is serious! I have misjudged her*.

Minette left our room, her heels rapping sharply on the stairs to waken those late-sleeping neighbors for whom Sunday-morning church services were not crucial. By this time I was dressed and ready to follow. My heart beat rapidly as a hunter's! I felt the thrill of danger, expectation. Haven House was mostly deserted at this hour. On campus, chapel services were to begin at 9 A.M. and a few girls were drifting in that direction. Shortly, the sonorous notes of the chapel's bell tower would sound. Minette was walking swiftly away from Haven House. I would keep a discreet half-block between us though there was little likelihood of my roommate glancing back to see me. Minette strode in one direction like a truck in forward gear, oblivious of her surroundings.

It was a very bright chill and windy December morning. Our breaths steamed. My eyes teared keeping Minette's sturdy figure in sight. My rumpled camel's hair coat swayed loose on me, purchased a few years ago several sizes too large. On my head I wore an unflattering wool knit cap, pulled down onto my forehead.

Beneath a row of plane trees whose burly trunks looked partly skinned

Minette crossed the quadrangle, head thrust slightly forward and handbag gripped tight in her gloved hand. Without a glance Minette bypassed the beautifully spare white chapel with its numerous stone steps, and stately old Elias Meade House tight-shut on Sunday morning. You could see, Minette Swift was eager to escape Schuyler College! She would leave through the ornamental front gateway, walking now in the road and not on the sidewalk; a car approached Minette from behind, made a wide berth around her to pass her; Minette appeared not to notice. The ground was covered by a gritty snow-crust and in the bright sunshine had the glare of an over-exposed photograph.

She isn't bad-looking, our daughter.

Fuck you Genna is beautiful! She has an ancient soul, you can see in her eyes. She may be the reincarnation of the original Generva Meade.

Tell it to your buddy Baba Ram-Ass. That "recycled" bullshit.

Following Minette Swift I was reminded of how, as a lonely child, as a sly inquisitive yearning child, I'd followed my parents from room to room in the house at Chadds Ford. My parents who were giants. My parents who were deities. In those days Veronica was very beautiful. Her bones did not jut against her translucent skin, her eyes were not bruised-looking. She had many admirers. Max was not yet bald, his dome of a head had not yet emerged but was covered in dark hair tufted and snarled and falling nearly to his shoulders, kept in place by a red headband. Mad Max, looking like an Indian! When he was Mad Max his eyes glared like an owl's, wonderful to see. His breath was fierce, hot. A kiss from Mad Max was "combustible." I ran to hide beneath the stairs. I hid amid soiled laundry. I saw them naked. I saw them naked together, and with others. And with the children of others. There were young girls among them and it was not clear to me if Genna was one of these or only the sly inquisitive lonely child who observed. There were baths in old-fashioned claw-foot tubs in "herbal" steaming water. There were words like music uttered by my parents (with lovers, with each other, over the phone to unknown parties) I would hear only in teasing fragments like moths throwing themselves against a windowpane at night.

Bullshit can be beautiful! God is ALL IN ALL you cold-hearted bastard.

I had to slow my pace, I'd been gaining on Minette. Her red-coated fig-ure had drawn dangerously near.

The old "historic" campus was bounded by an aged-brick wall with wrought-iron gates of Gothic intricacy. These gates were never shut. The buildings were a mixture of Colonial and "Gothic" and new buildings shrewdly designed to mimic the old except that their windows were plate glass and their interiors wholly modernized. It was a wealthy school founded by a wealthy man who wished to repudiate his wealth. Every-where were chiseled hedgerows, evergreens and ornamental trees. In spring there were banks of blazing azaleas. There were cascades of lilacs. There were stone benches, cul-de-sac walks, a stone wishing well endowed by the class of 1928. There was the Victorian gazebo/Temple of Minerva over-looking the Schuylkill. Outside the walled campus were playing fields, hik-ing trails, woods and open meadows stretching for miles into rural Montgomery County.

Even Max Meade who hated what he called conspicuous consumption had to concede, the college his grandfather had founded was impressive. *You have to ask: is beauty worth its cost? But if beauty exists, we may as well admire it.*

I knew that, for a while in the late 1960s, my father had hoped to wrest control of Schuyler College from its board of trustees and administrators. He'd wanted to "radicalize" the faculty and student body in the manner of purification of Mao's Red Guard. But he'd met only opposition. Among the trustees were older Meade relatives to whom Mad Max was a pariah and an embarrassment. In any case Max's energies had been deflected and scattered and now in the aftermath of the Vietnam Era he'd lost his bel-ligerent edge.

Ahead, Minette was still walking in the roadway, a defiant red figure. This was College Road which ran parallel to the river on our right. Minette passed Faculty Road and the predominantly Colonial and English Tudor houses in which senior faculty lived. Here were large spacious wooded lots. Beyond the northern edge of the campus the Village of Schuylersville began at the intersection of College Road and a two-lane state highway; beyond the intersection was Pierpont Avenue, a steep, quaintly restored block of small stores, shops, boutiques. Set back from the street was the landmark Schuylersville Inn. There was the Old Mill, an eighteenth-century lumber mill long since converted to upscale dining on the river. And there was the first of Schuylersville's churches: squat-built beige-brick St. John's Roman Catholic.

All these, Minette passed without a flicker of interest.

She began to descend a hill. I followed. At this edge of Schuylersville were less prosperous stores, older and more weatherworn buildings. There were woodframe bungalows in small lots. There were vehicles parked at the curbs. A gas station with a shuttered front window. The First Methodist Church of Schuylersville in an asphalt lot surrounded by cars, and more cars arriving. At first I thought that Minette would turn in here amid other churchgoers, but she continued on.

Her breath steamed. By this time she had walked briskly more than a mile from campus, now her momentum was slowing.

Church bells were ringing. It was nearing 9 A.M.

We passed a weatherworn gray-granite Lutheran church. We passed a red-brick Presbyterian church. And there at last, at the outskirts of town, was the First Baptist Church of Schuylersville, dun-colored clapboard, a steeple and a cross gleaming in sunshine. Almost, I saw the cross through Minette's eyes: the outward sign of the crucifixion and death of her Savior.

You had to lift your eyes to see. And the cross gleaming like gold outlined against a winter sky of glass-like clarity. I felt a small stab of emotion, in the region of my heart. I think I did.

Wanting to call impulsively *Minette! I understand.*

There was more activity at this church than at the others. Cars were being parked up and down the roadside, churchgoers were hurrying to church. Mostly these were women, and all were black. They were middle-aged and older though there were many young children. The women wore coats eye-striking and "stylish" as Minette's, quite a few wore extravagant hats. Gloves, handbags, high-heeled shoes and boots. In the fragmented speech of the churchgoers as they called greetings to one another I heard some of the cadences of Minette Swift's speech. One of the women, stout but energetic, wearing a lavender velvet hat with deep-purple cloth flowers, so resembled Mrs. Swift as I remembered her, for a confused moment I thought that Minette might be meeting her mother here. . . . But Minette had surprised me, she'd stopped on the other side of the road.

Impatient to leave Haven House, making her way unerringly here, now Minette paused, indecisive, guarded. With the heel of her hand she shoved her pink-plastic glasses against the bridge of her nose. She gripped the handbag tight. She stood unmoving.

This was so strange! I wondered if Minette was waiting for someone.

In a steady stream churchgoers were entering the church. The bell continued to sound. I waited for someone to notice Minette, to call out to her, but no one did. No one seemed even to glance at her, the impassive black girl in a red coat trimmed with leopard skin standing alone across from the church.

I thought *Minette is invisible here as I am.*

The bell ceased its ringing. From inside the church came a sound of choir singing. Minette turned away, walked very deliberately away, yet slowly, with no urgency. She crossed the road, she stumbled across an open lot, still moving away from town. It was a snowy-muddy place, her black leather pumps would be dirtied. I could not decide if I should follow Minette further, or let her go. If I should call to her, "Minette? What's wrong?"

Of course, I could no more call to Minette Swift in this public place than I might throw open her bedroom door when she was inside.

I followed Minette hesitantly now. At any moment I expected her to turn back but she did not, she continued downhill toward the river, to sit heavily on a park bench. It was a small municipal park, deserted and desolate in winter. Even the snow stubbled on the ground wasn't the pristine white of Schuyler College but a dispirited trampled mud-white. Even the "picturesque" Schuylkill did not look especially attractive from this perspective.

In the leafless trees close by a chorus of crows had gathered while others circled the air overhead, ungainly wide-winged and raucous in their cries. *Be here now! Be here now!* Minette glanced upward, distracted. I could imagine her forehead furrowed in annoyance. She fumbled inside her handbag, removed a tissue and blew her nose.

I could not believe that my roommate, so self-possessed and stubborn, should have come so far on foot, simply to sit by the river! This could not have been Minette Swift's plan for Sunday morning.

At a distance of about thirty feet, part-hidden behind a children's slide, I waited, and watched. My nose, too, was running. My eyes were leaking tears. For some time I stood undecided what to do. Minette Swift appeared so diminished, now. So alone. Even Crystal Odom would have pitied her. *Get on your feet, girl!*

I could hear the Baptist choir, faintly. Their singing was ethereal, eerie. I wondered if Minette heard it, or if the noisy crows and the wind from the river muffled the sound. In a movie, such faint teasing music would be the background of a "scene." After a suspenseful interlude Minette would glance around uneasily and see me: and recognize me: and I would have no choice but to hurry forward: smiling? But this was not a movie, there was no camera eye and no guidance; there was no script; what music there was dimmed and faded in the wind. My hands were shoved deep into the pockets of my camel's hair coat. My eyes brimmed with moisture. I was seeing the river through Minette Swift's eyes: the color of ditch water, blurred with tears.

The Schuylkill would not freeze over until January at the earliest. Now its oily-dark waters moved swift and turbulent as if giant creatures struggled with one another beneath its choppy surface.

I avoided Haven House for the remainder of that Sunday. I returned to our room at about 10 P.M. When I entered the room I saw that the overhead light was out, my desk lamp had been turned on. This was thoughtful of Minette. There was a band of light beneath her bedroom door, she'd gone to bed to work, probably. She would not acknowledge my arrival and I would not disturb her by calling hello. It had been more than twelve hours since we'd spoken.

All that day I'd been thinking of Minette. I was resentful, disappointed. *It was my chance! My only chance! I was cheated of it.*

Exiled to the college library, to work until my head swam. And an afternoon meeting of the literary magazine staff, for now I was a junior editor. And a meal at the student center with several of the editors. If Minette had gone into the First Baptist Church of Schuylersville, how very different this Sunday, December 8, 1974, would have been for us both.

As I entered the room I stepped on a sheet of paper that appeared to have been shoved beneath the door. I picked it up, brought it to my desk to examine in the light.

At first I thought it was a joke: a cartoon, caricature. Something from a tabloid paper.

Hottentot Venus! What was this . . .

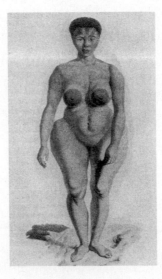

The obscene: that which, when you see it, in that instant you cannot not have seen it. And will continue to see it. And will continue to see it no matter if your eyes are gouged out.

Guts

When I was eleven years old I saw a man try to eviscerate himself with a paring knife. One of Max's old-young male disciples. It happened at the rear of the house at Chadds Ford, on the ruin of a flagstone terrace. It was a leaden-cold autumn day but the old-young man known as Ansel was naked. He'd torn off his clothes in what would be called an amphetamine rage. He was covered in sweat like tiny cheap jewels. His bristly spider-hair hung in his face and his wisp of a beard looked as if he'd been tearing at it. He stumbled from the house, onto the terrace. I saw, from one of the side doors. It was an accident of timing, I had just returned from Chadds Ford Middle School where I was a sixth grader. For it was a weekday in the world beyond.

But I am not seeing anything like this! my brain consoled me. So strangely, I did not run away but toward the staggering man. Because I saw that he had "hurt himself" and he "needed help" and I was a witness. I saw the knife, and I saw the blood, and I saw guts. I saw guts without realizing that I saw "guts"—"intestines"—as the paring knife sank into the belly, and was twisted.

I saw the snaky glisten of guts through the man's fingers, and I heard the yelping cry that was more surprise than pain. *But wouldn't you know it would hurt!* I thought for I was a practical-minded child mature and canny for my age.

Often I spied upon the adults in the house at Chadds Ford. For I was invisible to them, as I was invisible to myself. But this day, a weekday after I'd returned from school to an empty-seeming disordered house whose air was highly charged as the air before an electrical storm, I had not intended to spy on anyone. Yet it happened.

In the way that in those days things happened with no clear precedents and antecedents. Like a scene illuminated by a flash of lightning. Then the deafening thunderclap, and silence.

Like a dream that erupts out of nowhere, and vanishes. You feel its aftermath pounding in your skull though you have lost it.

His name was Ansel, I knew "Ansel." Later I would learn his surname he had renounced: "Trimmer."

He'd come to stay in the house at Chadds Ford for a day, a night, a week, six weeks. He was not alone, there was a shifting population of others: male and female, though mostly male. And mostly young, in their twenties. They were in protest of the U.S. armed services draft and they were in protest of the U.S. military presence in Vietnam. I would learn one day that they were "extremists"—"radical activists"—"terrorists." I would learn that my father Max Meade was a "charismatic radical theorist"—a "brilliant defense attorney of the Left." The language of the enemy, Max said. Ignore!

The paring knife: Ansel must have reached blindly into the sink, into cold scummy water in which cutlery, dirtied dishes and glasses were soaking in our kitchen. Possibly in the amphetamine rage he could not accurately gauge the sizes of objects. A paring knife hardly five inches in length. You would need a longer, much sharper knife. You would need a better grip. A paring knife could not possibly be made to sink deep enough into the belly as required even if his grip on the handle hadn't faltered, slip-sliding in his own somehow unexpected and astonishing blood.

It wasn't warm, I'd worn a jacket to school. But Ansel had torn off his clothes because he'd been pouring sweat. Inside his clothes, his T-shirt, denim jacket, jeans he'd had a warrior swagger but naked he was boy-thin, you saw his rib cage, spine, pelvic bones straining against his papery skin and you wanted to look away, embarrassed for him. Except for patches of flushed, mottled skin he was very white. He was of that pigment scorned as Caucasian, imperialist, and blind. Dark hairs grew sparsely on his narrow chest, more fully at his groin. His penis was a bobbing rubbery skinned-looking piece of flesh. And his slashed and bleeding belly, and a spill of "guts" held back by his fingers. . . .

It must have been, Ansel had quarreled with Max. Ansel was one of Max Meade's disciples who quarreled with him. Those disciples who loved Max Meade most passionately were likely to be those who quarreled most bitterly with him. They were sons wanting to devour the man's living heart.

Ansel's intention on this leaden-sky afternoon in Chadds Ford, Pennsylvania, in the fall of 1967 was to commit *hari-kari*—the classic Japanese way of ritual suicide. To capture the permanent attention of Maximilian Meade as other protegés of Maximilian Meade would not, ever. *Hara-kari* was an act requiring the most rigorous spiritual discipline as well as unfathomable physical courage and clearly it was an act not casually tossed off, an act to be performed flawlessly the first time for very likely there would not be a second time. It was an act not to be rehearsed except in fantasy. Another way that might have appealed to Ansel Trimmer was self-immolation of the kind performed by Vietnamese Buddhist monks protesting the American military presence in Vietnam and played and replayed to ghastly effect on TV news. Yet the paring knife was snatched up in Ansel's eager fingers, and would have to do.

Now I know, as I could not have known as a child, that the wish to commit suicide is not invariably the wish to die. The wish to commit a showy suicide, a suicide to make a statement, is certainly not the wish to die. Ansel Trimmer was twenty-six at the time: one of those children of the well-to-do, Max Meade's own class, who believed himself exiled from America; the repudiated son of the American capitalist/manufacturer of high-quality sinks, bathtubs, toilets George Trimmer, a major contributor to Richard Nixon's presidential campaign, headquarters in Minneapolis. Ansel Trimmer may have been one of Veronica's bearded boy-lovers. His rich-boy teeth had lately become stained, rotting in his gums out of his indifference to personal health, grooming, diet as bourgeois preoccupations in a time of political crisis. For had not Chairman Mao himself scorned to brush his teeth that turned scummy-green in his mouth as they rotted into his gums. For to realize your life you must throw your life away. The individual is one of teeming millions, billions. Max Meade had taught the Kierkegaardian principle of search for *the truth for which I am willing to live and to die*.

Ansel Trimmer would not die of a botched hari-kari but would survive. He would renew his commitment to the revolution. He would follow Max's most valued disciples who had repudiated the adolescent exhibitionism and adventurism of the publicity-minded Weather Underground (wishing always to be identified with their acts) by insisting upon anonymity. This was a higher calling, like sainthood. Three years later, following the bombing of the Dow Chemical plant in Niagara Falls in March 1970 and the death of a night watchman, he would disappear underground with his comrades. He would become "John David Donovan" equipped with a counterfeit I.D. seemingly issued by Pennsylvania State U. in 1968. The miniature photo of "John David Donovan" on this plastic card was of an old-young man with hair trimmed short, glasses with thick black frames, jaws now beardless and weak receding chin now bravely exposed. The birth date of "John David Donovan" was not the birth date of Ansel Trimmer but a reasonable birth date, 1949. The birthplace of "John David Donovan" was not the birthplace of Ansel Trimmer but a reasonable substitute, Scranton, Pennsylvania. For the fugitive would disappear into a *safe house* somewhere in Pennsylvania, or across the state line in Maysville, West Virginia. Always the counterfeit I.D. bore, beneath its laminated coating, the likeness of "John David Donovan": a tense-smiling old-young man with a painfully narrow face looking as if it had been squeezed in a vise, and twisted.

"Oh, why did you do that? Oh, doesn't that h-hurt . . ."

I was shy of Ansel Trimmer as I was shy of all adults yet somehow I heard myself stammer these words. I was thinking *This is not real—is it?* for in my confusion and panic I might have believed it could be a movie scene, or something on TV denounced by my brother Rickie as "phony." Only a few inches from the stricken man, now I saw the blood, and I saw what Ansel's shaking fingers were trying to hold inside his slashed belly, and I smelled a sudden stench so powerful it made me gag. Ansel was on his knees, swaying. He was moaning and whimpering to himself as in an exotic prayer. His eyes were shut, his squeezed-together face had gone deathly pale. I was calm thinking I would run to get the first aid kit from the downstairs bathroom where such supplies were kept in a sliding-door closet. I had learned this past summer to savor the smell of Mercurochrome and the textures of gauze and adhesive bandages. I thought *Daddy will be proud of me* though it wasn't clear that Max was even home. You could not always depend upon Max Meade to be a witness of his protégés' displays of emotion, bravado. Though others had come to witness, out of the house stunned, slow-moving. And among them Veronica pushing through crying, "Ansel! What is it!" You had to be close up to see what Ansel had done to himself, how his fingers clutched against his slashed belly.

The rear of the house at Chadds Ford had lapsed into a slow ruin. Flagstones were cracked, edged with grasses gone to seed. Blood was spilling onto the ground from the raw wound. I was shivering badly now, my teeth were chattering. I opened my mouth to speak but could not and suddenly there was Max rushing at us, his strong fingers shut about my upper arm yanking me back as he shouted at Veronica in his hoarse, broken voice: "She can't see this! Take her away! Shut her eyes! *Take her.*"

Later when they'd driven Ansel to the hospital I returned to the terrace with a flashlight, for now it was dusk: and there was the blood on the cracked flagstones, and there was the paring knife where it had fallen from Ansel's fingers, still wet with blood. So it had happened, it was real.

And the thought consoled me, as it does now: everything you believe you have imagined is real. You have only to outlive it.

The Enemy

Knowing nothing of what had been shoved beneath our door and yet: what she did not know but must have sensed made her sick. For on Monday morning, Minette woke with a fever. Through the plasterboard wall between our bedrooms I heard her coughing. Later she staggered to the bathroom to be sick to her stomach. Protesting she never got sick, hadn't missed a day of school not hardly ever. Without the pink-plastic glasses Minette's eyes appeared strangely naked, heavy-lidded and dazed. Her fleshy lips looked dry, cracked. I said, "There's flu going around, Minette. It isn't a sign of moral weakness or anything. Why don't you go back to—"

" 'Scuse*me*! No."

Minette quivered with disdain. She was one whom illness frightened. The flu was just some "bug" going around, she said. She had too much work to do, classes to get to, biology lab . . . Her eyes were shiny with moisture, not quite in focus. I saw that she was trembling. Inside the tight-belted navy blue bathrobe her fleshy body seemed turned in upon itself, cringing.

Minette had gained maybe fifteen pounds since she'd arrived at Schuyler. Breasts, thighs, fattish-muscular legs. Still her face was that of a twelve-year-old girl, tough, stubborn, sullen about the mouth. In the aftermath of her feverish sleep she smelled of her body, yeasty and just perceptibly sour.

"But if you're sick, Minette—"

Hotly Minette reacted, "You hear me, I don't get *sick*."

She would have pushed past me, unsteady on her feet, except she succumbed to a fit of coughing. I dared to take her hand that was burning-hot, and very dry. "Minette, come on! You will only get well if you keep warm, and sleep." I had never spoken like this to Minette, I had never touched her. I, who was careless of my own health, who often pushed myself to exhaustion as a kind of punishment for my shortcomings and half-welcomed that tinge at the back of my skull that signaled the onset of a headache, felt strongly the wish to protect my roommate from such folly.

" 'Scuseme I just *can't*."

Minette spoke less certainly now. Almost, she was pleading, anxious.

" 'Scuseme, Minette: you *had better*."

Weakly Minette laughed. My uncharacteristic forcefulness startled her. She began coughing, shivering. Hugging herself as if her ribs ached. She had no choice but to return to bed before her knees buckled. I would bring her fruit juice, buttered toast, small boxes of sugary cereal and jelly donuts from the dining hall. I would make her cups of tea, cocoa, bouillon on Dana Johnson's Pullman stove (no undergraduate residents of Haven House were allowed even hot plates in their rooms); I brought her aspirins, cold tablets. I even brought her mail upstairs: helped her open a fastidiously wrapped package from her mother containing a pair of hand-knit gloves, corn bread, and chocolate fudge which Minette tried to eat, but could not keep down. I ran around campus to speak with Minette's professors explaining that Minette was ill; I got her assignments for her, went to the library to take out books for her, cut classes of my own to attend her classes and take notes. "What a good roommate you are, Genna. Wish I had a roommate like *you*." Crystal Odom winked at me in passing.

I understood, I was talked-of, resented. I felt eyes upon me. I thought *Minette Swift's enemies want her to fail. But she won't.*

I had shielded Minette from the racist drawing. She knew nothing of *Hottentot Venus* for I'd quickly destroyed it, ripped it to pieces within minutes of discovering it on the floor of our room.

Whoever was responsible, whoever hated Minette Swift, certainly lived in Haven House. It might have been, must have been the same person or persons who'd taken her Norton anthology and damaged it. No one else would have such access to our room on the third floor of the residence, and no one else would feel such animosity for Minette. I had learned that, in Bob-o-links, Minette had been considered "rude"—"haughty"—the director Miss Bidelman wasn't the only person she'd quarreled with—yet still the enemy had to live in our residence. I knew this! I knew, as certainly as if I'd seen one of the girls make her stealthy way along the third-floor dim-lighted hall, stoop and shove the photocopied page beneath our door and hurry away . . .

I could almost see that girl's face.

One of the revered traditions of Schuyler College was the honor code. You signed an oath, you vowed you would not cheat and you would not shield others who cheated. It was nearly as grave a violation of the honor code to fail to report cheating, as to cheat. Students who violated the honor code were severely disciplined, at least in theory. And so it may have been wrong of me not to report the racist drawing. I had reacted impulsively, without thinking. I could not possibly have shown it to Minette, and I did not want to show it to Dana Johnson. I'd torn the paper to pieces, and flushed them down a toilet. I was upset, agitated as if the insult had been directed toward me.

A racist, or racists, in Haven House: was it possible?

Enemies of Minette Swift, in any case. That was obvious.

I thought of the photograph of the lynching, in my father's father's study. That too was the obscene.

Though the drawing had been destroyed, still I might have reported the incident to Dana Johnson. But I did not. As days passed, I had time to think the situation through, to analyze it and to determine what behavior on my part was most appropriate. I think that I had not wanted to share such ugliness with any other person: a white woman like Dana Johnson, for instance. Nor did I want to be the one to cause upset, mortification to Schuyler College. I did not want so isolated and perverse an incident to be taken up by the media like similar racist and anti-Semitic incidents at other colleges. I did not want to give the enemy so much power.

Above all, I had not wanted Minette to know. I did not want her to be hurt. I did not want her to recoil in anger, disgust. I did not want her to think *white racism*. I did not want to suddenly discover myself, as in a nightmare of reversals, made by Minette into one of the white enemy, who knew herself Minette Swift's only friend at Schuyler College.

I did not want Minette's parents to know: I feared Reverend Virgil Swift's wrath.

I would wonder if the act hadn't been purely personal, aimed against Minette Swift as an individual, and not "racist." Yet how swiftly and crudely the personal becomes the racial! As if, beneath ordinary hatred, there is a deeper, more virulent and deadly racial hatred to be tapped. As the nineteenth-century British looked upon the "Hottentot Venus" (a naively trusting young South African woman who had cooperated with her exploiters, I'd discovered) as a crude sexual spectacle, a brute and not a human being to be ogled, displayed in a carnival, eventually dissected for "scientific" purposes. It was sickening, such cruelty. Yet exhilarating to know for always there is power in knowledge.

Racists are not hypocrites Max Meade once provocatively said. *Unlike some liberals.*

How I wanted to speak with Max about this incident! Someday.

A nasty strain of "Hong Kong flu" had struck campus. After two days in bed, Minette wasn't recovering and was advised to check into the infirmary. So weak, so sick, Minette hadn't the strength to resist. Dana Johnson would drive us in her car. I helped Minette put on warm clothing over her pajamas, I packed her toiletries for her. I had no care that I, too, might succumb to flu; I seemed to feel that caring for Minette gave me immunity.

As I helped Minette out of our room, along the corridor and down the steep stairs to where Dana Johnson awaited us, I was aware of being covertly observed. I understood that Minette's enemies would dislike me, too, for my loyalty to her. Already I'd been mocked when they'd taken her book to toss into the mud and mutilate.

Max'milian Meade's daughter what can you expect?

No one spoke to us as we slowly descended the stairs, Minette leaning heavily on me. But as we were leaving the residence with Dana Johnson, there came Lisane into the foyer, breathless with running; seeing us, she stopped in her tracks and stared, smiling nervously. "Minette is sick? Going to the infirmary?" In the Korean girl's creamy-pale, plain-pretty face there seemed to me a look of regret, or guilt.

Minette was in the infirmary for several days. She had plenty of company there, nearly every bed was taken. I ran over to see her often, I even spoke on the phone with her mother when Mrs. Swift called each evening. Phone calls were not allowed in the infirmary and so I assured Mrs. Swift that Minette had only the flu that everyone seemed to have, a sore throat and a very bad cold. Mrs. Swift was grateful to speak with me though clearly she'd never heard my name or anything about me from Minette.

I told her that Minette was improving daily. I told her that I hoped to meet her sometime, and her family. I told her that I had never seen such beautiful hand-knit gloves as she had knitted for Minette, that rich coppery color, a diamond pattern at the wrists in dark brown.

O Come Let Us Adore Him

"Remember me, your hippie-mom? The one who burnt the turkey?"

On the phone Veronica laughed like one eager to share any joke, even one at her own expense.

It was December, the pre-Christmas season. A tunnel of rapidly accelerating time when day narrowed to night by 4:30 P.M. Faithfully and naively I awaited my father's (promised) telephone call (for hadn't Max said he wanted to visit the Elias Meade House he had not seen in fifteen years, hadn't he expressed a wish to meet my roommate Minette Swift) but in his place my mother called instead.

My nightly conversations with Mrs. Swift had abruptly ceased when Minette was discharged from the infirmary. Minette never spoke to me of her mother, as she never spoke to me of anyone in her family, and I had to wonder if Mrs. Swift ever spoke to Minette of me.

We'd become friends, I had thought. On the phone.

I don't believe we've formally met, Mrs. Swift! I'm Genna Meade, Minette's roommate.

I promise: I will protect Minette. I think that I have protected Minette already.

Through the darkening days of December I continued to await Max Meade but Veronica Hewett-Meade arrived instead, one Saturday at midday. Hoping to meet my roommate but I'd made excuses for Minette: too busy, too shy, never eats lunch, doesn't have time for a two-hour dinner at the Schuylersville Inn where only the busboys were dark-skinned. I squirmed in misery at the thought of Minette and my mother meeting: Minette staring with her look of faint incredulity and disdain at the middle-aged white woman smiling so eagerly at her, drawing back as Veronica leaned forward. If, as she chattered nervously, Veronica made the mistake of touching Minette's wrist or arm, Minette would shrink visibly away. *'Scuseme!*

This nightmare did not happen, Veronica was spared and I was spared.

Instead, Veronica drove us to the newly opened Valley Forge Mall thirty miles west and south of Schuylersville. It was a mother/daughter outing in the pre-Christmas season. When I'd lived in the house at Chadds Ford I'd rarely gone shopping with Veronica and so it seemed very strange for us to be drifting amid frantic/festive shoppers most of them Caucasian, female, affluent; very strange to be wandering in and out of the high-priced stores I had been brought up to despise, and did despise. Strange, a ritual-remnant from a long-ago religion in which neither of us believed, yet there was a logic to it, for only in the Valley Forge Mall climate-controlled and illuminated by a galaxy of lights like a giant spacecraft making its way through the emptiness of space, only in this improbable setting new to us as a brightly lighted stage upon which we'd been, mother/daughter, Veronica/Genna, hastily pushed to enact a scene unscripted and unpre-pared by either, might Veronica have suddenly confided in me, with a tug of her fingers on my wrist, how lonely she was, and how restless in her lone-liness, and how when she was restless she looked for someone to blame: "It's my failing. My wounded soul. I come from a 'wounded' class: ex-ploited, but unconscious of being exploited. Identifying with their oppres-sors. How can I expect Max, or any man, to heal me! Healing must come from within. Better to be proudly raw and wounded, and never to heal, even to fester, than to hope for healing from 'without.' I believe this." Veronica spoke breathlessly, with a lurching sort of conviction, like one re-peating the words of an ancient prayer. "He must have his freedom. He has given me mine. He is the most extraordinary human being I have ever known and of course no one can 'possess' him."

Veronica's voice quivered with humility. And the rage beneath humility. I heard, but would pretend not to hear. I was frightened of both.

"It's futile, you know, to say 'my husband'—as you and Rickie can say 'my father.' One is a biological fact, the other is just a legal term. So futile."

"But 'my father' means possession, too. Like 'my mother.' "

I was playing the bright-bratty schoolgirl. Quick in debate, provocative.

I had not meant to wound, exactly. *My mother.* Hadn't I been discouraged to call this woman any name other than *Veronica*?

Veronica laughed, sharply as if she'd been stung. We were walking swiftly though in no clear direction. Past gaily decorated store front windows, beneath garlands of evergreens, red-and-green winking lights. I understood from frequent glances in our direction that my mother was conspicuously dressed though I had not wished to examine her too closely. I wanted to ask if she and my father were separated, if that was the explanation for Max's protracted absence from Chadds Ford. I wanted to ask if she and my father would be divorced. If, for all I knew, they were already divorced! I could taste the bitter satisfaction, my wishes as a daughter had nothing to do with my parents' private lives.

Instead I spoke of Max having called me at Haven House, his promise to visit me soon. My words were vaguely boastful to suggest that Max called me frequently. Just the other evening . . .

"Yes! Max will see you, Genna. He will make it up to you, these past few months. He loves you." Veronica spoke urgently as if she'd been entrusted with a message she might forget. "He will be proud of you 'one day'—he has said."

"Proud of *me*? Why?"

I laughed, I was so stricken. Mad Max reaching into my rib cage to grab my beating heart.

But Veronica insisted, "Of course, your father is proud of you now. But he looks to the future, you know Max: 'the future will redeem us.' He says, you don't have the personality to be a political activist, or a lawyer like him; but you have the intelligence and patience to be a historian, and the depth of character to 'mold future minds.' Max has said."

Max has said. These oracular words uttered by my hippie-mom as if they were nothing out of the ordinary. As she paused to peer nearsightedly into the crowded interior of a women's shoe store advertising PRE-CHRISTMAS SALE! BARGAINS 10–30% OFF!

When I asked Veronica what Max meant by this, was he serious, when had he said these things, she became vague, defensive: "Genna, I don't know! He will tell you. I think it had something to do with—research? In a library? 'Archives'? You could do research into the 'original' Generva Meade. In the Schuyler library special collections there are all sorts of letters, a journal . . . The material is restricted but you are the woman's great-granddaughter, you would have the right."

A historian? Of my own namesake? This sounded like one of Veronica's extravagant flights of speech.

"I don't want to be a 'Meade.' I want to make my own way."

Veronica shrugged. In her soul she was indifferent to the Meades, untouched. "But this way, Max thinks, would be a way to be respected."

We were losing our momentum, in the Valley Forge Mall. I saw that my mother was a "sight": the sleek dyed-black hair wasn't twisted into a top-knot today but spilled over her shoulders like a young girl's hair. With a defiant sense of style she wore leather gaucho pants, a black serape of some dense-knit wool threaded with gold that shifted and swirled about her. And tight sexy knee-high black leather boots with stiletto heels upon which she teetered like a large ungainly exotic tropical bird.

I wore my rumpled camel's hair coat over faded jeans. My boots were salt-stained from the previous winter. No makeup! My face was fierce-plain and pale like scrubbed soapstone. On my head the wool cap yanked low on my forehead so that I more resembled a middle school boy than a Schuyler College undergraduate woman.

We drifted in and out of stores. Veronica made several spontaneous purchases, paying in cash. We were pursued from store to store by piped-in Christmas carols: "Jingle Bell Rock" was a favorite. There was "O Come Let Us Adore Him" buzzing about our heads like gigantic flies. Veronica insisted upon having lunch at a vegetarian café on the mall though she ate very little, twice lighting up cigarettes and crushing them out with a stammered apology. In Lord & Taylor at a crowded handbag counter she selected a "pre-Christmas" present for me: "You can use this, Genna! Don't make a face. Toss away that ratty old bag you've had forever."

I shrugged. I gave in. The new handbag was Italian leather, very attractive. The price was absurdly high but Veronica took pleasure in counting out bills onto the palm of the politely smiling salesclerk. The bag was the size of a briefcase, with a shoulder strap. Minette would (possibly) notice it for she had a sharp eye for such things but would she remark upon it? probably not.

As if reading my thoughts Veronica asked if I would be buying my roommate a present. I frowned and mumbled what might have sounded like *yes* but did not pursue the subject.

Xenogeneic. It was a term from biology. Meaning a curious break between generations. Offspring "significantly different" from a parent or parents. In gigantic frosted mirrors along the mall "promenade" I observed us.

I'd begun to feel light-headed, floating. It was a sensation that came over me sometimes when I'd been reading, working late into the night. Or secluded away in an area of the library where few others ventured for hours at a time thinking *Why? Why am I here, and not somewhere else? And where exactly is here?* This woman who was my mother and whom I was obliged to love, to feel very sorry for and to love, to be embarrassed of, ashamed of, impatient and disgusted with yet to love, this woman and I were—what were we doing?—gazing upward in a pretense of awed admiration at the most gigantic Christmas tree either of us had ever seen, in the courtyard at the heart of the Valley Forge Mall: synthetic, satiny-white, covered in twinkling baubles and candy canes and winking blue lights. Close by this tree was a fattish Santa Claus, mechanical in behavior but evidently human, an eager queue of children waiting to clamber onto his lap. One of Santa's more aggressive dwarf-elves in wig, whiskers was shaking his bell at passersby, who gave him a wide berth. Veronica was chattering about what we might do at Christmas, who might visit us, I did not hear Max's name and did not intend to inquire wanting suddenly to laugh loudly, to turn on my heel and walk away from my mother in the serape and stiletto heels, in my mind's eye I was seeing *Hottentot Venus* which was the emblem perhaps of all women, it was a pornographic image rendered in derision, disgust, loathing, *Hottentot Venus the Toast of London 1815.* Never had I seen any image so grotesque and so fascinating, close up. Never held the evidence of hatred in my hand. I wished now that I had not destroyed the drawing, for now I had no proof that it had ever existed.

I interrupted Veronica to ask, in the way of an adolescent daughter trying to recall something long-ago and uncertain: "Is Daddy still in contact with, what was his name . . . You had to take him to the emergency room, he'd ripped open his belly. Is that where Max is, with him? 'Ansel Trimmer'? Somewhere in Altoona, or . . ." My voice trailed off in vague innocence as Veronica turned to stare at me.

"Genna, what are you saying? I've never heard of that—name. Either of those names. I don't know what you're talking about."

I would have shrugged and walked on, except Veronica seized my wrist. This was not the light flirtatious touch I had imagined for Minette, this was a talon-grip.

In my ear Veronica said hotly, "Max has no contact with whatever you are hinting. Whatever name, I've never heard that name."

Quickly I nodded, yes. I was trying not to be frightened.

"Your father is an officer of the court. He has sworn to uphold the law of this country. He has never violated the law. You know that, you are the man's daughter."

The sensation of light-headedness seemed to rush at me, from all sides. I was feeling faint, panicked. Santa's antic dwarf-elf had overheard something of Veronica's words and grinned at us with glittery eyes. Harder he rang his bell in our direction, as if to goad my mother on.

I tried to pull away from Veronica, who would not release me. Together we stumbled like drunks. *Nice-Mommy, bad-Mommy* had me in her talon-grip. Out of nowhere moving stairs erupted from the floor as in a child's nightmare, Veronica would have blundered into the escalator except for my vigilance. Her Cleopatra eyes were not coquettish now but sharp, glaring. Her delicate thin nose was a raptor's beak. "You! What do you know! Nothing of Ansel, and nothing of any of that time. It is all so complicated, you can't guess! Ansel was an innocent, he meant to injure no one. None of them did. No one knew there would be a guard there. It was not intentional, it was an accident of history." Veronica was breathless, now sarcastic: "Oh yes, looking back it's easy to say 'Of course there would be security guards, there would be a night watchman.' But then, you targeted the enemy. There were many enemies deserving of punishment and so you targeted the most vulnerable. You concentrated your energies on expediting your goal. Dow Chemical was the target. This was a target that deserved annihilation. You, looking at me like that, you little shit, who are you to judge? Look at me like that who the fuck d'you think you are? You could argue, anybody on the payroll of those fascists manufacturing napalm was risking his life. Legs blown off. Even a black security guard."

Startled shoppers observed us: a derailed mother/daughter pair stumbling along the "Grand Promenade" of the Valley Forge Mall with no evident awareness of our surroundings. How rapidly my hippie-mom had changed. How furious, and radiant in her fury. I realized her contempt for me, in my naiveté I had imagined it was I who felt a mild daughterly contempt for her. Recalling how long ago when I'd been a little girl there was nice-Mommy and bad-Mommy the one hidden inside the other like a jack-in-the-box. I had not liked surprises as a child. I had not liked toys that sprang up into my face. I had not liked toys that erupted in noise. Inside the camel's hair coat I was sweating, in the knit cap pulled down low over my forehead to disguise my face's resemblance to the ruined-beautiful face of Veronica Hewett-Meade I was sweating. Veronica slapped at me, but did not release me: "Ansel is nowhere we know. He is not in the United States. Max is not in contact with him or with any of them from that time. It is all behind us, that time. I was never one of them, they scorned me. I was too weak, they were right to scorn me. Poor Ansel he'd meant to commit hari-kari—but wound up instead with dozens of ugly stitches in his belly. A long nasty scar twisted like a corkscrew. A 'miracle' they said at the ER, that they could save him. Trimming trees out in Chadds Ford, an accident, freak accident with a chain saw—"

Veronica's mad rush of words abruptly ceased. She'd been drawing attention. She'd said too much, teetering on stiletto heels and her dyed-black hair dragging in her face. The burnt–orange peel smell lifted from her skin. Whatever powerful medication had fueled her frantic energy, inspiring her to drive not only to Schuylersville from Chadds Ford but to

Valley Forge from Schuylersville was rapidly departing from her, like water swirling down a drain.

The Christmas carol tape had looped back: perky-demented "Jingle Bell Rock" giving way again in a few short beats to sappy-reverent "O Come Let Us Adore Him."

Veronica whispered what sounded like *Oh Genna. Help me.*

I helped her to a bench near one of the mall entrances. She was so exhausted, she could barely walk and leaned heavily on me, breathing into my face. *Oh Genna, Genna. Oh help.*

On this bench an elderly wispy-white-haired disheveled woman was also seated. As we approached she glanced up at us squinting as if expecting she might know us. In her distraught state Veronica regarded her with a look of terror. The woman's stumpy legs were encased in thick support stockings, her veiny face was slack and her mouth damp with saliva. Under her breath she was singing along with the Christmas carol. I knew that Veronica did not want me to leave her on the bench with the elderly woman, but I had no choice. I ran out into the enormous parking lot, to search for Veronica's car in a lightly falling snow. Only vaguely had I taken note of where we'd parked, it would take me nearly a half-hour to locate the car and bring it around for Veronica to hobble to, leaning on my arm and whimpering in my ear: "One day I will be that pathetic old woman. I will be singing to myself and laughing and crying and shitting my pants and no one will give a damn for why should they? Strangers will shrink from me as if I am a leper. One day that will happen to us both."

As I hadn't thought to note precisely where Veronica had parked her car, so I hadn't thought to bring my driver's license with me on the mother/daughter adventure. Still, I drove us back to Schuylersville while Veronica slept in the seat beside me, head lolling, crimson mouth agape. I would ask nothing further about Max and Ansel Trimmer. Never again would I speak of Ansel Trimmer. Never speak his name again to my mother as I would never speak it to Max. Thinking *Whatever I don't know, is not meant for me to know.*

Sick

And after that I was sick for a while and it would seem to me that the sickness had begun in the climate-controlled air of the Valley Forge Mall and that my mother had brought me there in stealth to be infected. For my head was wracked with pain like broken glass, my eyes leaked acid-tears. My bowels were fiery with diarrhea. Yet out of stubbornness I dragged myself to my classes where I succumbed to coughing spells, choking on clots of greeny phlegm the size of half-dollars. *Shrink from me as from a leper. One day that will happen to us both.*

In my bed I lay for hours neither asleep nor awake. The shade on my window had been pulled to the sill. It was no loss to me that the world veered on without me. Minette came frowning to the door, to peer inside and to scold. What comfort, in being scolded like a younger sister! In Minette's voice I heard the voices of Reverend Virgil Swift and Mrs. Swift. I knew that Minette would not let me die though she was impatient and exasperated with me, disapproving of sickness in others as in herself for wasn't it just weakness! the flu was just weakness! giving in when you should be strong yet Minette brought me fruit juice and toast, sweet rolls, waffles wrapped in napkins from the dining hall, fed me a piece of her momma's gingerbread that was so delicious I began to tremble. Naturally Minette was away from the room most of the day. Alone in the room I drifted, floated. My throat was sore as if scraped with razor blades. Yet I would not ask to be taken to the infirmary. So long as I floated, my bowels would not turn to liquid fire. I could not clearly recall the Dow Chemical bombing, I had been too young to care or to know or to make connections yet there came to me a memory blurred as damp newsprint the photograph of the black man killed in the blast, legs blown off and he'd crawled out of the burning rubble dragging himself as he bled to death, I was a ghost observing, I was a ghost blown about by the air-vent winds of the Valley Forge Mall hearing again Veronica's furious rush of words. Seeing again the raptor face. *You could argue, anyone on the payroll.*

In my fever wondering: how innocent had Veronica been? The outburst, the revelation. Providing me, Max Meade's daughter, with information I should not know. Had it been deliberate. Had it been scripted. As an actress who has memorized her lines forgets them in the emotion of the moment yet uttering what flies into her head reproduces these lines flawlessly. Had Veronica come to this very residence, to bring me to that place for a motive unknown to me, unimaginable. The climate-controlled spacecraft plunging through emptiness where she might reveal to me, her daughter, knowledge forbidden elsewhere. *And all revealed in that place she would repudiate at another time and in another place little shit you'd better know that.*

Notes on My Roommate
Minette Swift

Lost. Ohhh where was it! where was Minette's left-hand glove of the pair her mother had knitted for her, had she left it somewhere? had it fallen out of the crammed pocket of her jacket? had someone stolen it out of mean-ness, spite? We heard her stomping on the stairs in Haven House so angry! disgusted! frustrated! as if she wanted to bring the stairs down with her. Dropped her bookbag on the third-floor landing, had to trudge all the way back to the lecture room in Woburn Hall, could not find the glove in the row she'd been sitting in, or in any row, or on the floor, or on the stairs, so dis*gusted*. No choice but to trudge across the quad to the library where she'd dropped off books before her American lit. lecture, possibly she'd lost the glove there, always things are falling out of her pockets she has to stoop to retrieve, or somebody calls to her, hands them to her, this extra weight she's been gaining has made her short of breath, her clothes are tight and tugging at her, seems like even her eyeglasses are too tight for her face, and the lenses are weakening, smudgy and steamy half the time, Ohhhh she is so anxious to find that glove it's like every nasty old thing that has happened since coming to this place, every insult not-to-be-named, for Jesus has cautioned not-to-name evil at the expense of good, every nasty insult and loss is caught up in that glove, Momma's hand-knit glove *Ohhh where was it!*

Crossing the quad sighting the roommate, red-haired white girl so pushy-friendly Minette would duck away to avoid her except what's-her-name has seen Minette, approaches with a quickened step, a wave and a smile, Minette is stony-faced not intending to tell of the missing glove but somehow she does, and the roommate exclaims without thinking, "Oh

Minette. You didn't," and Minette flares up, "*I* didn't? *I* didn't? How'd you know what *I* did, and *I* didn't!" Minette laughs in exasperation wanting to make a joke of her loss, but it comes out confused, incoherent. Minette is panting: pudgy nostrils widening and narrowing. Shell-pink plastic glasses slip-sliding down her nose. Complaining, "I can't keep any darn thing. It's like some wicked old hole sucking things *in*." To make the staring room-mate laugh, keep her at a distance, Minette turns the crammed pockets of her jacket inside out: here's the lone remaining glove of the hand-knitted pair, a vivid coppery-color, here's a handful of tissues (fresh and used-wadded), a near-empty box of Smarties, sugar and ketchup packets from the dining hall. High-pitching her voice in mimicry of her mother: " 'Min-*ette*! Your face always in some book, you'd lose your head if it wa'n't stuck on your shoulders.' My momma is going to be dis*gusted* with me, losing this glove so fast. And she'd be right."

Minette laughs shrilly, swiping at her nose. Girls passing by glance at her: a stout black girl with an oily-dark skin, pink schoolgirl glasses. Minette takes up the sidewalk, seemingly unaware. Used-wadded tissues have fallen onto the walk, Minette kicks them away. The other items she has carelessly crammed back into her jacket pockets.

It's a hulking down jacket, dark green with a hood.

The roommate: small-boned very young-looking white girl with a bleached-out face covered in freckles like water drops tinged with rust. Her hair is rust-colored, too. Fine, frizzy-curly. Her eyes are luminous-gray, somber as stones. Eyebrows and lashes so pale, the eyes look naked. Like you can see into them too deeply, and you don't want that.

Minette goes silent, grinding her back teeth. Seeing the roommate so close. What's-her-name: Genna. The sudden wish comes over Minette to shove this white-girl Genna away with the heel of her hand, hard.

Quickly the roommate says, "Minette, I didn't take your glove . . ."

Minette blinks at the roommate as if she can't have heard this plain-tive remark correctly. " 'Scuseme *what*? Who'd ever said you did *what*?"

Scowling Minette shakes her head, she's never had a thought so fool-ish. *Yet I felt it. Saw it. Minette Swift biting her lower lip to keep from shoving me away.*

Somehow the roommate, wanted/unwanted, has attached herself to Minette to search for the lost glove. Two of them trudging across the windswept quad to the library where (Minette knows, resigned) they won't find the glove. Next, the gym? dining hall? retracing steps back to Haven House? Minette is in a sullen mood, knows she won't find the lost glove, not the first glove or mitten her mother knitted for her that Minette Swift has lost in her eighteen years, always Minette seems to be losing things in this place, or things are being stolen from her, like some magnet is drawing them out of her grasp and into a gigantic open mouth-hole at her feet. This mouth-hole chewingchewing, evil old thing you can almost hear in the night.

Lost. Minette's missing glove! I would discover it a few days later in the gutter outside Haven House, stiffened with dirt amid icy slush and mud. I had not been looking for the glove any longer, just happened to see it at the curb as I was crossing the street.

"Oh, Minette."

With some difficulty I extricated the glove from a tangle of icy debris. It was covered in filth, almost unrecognizable. Yet it was Minette's glove: I could discern the diamond pattern at the wrist, in dark brown. I decided to wash it, I could not bring it to Minette in such condition. I used Woolite and cold water, letting the glove soak, then washing it gently, slipping it on my hand. The glove was too large for my hand, for Minette's hands were larger than mine. The diamond pattern was less pronounced than I recalled. The coppery color had faded to a dirty beige. In the mirror above the sink my face appeared flushed, furtive. I was in the third-floor bathroom, outside our room; I would not have wished Minette Swift to enter the bathroom, to discover me with her glove. My lips moved in a whisper: "Minette! I didn't take your glove . . ." seeing again how strangely she'd stared at me, as if in distrust, dislike. Seeing again how Minette had edged away from me.

We were roommates, and friends. By slow degrees we had become friends. Yet Minette remained distant, aloof. You could say that our friendship was one-sided, yet I believed that Minette liked me, and accepted me. *Her only friend! Her only friend at Schuyler College.*

I hid away Minette's glove to dry. When I brought it to her, Minette stared doubtfully at it, and slowly took it from me. "It's all *shrunk*."

I explained that I'd found it in the gutter, I'd had to wash it. Minette forced the glove onto her hand, flexed her fingers. In the mock-southern-Negro voice Minette sometimes lapsed into for a harshly comic effect she said, " 'Scuseme, this ain't my glove."

"Minette, what? It's your glove."

I wasn't so certain, though. Minette was seated at her desk, I stood beside her. We examined the glove from all sides as Minette turned her hand slowly. "Naw. It ain't a match. Some ol' throwaway in the street. That's what this is."

"Where's the other glove, Minette? We can check."

"Don't need to check. I said this ain't my glove."

Minette's face had gone sullen. She'd been in an irritable mood, I should not have interrupted her: hunched at her desk working on calculus problems, fidgeting and sighing. From time to time she slid open her desk drawer, to break off pieces of a peach crumb cake her mother had sent her; eating as she worked, scattering crumbs onto her papers, her clothing and on the floor.

Minette laughed. "This ol' glove fits you, *you* take it."

She peeled off the glove and tossed it in my direction, in the manner of a bullying older sister. It seemed to me a gesture of familiarity that assumed affection, of a kind; I did not want to think that it assumed contempt.

Since *Hottentot Venus* Minette had been sulky-angry, unpredictable in her moods. (Though she could not have known anything about *Hottentot Venus* shoved beneath our door.) Since that Sunday morning I had followed her to the First Baptist Church of Schuylersville and left her sitting alone at a bench above the river. (Though she could not have known that I'd followed her.)

The day following the glove incident, Minette apologized: admitting she'd thrown out the remaining glove in disgust, so she hadn't anything to compare the found glove with. She'd been embarrassed to tell me. She'd been feeling bad, always losing things. Oh she was "sorry to be rude"—"hadn't meant to be rude." Minette's thick-lashed eyes, slightly magnified by the lenses of her glasses, were downcast and evasive; her voice was nearly inaudible, a low earnest murmur, all humility now and utterly different from the mockery of the Negro drawl.

The revelation came to me *This is Jesus speaking. Jesus is the one to love his enemies.*

Now I began to worry that my father would call, and come to see me, and he and Minette Swift would meet at last, and the meeting would go badly.

Minette would turn very quiet if Max questioned her too closely. As he'd questioned my friends from prep school, so he would try to draw Minette out as a "black American"—an exploited, colonized victim of Caucasian/American imperialism. And Minette would resent this, of course. For Minette was supremely herself.

Max would be disappointed in Minette. He'd been involved with Black Panther cases, Angela Davis. Minette shuddered in disdain of such "Communists." I could not bear to have my father learn that Minette Swift scorned jazz and claimed never to have heard Billie Holiday sing.

Still, I awaited Max's call. I think I did.

Genna? Give me a call, it's lonely here. V.

This pink slip in my mailbox. It wasn't marked URGENT.

With a group of girls from Haven Hall, I went to the Christmas Bob-o-links concert in the college chapel hushed and candlelit and beautifully decorated with white-streaked poinsettias. I heard Crystal Odom sing her solo flawlessly. I felt the loss, that Minette Swift was not in the choir; that she'd cut herself out of the singing group she had so much prized. Another girl with a powerful alto voice had been selected immediately to take Minette's place.

The girls of Bob-o-links were very talented. All their songs were a capella, ingeniously harmonized. They could jive up "Silent Night" and they could make unexpectedly dreamy and seductive "Let It Snow." Even the most mawkish of their songs were very skillfully rendered.

Bob-o-link! Bob-o-link!
Roused by dawn's first gold!
Sing of spirit mysteries yet untold!

Out of loyalty to my roommate I hadn't intended to hear the concert, then out of loyalty to my roommate I would not mention to Minette that I had.

Leaving the dining hall, with Minette. And approaching us were a number of girls from Haven House including Crystal Odom. I saw their eyes move onto us, their facial expressions stiffening. I was on friendly terms with these girls and exchanged greetings with them but Minette stared past them as if unseeing. Crystal smiled at me, and winked. I'd congratulated her the evening before, at a lavish reception hosted by Bob-o-links alums after the concert, and I dreaded her saying something now, to spite Minette.

Head-on and brooding Minette trudged in the middle of the sidewalk, in her bulk down jacket with the hood drawn up. Anyone who approached us had to give way, and walk on the side. Very possibly Minette hadn't seen the girls from our residence, had not noticed Crystal Odom with her insolent smile all but mocking her in passing.

In that instant I thought *She is the one: Crystal.*

My heart beat hard, with the revelation. I knew! It was the most subtle cruelty. For no one would suspect a black girl of harassing another black girl with ugly racist/sexist material. No one would suspect beautiful Crystal Odom of even wishing to harass unbeautiful Minette Swift.

Sunday mornings, Minette still dressed as if for church, primly descended the stairs and crossed the quad in the direction of Schuylersville. I did not follow her of course. I had no idea if she was going to church now, or if she simply stayed away from the room for a while. I thought, this would be Minette's secret, I would never reveal it.

I'd ceased imagining that I would attend church with Minette. I had no wish to attend any church without her. Sometimes alone in the room I leafed through copies of *The Beacon* on the windowsill, glancing at such articles as "The Power of Prayer," "When Jesus Calls." Once, I saw a photograph of a stern-smiling young black woman who resembled Minette Swift to an uncanny degree, but she was a stranger: an "overseas missionary for Jesus."

I leafed through the gilt-edged pages of Minette's Bible like a skeptic tossing dice.

> Then he said unto the disciples, "It is impossible but that offenses shall come: but woe unto him, through whom they come."

He has never violated the law. You know that, you are the man's daughter.

On Pierpont Avenue searching for a Christmas present for my roommate Minette Swift. Wanting to buy her something though knowing that probably Minette wouldn't have anything for me. I did not want to embarrass Minette, or myself. Yet I yearned to surprise her, to make her smile who so rarely smiled lately.

It was like me, a criminal lawyer's daughter, to so obsessively plot a small maneuver: on the final day before Christmas break I would give Minette the present, perhaps I would leave it on her desk. And if Minette didn't have a present for me, she would be spared the embarrassment of my presence.

I vowed not to be hurt, if Minette had nothing for me. I told myself I did not expect it, our friendship did not depend upon such exchanges.

Yet nothing I could find in the stores, shops, boutiques of Pierpont Avenue seemed quite right for Minette. It was my hope to replace the "lost" gloves with new gloves, but such a maneuver would have to be executed with finesse. If I gave Minette gloves inferior to those her mother had knitted, Minette would crinkle her nose *'Scuseme, what's this?* If I gave Minette expensive gloves, this too would be offensive. Only knit gloves would be appropriate but those I found were machine-made, ordinary. And none of the colors was right.

In Alyce's Gifts, a boutique selling handmade crafts, jewelry, clothing, there were beautifully hand-knit mittens, but no gloves.

A middle-aged woman with striking white hair hovered near, perhaps this was Alyce herself. She wore a gorgeous hand-knit cardigan made of heather-colored yarn. She was friendly, meant to quiz me about what I wanted or thought I wanted, but I only just thanked her and drifted out the door. "Thank you! Come back anytime." The woman's words were utterly sincere, not ironic. She was nothing like Veronica in appearance or manner and yet I was reminded of my mother, suddenly I was short of breath and needing to escape.

Little shit. Who are you to judge.

Here was a coincidence: the day after I'd been shopping on Pierpont Avenue, Minette asked in a low embarrassed murmur if I would come with her "to the downtown" to buy a few things. She had Christmas presents to buy, she said. I wondered if she knew that Pierpont Avenue stores tended to be high-priced.

Only two or three times since we'd become acquainted had Minette

Swift and I gone together to Pierpont Avenue, and then only to the college bookstore.

In Minette's company, in Laura Ashley, in Saks, even in Merrick Stationers, I was made to feel acutely self-conscious. At once eyes shifted onto us, and snagged. Minette's presence in a store seemed to trigger small frissons of attentiveness, vigilance. In her bulky down jacket and clumsy boots, with her oily-dark skin, face impassive, unsmiling, Minette must have struck the Caucasian salesclerks as a figure of threat and suspicion, and in her company I had taken on something of that aura. Even when Minette was examining items like wallets, belts, candles that could not possibly be contaminated by her touch, a clerk or clerks hovered near. Repeatedly we were asked, "May I assist you?" and each time Minette shook her head no, and edged away. The clerks were female, straight-backed and impeccably groomed. No one seemed to recall me from the previous day: their expressions were stiffly polite, and their eyes never left us.

I wondered: was it Minette's blackness, or was it Minette's person? Would Crystal Odom be so viewed, with such suspicion? Traci Poole, light-cocoa-skin and Caucasian features and very stylish clothes? There were numerous other dark-skinned girls at Schuyler College, many "foreign"-looking girls, but few of them dressed and behaved like Minette Swift who looked as if she'd come by bus from South Philly . . . Thinking in this way made me uneasy, self-doubting. For wasn't it racist, such reasoning? *The others can be perceived to be middle-class white girls, despite their dark skins, and therefore welcome in white stores; Minette is in no way white. And in no way welcome.*

Yet, in each store, Minette moved about with her usual stolid self-possession, frowning and muttering under her breath. If she saw something she liked, it was invariably too expensive: " 'Scuse*me*! Who'd pay this! Have to be real rich or real dumb."

As our shopping excursion proceeded, Minette's laughter became by quick degrees shrill, derisive. We laughed together. We drew attention to ourselves, laughing. I who was ordinarily unobtrusive in any public place, well behaved to the point of invisibility, felt now the impulse to behave rudely. A kind of wildness came over me, a wish to cause upset. The genteel Caucasian-female eyes would widen in fright, if Minette and I began to misbehave in the way it was feared we might misbehave.

In our wake, as we left each store, I imagined exchanges of glances, relief! Though neither Minette nor I had committed any discernible act, let alone any act of vandalism or desecration, it would require some minutes for the shock waves to subside.

So black is Minette Swift, her blackness spills over onto a companion and the two of you become black.

Was this funny? Was it tragic? Maybe this was what Minette was laughing at, instinctively.

I tried to talk Minette into buying something at the college bookstore where we'd have been treated much more hospitably, but Minette shrugged me off: "Any book I get for Jewel, she won't read 'cause I got it for her. You can't push that girl's face in anything, she's stubborn." Minette spoke with a kind of proud exasperation.

I told Minette that I'd met Jewel, briefly. Minette turned to stare at me in disbelief.

"*You* did? When?"

"In the Elias Meade House."

" 'Scuseme what house? Where's this?"

We were crossing a street. In the fresh, cold, wet air of December, we were not so inclined to hilarity as we'd been inside the stores. I was trying not to feel disappointed that Minette seemed to remember neither me nor Elias Meade House itself, from that day in September.

"The old red-brick Federalist house on campus. You know, the 'historical' landmark where Elias Meade lived."

" 'Elias Meade'—who's that?"

"The founder of Schuyler College." I tried to sound neutral, indifferent. But my heart beat hard in disappointment. Had there ever been anyone so lacking in curiosity, so self-absorbed as my roommate Minette Swift! "It was his house we were taken through, on the guided tour."

Minette seemed only vaguely to remember the guided tour. Clearly it was confused in her memory with the numerous other events of that overscheduled Orientation Day. When I mentioned that I'd first seen her there, with her family, though of course we hadn't known each other then, Minette crinkled her nose in disbelief: "*That* old house? Like a pioneer museum? You were there? You never were!"

But I was, I told Minette. It was rare for me to surprise my roommate, let alone astonish her. She was looking at me, regarding me, with genuine interest.

I told her that her sister Jewel and I had climbed together up the secret staircase behind the chimney.

" 'Secret staircase'—?"

"The Elias Meade House was a stop on the Underground Railroad."

" 'Underground Railroad.' "

Minette spoke these words in a vague neutral voice. I could not determine if she knew perfectly well what the Underground Railroad had been or whether the phrase triggered only an indistinct memory associated with that sacrosanct subject *American history*.

I described the kitchen of Elias Meade House, the large fireplace and chimney, the "storage space" in the wall, how Jewel poked her head into it and before anyone could stop her climbed inside, and Minette interrupted with maddening certainty: "Jewel wasn't there. It was just my parents and me, and we didn't stay."

"Minette, no. Jewel was there, we climbed up the stairs together . . ."

"I don't remember any stairs. I sure don't remember Jewel climbing up any stairs in any old museum-house."

"Well, you couldn't actually see her, or me. We were inside the wall, in this secret space. We climbed all the way up into the attic and scared ourselves in the dark and then your mother called Jewel back down . . ." I wasn't sure if this had been so, but it seemed plausible.

Yet Minette shook her head, unconvinced. I thought *Why are you so stubborn! So blind!*

I wondered if it was a racist expectation: that any black would be more perceptive than any white, in such a situation? Or could a black be as stubborn, as blind, as any white? I wished that Jewel were with us, to bear witness to my testimony. Jewel would remember me!

It was pointless to reason with Minette, she refused to listen. I did not want to think that in some nightmare fashion I might be mistaken, myself; maybe I had climbed the stairs with the younger sister of another black girl, and had subsequently confused this girl with Minette Swift . . . I'd forgotten my own mother, after all.

A car horn sounded sharply. I'd stepped out distracted into traffic, oblivious of a red light. Minette seized my arm and with considerable strength yanked me back, hard.

" 'Scuseme!"

I was chastened. I was embarrassed. I'd almost been struck by a car, Minette had saved me.

We walked on, in silence. Minette's breath was panting, steaming in the cold air. It was the first time that Minette had touched me. There was a slight tension between us. I would not even try to dissuade Minette from entering Alyce's Gifts, the most exquisite and expensive of Pierpont Avenue boutiques.

A bell tinkled daintily above the door, to signal our arrival. We were the only customers in the boutique. Quickly there appeared the straight-backed white-haired woman in her gorgeous hand-knit cardigan except today the woman's arms were folded tight across her bosom and her concerned gaze bypassed me entirely. With a look of something like dismay she was staring at Minette. "May I—may I assist you? Is there anything in particular you wish to see?"

Minette was in a truculent mood, scowling at clothing, handbags, jewelry displayed differently than merchandise was displayed in more conventional stores: hanging in small clusters, neatly folded and fanned out on top of polished lamplit tables, in stacked Plexiglas cases like works of art in a gallery. Silks, satins, velvets; knitted and crocheted and embroidered goods; long dresses and skirts, lace blouses, cashmere coat sweaters and elegant fringed shawls; hand-crafted jewelry that seemed to float in the air, illuminated. Minette moved impatiently about, rifling through the hanging clothes, pawing through the neatly folded items of apparel on tables, and the white-haired woman hovered near with a look of pain.

"Ssssh!" Minette held up a hand-knit cardigan sweater in rainbow colors. It might have been ideal for her younger sister Jewel except, as I knew from having priced it the previous day, it cost nearly two hundred dollars. Minette snorted in derision, and let it fall; it slid from the table to the floor, where, as if reflexively, without thinking, Minette gave it a kick.

The white-haired woman gave a little cry: "Excuse me! I am so sorry, I must ask you girls to leave. I'm closing up early this afternoon . . ."

The woman's voice shook. I felt sorry for her, she was so very anxious for her beautiful things. For Minette was stalking about the small boutique heavy-footed, scowling and muttering to herself as if she hadn't heard the woman's words, or, having heard, was choosing to ignore them for as long as she wished. I tried to draw her away but she shrugged me off with an irritable " 'Scuse*me*!" Minette's face looked like something carved out of a dark-stained wood, ageless and sexless and impervious to appeal as a wooden idol would be impervious to appeal. The thought came to me *If this woman calls the police! If we are arrested!*

I would call my father, for help. Except I had no idea where my father was.

At last, Minette relented and stalked to the front of Alyce's Gifts. Like a mischievous child she jiggled the door to make the bell tinkle frantically and in a voice heavy with adolescent sarcasm she said, "Ma'am, Jesus loves you anyway."

In a headache-haze I followed Minette out of the boutique. I could not bring myself to apologize to the frightened white-haired woman. In our wake she hurried to the door, to shut it hard and to lock it. I imagined her trying to recover her breath as her heart beat dangerously hard. She was not Veronica's age but twenty years older at least.

I thought *Now she will fear and hate black people forever. This is Minette Swift's revenge.*

Disgusted, Minette had given up looking for clothes. Still, she intended to buy Christmas candles. This was a relief for Minette could buy candles in Woolworth's Five-and-Dime where black customers were not made to feel self-conscious.

Candles! Strange to see such a variety, not just Christmas candles but every kind of candle. I was struck by Minette's interest. Where she'd been irritable and bad-tempered in the higher-priced stores, now she took her time carefully selecting her purchases: elegantly long tapering candles with an "evergreen" scent; cream-colored candles with a "flower" scent; red candles sparkling with tinsel; squat green candles with little silver handles. There were candles shaped like Christmas trees, and candles shaped like angels. This time of year, Minette said, swiping at her nose, she was missing home "real bad" because they'd have their tree up by now and she'd always helped decorate the tree with some of her special ornaments she'd made herself in Sunday school when she'd been a little girl. "And all that was happening back home and I wasn't there, stuck up here in 'college.'" In the windows of their house upstairs and down there were lights meant to be candles burning, and in the Temple Vale there were candles, and her favorite aunt Florence who'd been a missionary in the Philippines until she got sick and had to come back to D.C., had this custom where each Christmas she "honored Jesus" with candles in her living room forming a cross that measured twenty feet the long way, and five feet across, and on Christmas eve all the relatives came to Aunt Florence's house for a "prayer vigil" from eleven o'clock until midnight. "You can be filled with strife and hate and still Jesus will come into your heart. You can be mean, low-down mean talking trash and acting evil like the worst kind of sinner, still Jesus will come into your heart if you allow him. If you a sinner, and cruel to people, like I know that I am cruel to people sometimes," Minette confided, her voice catching, "still Jesus loves you. That's why I said that to that woman back there, Jesus loves her and maybe Jesus loves me, too. That is the message of Jesus and why He came into the world on Christmas eve." Minette spoke with a strange childlike sincerity. You would not think that this was the same girl who'd been rude and threatening to the woman in Alyce's Gifts only a few minutes before.

Inspired by Minette, I bought several candles myself. Not the heavily scented ones but scentless, and dripless. I told Minette that a "candle vigil" sounded very beautiful, and spiritual. Though I was hoping that Minette wouldn't light any of her scented candles in our overheated room, for even unlighted the candles made my nostrils constrict, like cheap perfume.

And had I seen him watching us. Following us with his eyes on Pierpont Avenue. Following us into Woolworth's where Minette bought candles. A stranger, a dark-skinned man. A glint of eyeglasses.

Yes I saw but no, I did not see. My eyes saw, I took no notice.

A week before Christmas break there was Minette Swift sighted on campus walking with a dark-skinned man!

And in the coffee shop adjoining the bookstore, Minette Swift seated at a window table with a dark-skinned man, the two of them talking earnestly together.

"Can you believe it? Minette?"

"What's he look like?"

"He's older, maybe thirty. He wears glasses. He isn't tall. Sort of ordinary-looking. Dresses like a schoolteacher."

"He's black?"

"He's black."

"Somebody from Minette's church, maybe."

"What church?"

"People think Minette goes to a church in town, probably the Baptist. You see her, Sunday mornings."

I'd heard this before I actually saw them together. Disbelieving I'd heard from girls in Haven Hall. I smiled, to show that I was not shocked. I smiled, to show that I was not jealous. I smiled, though my face hurt.

In our room Minette hummed loudly under her breath. She was excited, distracted. When the telephone rang outside on the landing, she glanced up frowning and alert.

I thought *Why won't she tell me!*

I thought *Maybe he isn't a boyfriend. It's something else.*

Eventually, I saw them together. Minette Swift in the company of a youngish black man, listening as he spoke to her, tentatively smiling, shy in her demeanor; wearing not the bulky down jacket but her attractive red coat with the leopard skin collar. On her head she'd knotted the white angora scarf. Her fleshy lips shone with magenta lipstick.

I wondered if those lips were swollen from kissing. I did not want to imagine Minette Swift kissing, and being kissed.

Minette and her new friend were standing on the sidewalk in front of Haven House. I saw that they were not holding hands. I saw that the black man looked familiar to me: why? There was little distinctive about him. He was taller than Minette by only two or three inches. He wore tortoiseshell glasses, his head was covered in dull-dark nappy hair. His torso was thick, his neck thick. His legs appeared foreshortened. He wore a beige tweed overcoat, polished brown shoe boots. *In Woolworth's. He was watching us.*

He'd sighted me. Even as I was turning away, pretending I had not seen Minette. He spoke to her, and Minette glanced around at me, but already I was turned away, walking swiftly away, I would pretend not to hear if Minette called me. I would not glance back.

Why was I upset! I was not upset.

Thinking *Minette Swift saved my life. Saved me from injury at least. On Pierpont Avenue. It happened too quickly to be acknowledged and we will never speak of it, I have never thanked her. She has probably forgotten. She would be embarrassed to remember. But it is so.*

Thinking *If she loves him, she will be happy. I want Minette to be happy.*
Thinking *But if he hurts her?*

My snobbish fears were ungrounded, Minette did not light a single scented candle in our room. She'd put them away to take back with her to Washington, D.C. The candles were important to her, she would not waste them on me. Only faintly could I smell them layered in wrapping paper in one of her suitcases.

As I'd planned, I left Minette's Christmas present for her in a way to spare her embarrassment if she didn't have anything for me. My present was the exquisite Italian leather shoulder bag Veronica had impulsively bought for me at the Valley Forge Mall, gaily if somewhat clumsily wrapped in bright red tinsel paper. On a card I'd written

Merry Christmas, Minette!
Will see you in the New Year.
Love,
Genna

Love, Genna! It was risky of me to write something so intimate to my roommate Minette Swift who so disdained "familiarity."

I stayed away from Haven House until I knew that Minette had left for Washington, D.C., via Greyhound bus. When I returned I saw the red tinsel paper crumpled in Minette's wastebasket and the Italian bag prominently on top of her bureau. In apparent haste Minette had prepared a modest present for me: two of the scented evergreen candles left on my desktop with a Santa Claus card that read

Happy Christmas
Sincerely Yours,
Minette Swift

Part / III

Happy Christmas

Between mother/daughter was the unspoken understanding that in the Valley Forge Mall amid piped-in Christmas carols *I had heard nothing, knew nothing. Guessed nothing.*

Between us the understanding that no one had hissed at me *You little shit! What do you know.*

Holidays

We were popular it seemed. Among lonely elders it is not difficult to be popular. Somberly Veronica joked: "Used to be, I'd flirt with men. Now I flirt with old women."

We were invited to stay with wealthy Meade relatives in Philadelphia. We were invited to stay with wealthy Meade relatives in Wilmington. We were invited to stay with wealthy Meade relatives in Manhattan. We were invited to stay with wealthy Meade relatives in Midnight Key, Florida, on the Gulf of Mexico.

A gay and giddy time! Veronica meant for mother/daughter to keep in motion, cast no shadows.

In each of these households there were beautifully decorated Christmas trees. There were glittering ornaments on the trees, the evergreen needles gave off their dark potent fragrance. I shut my eyes not wanting to be observed crying.

Not wanting to be observed in pity *That poor girl! She misses her father at Christmas where on earth is that man and what is his excuse this time!*

In each of the households we opened beautifully wrapped presents.

New Year 1975

. . . waking in my bed in the house at Chadds Ford hearing through the plasterboard wall (but there was no plasterboard wall) a low desperate sound of back teeth grinding. Mumbled near-inaudible prayer *Our Father! Who art! in Heaven! Hallowéd* . . .

Testimony

"*Gen*-na! Your father."

Late afternoon of New Year's Day 1975 and Veronica called up the stairs to me in a quavering voice.

Since morning, snow had been falling in soft wet clumps like cotton batting. Covering the hilly terrain, the wooded acres surrounding the house at Chadds Ford.

We had avoided the house at Chadds Ford for many days. We had not wished to spend "the holidays" here. Late the previous night we'd arrived, mother/daughter exhausted from the gay and giddy effort of keeping in motion, casting no shadows.

I picked up the phone in my room. Eagerly?

In fact reluctantly. In fact with dread.

Shut my eyes trying to recall his face. There came the famous hoarse voice like sticks crackling in flame.

"Genna, darling! I've been missing you."

I murmured yes. It was a way of saying *I've been missing you too, Daddy* without exactly saying the words.

"These past months! But soon . . ."

Attentively I listened. I held the receiver tight in my perspiring hand pressed tight against my ear as a child might hold a receiver to her ear anxious that not a single syllable of a precious word tumble to the floor and be lost.

". . . definitely not 'separated' from your mother. Or from you, honey. Only just there are 'complications.' Not personal but professional, legal. I can be in despair of how the law is interpreted and enforced in this country but I never lose faith in law as the first principle of civilization and so—sometimes!—there are complications when clients want me to bend the law a little to help them, and I can't. Someday, I will explain." This small speech was passionately and seemingly spontaneously uttered, it wasn't unlike Max Meade to speak this way even intimately and yet the thought struck me *If this conversation is being taped my father is giving testimony in his own behalf.*

There was a pause. "Genna? Are you there?"

I murmured yes Daddy.

I laughed, flirtatiously. Where'd you think I would be, except here Daddy.

We would talk for approximately forty minutes. Max would ask me those questions you would expect. What were my courses at Schuyler, did I admire my instructors, who were my friends, what were my "activities" and "interests." What was I reading, and more importantly what was I thinking?

It was a question my father would often toss at my brother and me: *What thoughts are you thinking?* The question was casual and yet not so casual. For the wrong answer was *Nothing!*

Eventually, Rickie refused to answer. Always I answered in my bright schoolgirl voice wishing to please my father Max Meade who was not easily pleased.

Yet when I told Max about my college courses, when I described one or another of my instructors, trying to be witty, amusing, provocative, I sensed that his attention was wavering. What did Maximilian Meade who'd been trained as a historian care for the amateur efforts and naive discoveries of an eighteen-year-old "doing research" into the life and work of Henry Adams . . .

"You're the descendant of heroic individuals, Genna. Your great-grandfather Elias, your great-grandmother Generva. I hope you're not overwhelmed by their example but you shouldn't take them for granted, either."

My heart beat in resentment. It wasn't likely that I would take the illustrious Meades "for granted" and yet: how could it possibly matter if I did, or did not?

I couldn't think how to reply. Perhaps there was no reply. My father had never spoken to me in quite this way. He was sounding older, more somber. Not Max who would have mocked such solemnity but Maximilian Meade, historian.

My voice faltered. I was obliged to ask Max those questions you would expect a daughter to ask her father in such circumstances: how was he, where was he, what was the case he was working on, when would I see him, when would he come to visit me at Schuyler? My questions were sincere though I knew (I knew!) that Max would not answer most of them directly.

It had been in the public press, in fact in the *Philadelphia Inquirer*, that Maximilian Meade was one of several activist lawyers involved in appealing the lengthy prison sentences of several anti-war protestors who'd been convicted of a series of bombings in the late 1960s and 1970–71 and it was rumored that Max Meade was in contact with other protestors who'd jumped bail or managed to elude arrest and were believed to be living in the United States under assumed identities. One of these "fugitives from justice" was Ansel Trimmer but I knew not to ask about Ansel Trimmer. *Whatever I don't know, is not meant for me to know.*

This is wisdom, I think. Daughter-wisdom.

Not the wisdom of the historian. That would come later, in a colder epoch.

For a historian can't be daughter, son. A historian must be an orphan. No inheritance.

". . . this roommate of yours, this young black woman you've mentioned? I do hope to meet her soon."

Minette was fine, I told Max. Home in Washington, D.C., for the holidays.

"How do they treat blacks at Schuyler? Pretty well, I'd think?"

I hesitated. Pretty well, yes.

I was reluctant to bring up the subject of the racist drawing shoved beneath our door. For Max would become immediately alerted, lawyer-like he'd wish to quiz me, possibly he'd contact the president of the college within the hour! Arousing Max Meade was like tossing a lighted match into flammable material. I could not tell him that I secretly suspected another black girl behind the repulsive *Hottentot Venus* for of course I had no proof, and would never have proof; and there had been no further harassment. (So far as I knew.) It would be irresponsible to suggest to Max that there was "racism" at Schuyler College for truly I did not think that there was.

"Your roommate has one of Alden's scholarships, right? 'Merit.' "

Yes. That was so.

"So she's smart, eh? Those scholarships are competitive."

Yes. That was so.

"You've met her family, Veronica says? The minister?"

Vaguely I murmured yes. I knew the Swifts.

"Veronica was telling me that you and this Minette have become extremely close and that she, Veronica, sees a 'definite change' in you this fall."

This was news! I laughed, annoyed. Nearly everything Veronica reported of me to other people was laced with inaccuracies like rot. I asked what was this "definite change" Veronica claimed to have seen in me.

"She says you're becoming more 'religious'—'spiritual.' You suggested going to church services on Christmas eve?"

But not seriously! It had only been tossed out, a remark.

"You know how I feel about religion, Genna. But if Christianity has some appeal for you at this stage of your life, that's fine. I respect your quest, sweetie—'Let a hundred flowers bloom.' I had a religious phase of my own when I was a kid, a few years younger than you. Back in 1937 before the 'Christian' Nazis when you could still take the religion seriously."

I felt the sting of Max's words. How like a whip lightly glancing across my bare skin, drawing blood though hardly leaving a mark. It was cruel of my father to speak of me condescendingly as if I were a retarded version of himself.

"Veronica exaggerates, Daddy. Depending upon her drug dosage. You know that."

"Honey, don't I know! But there's some truth to this, I think."

I resented Veronica, too. Talking about me behind my back to my supremely rationalist father, to ridicule me.

I confessed that I'd wanted to go to church with Minette but she had not seemed to want me: "I even followed her one Sunday but it didn't turn out. I was very disappointed." Suddenly my words came in a rush, startling to me. My voice that had been poised became reedy and thin, and tears of indignation stung my eyes.

"Minette doesn't seem to want to 'convert' me. I think that I must be just a white girl in her eyes, I can never be a sister."

"Well, honey. There's a sense in which that's true."

"But I *try*. I *try*, Daddy. 'I stand outside the white race'—you've said. I *try so hard*."

Max laughed uneasily. He was one to hate hearing his own words flung back at him by disciples for no one could utter such words with the flair of Maximilian Meade. The rest of us were but caricatures, cartoons of him.

"I made that remark years ago, Genna. It was in a speech at a Black Panthers fund-raiser in Chicago. I meant it at the time and in a way I mean it, still: 'I would wish to stand outside the white race for I am ashamed of the white race.' In fact, I am white, I was born white, this is the hand I was dealt and I must accept it. The Black Panthers repudiated their white sympathizers and expelled them from their rallies, and they had a point. Maybe this Minette Smith—"

"—Swift. Her name is Swift."

"—doesn't believe quite the—"

"Minette is not a Black Panther, Daddy! Minette is a Christian."

"Yes but maybe she doesn't want you as a 'sister.' That's her prerogative, honey."

"But that's ridiculous. That's unfair."

"It may seem unfair to you but this girl has the right not to 'like' you regardless of how much you like her. If she wants, she can dislike all of the white race. You aren't going to change her."

"Daddy, what are you saying! I thought you were an activist, I thought you believed in change. I can, and I will."

"No. You can try."

"This is ridiculous! I can't believe that you, Max Meade, are saying such things. We all have to try, we have to do more than *try*. You know that."

Max paused. I could see him frowning. Lawyer-like he could not tolerate being contradicted.

"Well. We can talk about this another time. You're speaking irrationally, Genna. You've been under some strain."

"Daddy, I am not *irrational*. I am—am not—any judgment you make about me from your superior perspective because *you don't know me*."

Now it was out. I had accused Max Meade of ignorance.

Calmly he said, "All right, honey. We'll talk another time."

"This is the 'other time,' Daddy! Remember you'd called me back in October. Promising to come visit. The fact is, you don't know Minette Swift, and you certainly don't know me. You have no right to pass your smug fascist white-daddy judgment."

Now, now it was out! My voice shook in the effort not to break into derisive laughter like Minette Swift in the Pierpont Avenue stores.

"Genna, you are correct. I have no right. I'm going to hang up now, honey. You're angry with me and I don't blame you but I need to hang up now."

"Hang up, then! Jesus loves you anyway."

It was utterly irrational, my parting shot. It was delicious, thrilling. Quietly I broke the connection and listened to the dial tone and the consoling thought came to me *If this conversation was taped we both gave testimony in our own behalf.*

New Year

Eager for reading week, final exams, and the new spring semester I returned to Schuyler College two days early. Minette Swift returned three days late, just in time for her calculus exam.

Minette's first response of the New Year, to my cheerful query of how her Christmas break had been, was a shrug.

I was so disappointed! I had envisioned a very different sort of reunion after twenty-three days apart.

But Minette hadn't much wanted to return to Schuyler, it seemed. There was resentment and heaviness in her step. She muttered to herself, she sighed. She had exams to study for, final papers to hand in. Biology lab reports to complete. From remarks she made I gathered that her grades had been improving but only after much effort and Minette seemed to resent the effort required: " 'The lilies of the field, they toil not.' Wish I was one of those."

"It wouldn't be much fun being a lily, Minette. Somebody would come along and pick you."

Minette sighed, swiping at her nose. Muttering what sounded like *Wish they would!*

Minette had a new habit of stomping up the stairs, entering the room breathless to drop her books onto her desk in a clattering cascade. If I glanced up wincing at the noise, she muttered a near-inaudible *'Scuse me.*

I had thought we'd parted on friendly terms, in December. Yet now in January Minette was distant, moody. When I spoke she sometimes didn't seem to hear me and if she replied it was tersely, without feeling, as if speaking to me, uttering words at all, were too much effort. She'd gained weight over the holidays, and appeared older.

In D.C. she'd had her eyes examined and new lenses prescribed, and new glasses: the shell-pink schoolgirl frames were gone, now Minette wore tortoiseshell frames with a thicker lens.

I was reminded of the glasses worn by the stout black man who'd been seeing Minette in December but who hadn't yet appeared, in January.

January was very cold. Each day Minette wore the same approximate clothes: shirt with a button-down collar and a V-neck pullover sweater, woollen slacks, the bulky and graceless down jacket with a hood. She had new gloves, sheepskin-lined for warmth. They made her hands look gigantic. She had new waterproof boots with sturdy reinforced toes that gave her feet the authority of hooves. Sunday mornings Minette dressed in her church-going outfit but perversely carried her old middle-aged-lady handbag.

What had Minette done with the Italian bag? This was a mystery!

When I'd returned to the room in January there was the bag exactly where Minette had left it, on her bureau top. A few days later, after Minette returned, it had disappeared. (Into Minette's closet?) Minette never once alluded to the bag, and I would never ask.

The scented evergreen candles Minette had left for me I'd taken home to Chadds Ford and one evening when Veronica and I were having a rare dinner together I lit them but the incense-smell was too strong even for the former flower child.

Veronica shuddered: "A nasal acid-trip! I'm too old."

Veronica asked about the Italian shoulder bag. Seeing that I was still carrying my ratty old bag. I told her the truth: I'd given the bag to my roommate Minette Swift for Christmas. Veronica recoiled, hurt. "But that was my present to you, Genna! You had no right."

My face was hot. I would not defend myself.

"I hate 'material' things. They only remind me of what I can't have."

Now in the new year 1975 when the phone rang on the third-floor landing outside our room in Haven House, Minette froze. Sometimes, at her desk, she hunched forward pressing her knuckles against her ears in a childish cringing gesture.

Inevitably, the call was for someone else. Sometimes even for me.

Minette sighed heavily. Shifted her buttocks so that her desk chair creaked, slid open her desk drawer to rummage for a stealthy snack. Sometimes, for my benefit, she smacked her lips noisily in self-mockery.

"Piggy-*piggy*! That's ole Min-*ette*."

Except for Minette's parents, who called frequently in the early evening, no one seemed to call Minette Swift. By mid-January/exam week, the young black man with the tortoiseshell glasses had not reappeared. Others in the residence asked me what had happened to my roommate's "boyfriend"—if Minette had told me anything about him?

"Minette doesn't talk about her private life. She has too much pride." I'd meant this to be in defense of Minette but it sounded wrong.

Of course, Minette had told me nothing. Nor had I asked. I would not have dreamt of asking! Except one evening near the end of exam week, when Minette had been turning the gilt-edged pages of her Bible for some time in a leaden, open-eyed trance, she said suddenly: "He wanted to meet you, I think. 'Is that your roommate?' he asked me."

I was astonished by this remark out of nowhere. Minette spoke flatly and coolly as if bemused. She continued to turn the pages of her Bible.

There had been much commotion in Minette's life, in the past forty-eight hours. She'd staggered out of our biology exam in a panic and had to be taken to the infirmary: she'd started to faint, she feared she was having a cerebral hemorrhage. Subsequently she'd applied for, and had been granted, a grade of incomplete in our American lit. course which meant that Minette would have extra time to finish her term paper, and would take the final exam sometime next semester. Incompletes were rarely granted at Schuyler except for reasons of health, family emergencies, "extreme duress." For days Minette had been anxious about these exams and now the pressure had lifted, at least temporarily. (I had offered to read through Minette's term paper and to study with her for the exam, which would include a section of identification passages, but Minette had haughtily declined: " 'Scuse *me*! I wasn't brought up like some old mule with four broke legs.") Now Minette sighed, and cast an inscrutable sidelong glance at me across the room.

"Who wanted to meet me, Minette?"

Minette shrugged. "Oh, him. You know. That guy was showing up here, last month."

"But why would he want to meet me, Minette?" I thought Minette must be teasing. It was like her to inveigle me into believing something unlikely, then laughing at me as you'd laugh at a younger, naive sister. Over the interminable Christmas break, in the guest rooms of one or another wealthy Meade relatives, I'd hidden away to read Richard Wright, James Baldwin, Ralph Ellison but still I could not comprehend my roommate Minette Swift.

" 'Hendrick Cornish.' Least, he said that was his name."

Hendrick Cornish. The name meant nothing to me. I recalled having seen Minette with the young black man, on the snowy sidewalk in front of our residence. He'd seen me, and said something to Minette, and Minette turned toward me, but I'd ducked away . . .

In her flat bemused voice Minette told me that this "Hendrick Cornish" was a first-year law student at Penn. He'd met her in the bookstore on Pierpont Avenue. In all, he'd called her five times and they'd talked on the phone and gone out together three times though always on foot, never in his car. "He said he would call me over the break and maybe he'd drive down to D.C. to meet my folks, he sure sounded sincere!—but he never drove down. Never called, either. I am so grateful I didn't tell any of them there, they'd be expecting him and Momma would make such a fuss. This way, I can forget him." Minette was turning Bible pages swiftly, impatiently. Her expression was scornful.

Awkwardly I said, "It hasn't been that long, really. Maybe something happened in his family, so much goes on at Christmas. He seemed nice . . ."

Nice was such a weak word, Minette cut me off impatiently. "See, I'm in the bookstore, and this guy comes over. He's real polite, friendly. He said he was visiting the college library investigating some 'Abolitionist archive.' Said he was writing a legal paper. He had a degree in history from Spelman. He asked would I like to have coffee with him so I said yes." Now Minette's words came in a rush. She seemed not to know if she was hurt, or angry, or dismayed, or perplexed; if she should be indignant, or might as well laugh.

"Now I have had boyfriends before. I have had boys call me and ask me out, boys from the Temple Vale mostly. But this wasn't any boy, Hendrick is a grown man, a 'law student.' He was the politest man! My daddy would be impressed who's always saying how Jewel and I have got to be real picky 'cause there's boys and men with the devil in them you can't trust, only a decent Christian you can trust if you can find him. Hendrick hinted he took his religion real seriously and asked me about my beliefs. Especially, he asked me about my father when he found out who Daddy is. Maybe I talked too much about myself but he was the one asking! Sssssh." Minette had the air of one turning a curious object in her hand examining it from all sides, not knowing if she should toss it away in disgust.

"What did he say, the last time you talked?"

"Well! We had a nice talk, I thought. We were walking by the river mostly. That's when he said he hoped to call me over Christmas break. He was *so friendly*, Genna! These other guys I know, back home, they are not what you'd call smooth talkers. Hendrick was like some radio voice. Now I know, he wasn't all that good-looking and sort of bandy-legged but he was very intelligent, for sure. Daddy would have been impressed! Hendrick is asking me about my family background which happens to be South Carolina and he says that's a coincidence, his mother is from Charleston, and he asks me how do I like going to school 'up north' and I tell him I love it here 'cause it is a real challenge, not like the schooling I had back in D.C., and he asks how do I get along with the other girls and I say pretty well and then he asks about my roommate." Minette paused. She was turning Bible pages without a pretense of glancing into them.

I laughed, uneasily. "Your roommate! That's strange."

"I thought it was strange! Next he's asking if I met your parents and I said no. Asks about your father who is some kind of lawyer, I guess?—and I tell him I don't know anything about your father, not one thing. So he drops the subject. For a few minutes. Then comes back to it saying, 'When you visited your roommate's home, did you meet your roommate's father?' and I tell him sort of sharp, I did not meet that man! Didn't even know his name till Hendrick said it: 'Max'mil'an Meade.' Then he drops the subject, I thought, except, back at the house here, he sees you, and he says sort of excited, 'Is that your roommate, Generva Meade?' and I see it's you, and he wants to be introduced, but you went off and it didn't happen. So he makes me promise I wouldn't say anything to you about him asking questions and I tell him 'Yes I promise'—so I have broken that promise, I guess." Minette laughed harshly.

I was shaken by Minette's rush of words. Through the buzzing in my ears I wasn't sure I'd heard clearly. I said, "Did he—did he say why he wanted to meet me?"

Minette looked over at me, incensed. Her eyes glared whitely out of her blood-heavy face. In a final savage gesture she slammed shut her Bible. "Why? You playin dumb, girl? Why'd anybody want to meet anybody? Thought you was good-lookin, maybe. Damn lot better-lookin than old fat-ass Min-*ette*."

Minette's self-loathing stunned me. The terrible image of the Hottentot Venus came to me in a flash.

Had I seen the young black man watching us? On Pierpont Avenue, and in Woolworth's? "Hendrick Cornish." Somehow he'd known what I looked like. Deliberately he'd approached Minette, to get to me.

To get to Max.

Here was another astonishing revelation. Almost, I could not accept it.

Yet now in a sick cold panic it came to me: hadn't Dana Johnson asked me pointedly about my parents?—that pinched little smile, ice-pick eyes. There had seemed something forced about her friendly questions, would I be spending Thanksgiving with my family at Chadds Ford? And what was my father, whose "work" she'd read, "working on" now? Dana Johnson hinted, with an awkward smile, that, if I were alone at any time over a break, we might have dinner together. Of course, Dana Johnson was an intellectual, a professor of anthropology; she was a feminist, and a liberal; it was only natural that she might wish to draw me out, encourage me to talk about my father's politics, his "activism"; allow me to think that she was sympathetic with Max Meade's radical clients including those wanted by the FBI.

And there was my sociology professor Dr. Ferris. Straggly-haired, bearded, in jeans, tweed sports coats, bare feet in sandals through October. Dr. Ferris was in his early fifties but sexy, slangy. Enormously popular. His lectures were laced with references to the Grateful Dead, Timothy Leary, Frantz Fanon, Malcolm X, the Jesuit Berrigan brothers, Stokely Carmichael, Huey Newton; on his office wall was the famous poster of the armed Bobby Seale and Huey Newton POLITICAL PRISONERS OF USA FASCISM. In our class, Dr. Ferris had several times called upon me with a strange smile: "Genna? Tell us what you think." *You, daughter of Mad Max Meade.* He'd asked me to speak with him after midterms, he'd given me a grade of A+ on a paper I'd written. Except that another student was waiting in the corridor outside his office, Dr. Ferris would have spoken with me at length; I was flattered that one of my professors should seem to care about my ideas; it would have been easy for him to determine if I was as radical as my notorious father; he might then have expressed sympathy with my father's "fugitive" clients; he would inveigle me into confiding in him, sharing what I knew . . .

"But I don't know anything. Except that Max Meade has never violated the law."

This, I believed. For hadn't I been told, many times?

I lay awake in my bed. My thoughts shimmered, shook, shattered like ice. I felt a thrill of pure resentment, hatred. Very likely, a number of administrators and faculty members at Schuyler College were in contact with the FBI. The dean of students, certainly. The president, and the provost. Perhaps it wasn't their choice, they were being coerced. Still, they would "cooperate." Even Dana Johnson, even Dr. Ferris.

It was widely known that the FBI kept extensive files on private citizens. Through the 1950s and 1960s people had informed upon one another to the FBI out of political paranoia, ignorance, spite. Max liked to boast that J. Edgar Hoover had a personal vendetta against him, there were "more than 3,000 pages" of documents in Max Meade's file in Washington. (How could Max know such a fact? Yet he made the claim.) Max had not won all of his cases against FBI prosecutors in federal courts but he'd won a majority, he had not yet been intimidated or discouraged.

I was grateful to Minette Swift for knowing nothing of me, and for caring nothing of me. To Minette, the name "Meade" had no significance, "Max'mil'an Meade" meant nothing. I believed that whatever Minette knew of me, however trivial and harmless, she would not have disclosed to "Hendrick Cornish." She liked me, she would defend and protect me. I believed this.

We are sisters. We might be sisters. Max is wrong.

In the morning I called the Law School of the University of Pennsylvania. I was routed through several operators. I asked if there was a student named "Hendrick Cornish" enrolled there and after some delay I was informed that no one named "Hendrick Cornish" was enrolled in the law school and, for good measure, no one named "Henry Cornish" was enrolled, either.

I would tell Max this! Except I hadn't Max's current phone number. Still I was waiting for him to call me and to "drop by" Schuyler College to visit. I was waiting.

Thinking *A secret is always of some use. If you give it away you have lost it.*

Niggr

After her death it would be asked: Why did Minette Swift remain at Schuyler College.

Why, in the midst of enemies. Why, when she was so unhappy.

Because it was a test? Because it was a torment? Because she could not give up, could not fail? Because Reverend Virgil Swift wished her not to fail? Because Jesus never ceased to love her, and to have faith in her?

"She wouldn't get away with it if she was white."

"Are you kidding? She wouldn't be here if she was white."

"It's all an act. What doctors call 'malingering.' Pretending to be sick, to get out of exams. To get sympathy."

In Haven House and elsewhere on campus there began to be resentment of my roommate Minette Swift. Somehow it was known that Minette had been granted not one but two incompletes. So petty, yet so resented! I was mystified how other girls knew, for Minette would have told no one except me, and I had told no one. Yet this confidential information was spread in the way that rumors are spread.

Sometimes I overheard these remarks, and sometimes they were directed at me. I tried to defend Minette: she'd really been sick, during exams. She had had some sort of panic attack, she'd nearly fainted and had to be taken to the infirmary. She'd seen a doctor, she had high blood pressure and excruciating menstrual cramps. She'd been scheduled to see a "counsellor" . . .

Anyway, I asked, what was wrong with sympathy? It was hard for

Minette to be at Schuyler where there were so few black students and almost no black faculty.

The word *black* stuck to my tongue like tar. For I did not really think of Minette as *black*, and she didn't think of herself as *black*. If she'd overheard me talking of her in this way, she would have been furious.

"Other black girls don't behave the way Minette does," a friend objected. "They're embarrassed of her."

But other black girls came from better high schools, I said. They didn't seem to be under the pressure that Minette was under.

" 'Minette, Minette'! It's always 'Minette'! Why the hell is she here, if Schuyler is so hard for her?"

No one knew of *Hottentot Venus*. But everyone would know of *Niggr go home*.

Numberless times in subsequent days, weeks, months and even years the witnesses would recount: how at about 4:30 P.M. of February 8, 1975, they'd been present when Minette Swift took her mail from her box in the foyer of Haven House, paused to tear open an envelope and to extract a sheet of paper and give a little cry—"like she'd been shot."

Judith Holman, Sheri Shearer, Audrey Williams. They'd been talking together and only peripherally aware of Minette Swift who had just stamped inside from the cold, breathing through her mouth, her glasses faintly steamed. There must have been something curious about the envelope in Minette's mailbox for she turned it in her hand, frowning; opened it, and pulled out the sheet of plain white paper, gave her hurt little cry and froze. By this time the girls were watching her, seeing how unlike Minette Swift she was behaving: not so much indifferent to them, certainly not aloof or haughty but rather stunned, paralyzed. Judith Holman said quickly, "Minette, what is it?"—knowing it must be something ugly. When Minette didn't seem to hear her, Judith took the paper from Minette's now trembling hand.

On a plain sheet of ordinary typing paper, in mismatched letters scissored out from a newspaper or magazine:

NIGGR   GO HOME

Minette had dropped the envelope. Judith stooped to pick it up. The envelope had no stamp or postmark. Here too were the mismatched cut-out letters with a look of mockery:

MIN SWIFT

Judith, and now the other two girls, were speaking to Minette, meaning to comfort her. But Minette seemed not to hear. Her face appeared to be crumpling, her eyes behind the lenses of her chunky tortoiseshell glasses began to well with tears. Judith hugged her, tried to comfort her. Sheri and Audrey, who had now seen the offensive message, touched and stroked Minette's arms, hands. The girls were shocked, sickened, deeply embarrassed. They would say afterward that it was like being present when someone was wounded, and you didn't know what to say, what to do. When other Haven House residents appeared in the doorway, these girls waved them back.

Minette, too, seemed deeply embarrassed. She tried to laugh, swiping at her nose. Then she was trying not to cry. Except that Judith had taken the racist message from her, Minette would have torn it into pieces. "We'd better show this to Dana Johnson, Minette. That's what we'd better do."

Judith walked Minette back to Dana Johnson's quarters. The other girls watched in silence as they entered the resident advisor's office, and the door was shut quickly behind them.

I wouldn't hear of this ugly incident until later that day when I returned from classes. It was like stepping into a burning hive. There was an air of indignation, upset. Even girls who didn't get along with Minette Swift were incensed on her behalf. "It's nobody in Haven Hall who did it. Absolutely not."

By the time I entered our room on the third floor, Minette had withdrawn to her bedroom. A light burned beneath her door but she refused to answer my knock.

"Minette? Please."

It had taken me ten minutes to make my way upstairs. Everyone in Haven House wanted to talk with me. (Except not everyone: not Crystal Odom, not Traci Poole, not the two other black girls in the residence.) I was upset, anxious. I did not want to think that my failure to report the racist drawing might have provoked this second attack.

"Minette, it's Genna. May I talk with you? I've heard . . ."

Niggr go home was what I'd heard. The curious spelling *Niggr*—what did that mean?

Several times I knocked on Minette's door. I did not think that she could be asleep. "Minette? Can I come in?"—but there came a quick, muffled reply, to discourage me. I was very upset. I had a dread of Minette blaming me, lumping me with her enemies. I could not imagine Minette wounded, broken. She'd been described to me—by Audrey Williams, one of the trio of demonic noise-makers who roomed beneath us—as "hardly looking like herself" but I could not believe this! Not my roommate Minette Swift.

Here is what I saw: Minette glaring at me, on the other side of the (shut) door; Minette's stocky figure on her bed, muscled knees drawn to her chest and arms hugging her knees in an attitude of defiance? anger? disgust? scorn? Minette's face hard and unyielding as a mask carved in dark-stained wood.

If she wants she can dislike all of the white race.

You aren't going to change her.

My voice had become hoarse, as if I'd been pleading with Minette for hours and not minutes. My eyes stung with tears of rage, frustration. "The hell with them, Minette. Let's get some dinner. Come on!"

But Minette Swift was too proud to be inveigled by such white-girl stratagems. She would not open the door to me, and she would not give me permission to open it myself.

"Genna Meade. If you know anything about this . . ."

Genna Meade! How strangely the resident advisor pronounced my name, as if it were an impostor's name. As if there were a *Genna Meade* not the stiff somber-faced girl who stood before her.

It was the second time in three months that Dana Johnson was obliged to summon the residents of Haven House downstairs to speak with her, one by one. Seventeen Schuyler undergraduates, most of them Merit Scholars, had become characters in a 1940s noir film of petty criminals, corruption and guilt. As Minette Swift's roommate, I was naturally the first suspect to be summoned.

I was sick with worry: that Dana Johnson would (somehow) learn how I'd destroyed the *Hottentot Venus* drawing, as if I'd meant to shield the racist enemies of Minette Swift.

It was the wisdom of the school yard, you must never "turn the other cheek" when struck. You must never passively accept injustice or injury as if you felt you deserved it. By destroying the evidence, I had only provoked more harassment.

". . . you will tell me. Immediately."

"But, but I . . . don't."

Ms. Johnson commanded me to be seated. We were in the room known as the resident advisor's parlor. On a facing wall were photographs of Haven House girls of bygone years, decades. You could see how, from the first, there were dark-skinned faces among the fair-skinned majority. These were a distinct minority but always they were present, like punctuation marks. I thought that, one day, I might count the smiles on the wall of Dana Johnson's parlor.

Ms. Johnson had taken no time this evening to prepare tea, set out a platter of cookies. It was true as everyone was saying: Ms. Johnson was "distraught." Like an exhausted runner she was breathing through her mouth. She spoke carefully as if each of her words stung. Clearly she was frantic with worry that a "racist incident" in her residence would ruin her career at Schuyler College: she would be known as the faculty advisor of a house in which a black freshman was being harassed. The slur *Niggr* was obscene, unspeakable. Though no one knew about *Hottentot Venus*, except the individual or individuals who'd pushed the drawing under our door, and me, who had torn it up, the unsolved mystery of Minette Swift's vandalized literature text was widely known. Obviously there was a pattern of "racial harassment" in Haven House, historically the most liberal/integrated of Schuyler residences, and Dana Johnson, assistant professor of anthropology, seemed incapable of curtailing it.

Instead of tea things, Ms. Johnson had placed on her coffee table the sheet of plain white paper and the envelope Minette had found in her mailbox. (Unless these were facsimiles. Wouldn't the originals be checked for fingerprints?) I had not seen these documents until now, and seemed somehow to have expected them to be larger. But the sheet of paper was of ordinary dimensions, the torn envelope ordinary and cheap. Ms. Johnson did not want me to touch, only to contemplate these items. Like a terse, enigmatic poem by Emily Dickinson whose riddlesome verse Minette and I had been studying in our American lit. class, the documents seemed to invite interpretation in their very simplicity.

NIGGR GO HOME

MIN SWIFT

There was a riddle here. That *Niggr* was misspelled by accident did not seem possible.

"Well, Genna? Do you know anything about this?"

Ms. Johnson was seated across from me, staring at me. I was sick with worry, she would see into my soul: she would see my guilt, and misread it. For I was behaving like a guilty person, my eyes welled with tears that made seeing difficult. I knew that I should tell Ms. Johnson about the *Hottentot Venus* drawing. It almost seemed that she was waiting for me to confess. I did not dare look at her, who was observing me from such close proximity. *She knows! Knows something.* I saw that the awkwardly mismatched letters were familiar to me: why?

Quickly I looked away, my face pounded with blood.

Sternly Dana Johnson was reminding me: I'd signed Schuyler College's honor code. I was obliged to "uphold honor" in all situations involving Schuyler College.

I shook my head, no. No!

A memory came to me, fleeting and grotesque, of a staggering naked boy-man trying clumsily to sink a paring knife into his belly.

Trying, and failing. The knife slipped from his fingers.

"Is this funny, Genna? *This?*"

I hadn't known that I was smiling. I bit my lip to keep from laughing. Dana Johnson stared at me incredulously.

"You seemed to have something to say, a minute ago."

"No. I didn't have anything to say."

"You have no idea who might have left this ugly material in Minette Swift's mailbox?"

"No, Ms. Johnson. I do not."

"The penalty for lying is expulsion, Genna. If you are found to have violated our honor code."

Our honor code! Dana Johnson was new to Schuyler College as I was. She had no right to speak of its tradition so familiarly. I would have liked to tell her: my great-grandfather founded this college. My grandfather gave millions of dollars to this college. My father is Max Meade, no one is going to expel *me*.

I could not bring myself to look again at the documents on Dana Johnson's coffee table. I must have been mistaken to think that I'd seen the letters somewhere previously, recognized the font. My eyes were awash with tears, I could not have seen clearly. I was sweating, miserable. Perhaps I would be expelled by the disciplinary committee. I was not the guilty party and yet I was behaving guiltily. Even as Dana Johnson was speaking to me, I was on my feet. Even as she was commanding me to remain, I was turning rudely away. I would run from the resident advisor's parlor on whose prim wall-papered walls generations of Schuyler College students posed together in rows of smiling light-skinned and dark-skinned faces. I would run upstairs breathless and bold and the first opened doorway I would enter uninvited, I would laugh wildly asking who'd like to come with me to the student center to see a film that evening, the Film Society was showing the 1956 Kubrick *The Killing*, the residents of Haven House were too nerved-up to remain in our rooms studying like the good-girl scholars we were meant to be, the mood of the house was edgy, mutinous. Three of us, five of us would hike in the cold to the student center, loud in our talk, loud-laughing, trooping noisily into the film theater where *The Killing* had already begun, a plot of masculine genius, a clockwork-plot, precise and doomed, and what pleasure in it, to behold. It would be a giddy evening. I would make at least one new friend. I would not return to my third-floor room in Haven House until nearly midnight. By which time the light beneath Minette Swift's door would be darkened and I would grope my way to my own bedroom, in the dark.

Bare

The windowsill where copies of *The Beacon* had been placed was now bare. I would never see copies of *The Beacon* in our study room again.

Minette's "special Bible" bound in soft white simulated leather stamped in gold-gilt, pages edged in gilt, remained prominently, conspicuously on her desk.

Some truths are lies. Some lies are truths. For all human utterances are pro-visional and expedient. And what we wish to believe to be REAL is but our political perspective and our political perspective is determined by race, class, social privilege from which we must be wakened to be free to throw off our skin-consciousness which is our collective blindness and sometimes that awakening must be violent for there is no other way.

In the Night

Like teeth grinding, your own back teeth clamped together and grinding. Not believing these fervent words of Maximilian Meade uttered at a peace rally in 1968 in Washington, D.C., and yet I could not tell the truth about my roommate Minette Swift though I had pledged to uphold honor at Schuyler College for *truth—honor*—even *pledge* came to seem to me questionable terms, terms to be debated, and yet I could not speak of them openly to anyone for there was no one whom I could trust, awake in the night exhausted by such thoughts, resenting such thoughts, in a paroxysm of self-disgust that I should be the vessel of such thoughts, toward dawn lapsing into sleep like flotsam washed upon a disfigured beach already littered with debris and wakened by the creaking of bedsprings, a muffled moan, a child's whimper in the night, through the cheap plasterboard wall the grinding of teeth.

The Incident

Whoever did it should be arrested.

Not just the college, the police should investigate.

The Pennsylvania attorney general should investigate! What was done to Minette Swift is a hate crime.

It was no one in Haven House.

It couldn't be anyone we know.

"Sssssh!"

Minette laughed inside her spread fingers, these girls *so nice* to her.

Damn hypocrites *so nice* to her in the dining hall, dragging chairs to her table. In classes sitting near her, or beside her. Where they'd used to snub her. In Haven House going out of their way like Minette Swift was some convalescent calling *Hi Minette!* smiles and looks-of-sympathy and asking if she'd like to go to the basketball game with them or some film or play or meeting she didn't have time for, these philistines she knew (she knew!) hated her guts and secretly thought she got what she deserved cast down in the dirt in her pride insulted and threatened NIGGR GO HOME in their eyes shining like skunk-eyes every time they saw her, and some of them (Minette saw, for sure) ducking away not wishing to be seen, embarrassed of Minette Swift, pitying Minette Swift and resenting her like it was her fault what had been done to her out of pure wickedness, evil. And all these meetings! And all these people discussing the "emergency situation" in Haven House, from which meetings Minette Swift was privileged to be excused.

Except Minette had gone to hear the president's address, in the college chapel. So many crowded into the chapel, they had to allow standing at the back and in the aisles. President Belknap, formerly a professor in the history department, an eloquent and impassioned woman of youthful middle age, gave a speech titled "No Tolerance for Race Hatreds in the 'New' America." In this forty-minute speech there were quoted passages from John Stuart Mill, W. E. B. DuBois, Generva Meade ("Our own pioneer champion for minority and women's rights"), the Reverend Martin Luther King, Jr., Whitney Young, John F. Kennedy, and Marian Wright Edelman whom President Belknap fondly referred to as her colleague and friend. In the first pew, directly in front of the raised pulpit, Minette Swift sat in her red cloth coat with the leopard-skin collar frowning up at President Belknap her face stolid and stoic and betraying not a flicker of emotion for the duration of the speech not even when, at its conclusion, everyone else in the chapel burst into applause. Minette was sharing the pew with a number of other dark-skinned young women belonging to the African-American Student League at Schuyler College except these sudden new friends Minette distrusted, why'd they make such a fuss of Minette Swift *now*? Where'd they been when she was hounded out of Bobo-links by that Jew Bidelman, where'd they been when her American lit. anthology was stolen from her and vandalized just outside her window? And her hand-knit glove her Momma had knitted for her? Where'd they been until just the other day swarming into Minette's room on the third floor of Haven House like some old vultures sniffing carrion? Damn philistines to wish to exploit Minette Swift for political purposes sounding like outright Communists. Reverend Swift had warned his daughter, up north in that "leftist" college be careful of Communists wishing to seduce. No respect for Minette's Christian beliefs. Jesus teaches *Love thy enemies. Turn the other cheek. Let he who is without sin cast the first stone*. You'd heard of fair-weather friends, these are foul-weather friends Minette scorns for how they look at her pitying and impatient like Minette is some crippled-wizened little monkey in a wheelchair.

Same with President Belknap having Minette Swift to so-called Friday afternoon tea in the president's swanky house. This "informal gathering" of provost, dean of students, (black) assistant dean of admissions, (black) assistant professors of English, history, economics, philosophy plus two six-foot (black) phys. ed. instructors plus a dozen "student leaders" including the (caramel-skinned) co-chair of something called Arts at Schuyler Weekend and the (ebony-black) vice president of the class of '75 Wendy Yardman who is Schuyler College's most recently named Rhodes Scholar whose proud-smiling photo has been featured in the *Philadelphia Inquirer* alongside smiling white-boy scholars from Penn, Princeton, Haverford. Amid the animated talktalktalk of these others, Minette Swift is lumpish, quiet. Not sullen exactly (for Minette has been brought up to be polite in the presence of all elders) but very quiet: eyes downcast behind the clunky tortoiseshell glasses and hands tight-clasped in her lap as if waiting for the ordeal to be over; or, at least, waiting for the silver tray bearing tiny pastries and bonbons to make another elliptical round in her direction. For this special occasion at President Belknap's house old and "historic" as the Elias Meade House close by Minette is wearing her purple jersey dress with the flared skirt that billows at her hips but, as if she couldn't be bothered, no stockings or high heels just black wool knee socks covered in lint and the wedge-toed boots she wears everywhere. No makeup not even a smear of magenta lipstick. And her hair is stiff with grease, gives off a pungent odor for Minette has not showered or washed her hair since the afternoon of February 8 (several days ago) when she'd returned to Haven House to discover NIGGR   GO HOME in her mailbox.

"These females cluckclucking like a henhouse, and know what?—I interrupted sayin 'Scuseme, I wasn't some old 'nigger' I wouldn't be invited here today I guess?"

The white roommate to whom Minette is recounting this stares at her. Pale freckle-face blotching over in a blush. "Oh Minette. You didn't."

" 'Ohhhh, Minette. You *did*n't.' How'd you know, girl, what 'Minette' did or *did*n't? You wasn't there, 'cause you wasn't invited."

(No one else from Haven House had been invited, in fact. Not even Crystal Odom who'd been to at least one previous tea at President Belknap's swanky house, for "high achievers.")

Minette Swift in her loud laughing mood. Stomping up the stairs hard enough to make the house tremble. Stomping into the room loud enough to make the girls in the room below tremble. Lets her books fall out of her arms, onto the desk and onto the floor. Since *the incident*, as it's called, Minette lapses into this mood, you can't predict. Laughing at her roommate Genna Meade who is so easily beguiled, tell this girl any old nonsense she'd believe it like Minette's Momma wide-eyed *Oh Minette you didn't*.

Making you want to laugh in their faces.

How'd you know what Minette did or didn't. You wasn't there.

Midwinter

Midwinter the windows of Haven House facing north were covered in ice-clusters like teeth, glittering.

Some mornings, when no sun appeared, my roommate Minette Swift dragged herself from her creaking bed and dressed in the sallow occluded light of dawn reluctant to do anything more in the communal third-floor bathroom than use the toilet. She could not shower any longer for someone had placed tiny slivers of broken glass inside the shower stall, knowing that Minette was about to use it. She had hardly time to gargle with mouthwash, to rinse out her dry, stale mouth. She dreaded another girl or girls coming into the bathroom while she was in it, and so her movements were furtive and quick. She could not leave her towels on any of the racks as the other girls did, knowing that those others would use her towels, for this had happened not once but several times and since *the incident* one of her towels had been smeared with dirt. She could not leave her bar of soap, her shampoo, her tube of toothpaste or toothbrush for all these had been used, defiled. Her toothbrush—bright blue plastic, thick-bristled, newly purchased in September—had been dragged in the accumulated filth where the linoleum floor met the wall and (perhaps, she had no evidence except its smell) it had been dragged along the underside of a toilet bowl and so she had thrown it away in revulsion and had not purchased another. Ohhh her teeth ached, sometimes! Jaws ached. In the infirmary the nurse who'd seemed to feel sorry for her though reluctant to touch her had given her powerful cold tablets that acted upon pain the way water acted upon tissue paper dampening and softening it and so Minette swallowed what remained of her cold tablets dry off the palm of her hand, like Smarties.

Humming beneath her breath as she fumbled to put on her heavy winter clothes that seemed now to fit the contours of her body like a kind of armor and to give off the smell of that body identifiable from a short distance: the wool slacks badly wrinkled at the crotch, the rumpled shirt beneath the beige V-neck sweater, wool socks stiff with dirt. In this way Minette prepared to leave for the dining hall and morning classes in her wedge-toed boots but outside on the landing a few yards from our room her footsteps slowed and when, ten or fifteen minutes later I went out, I might find Minette crouched and vigilant peering over the stairway railing into the stairwell her eyes wary and distrustful behind the thick tortoise-shell glasses and a trickle of perspiration on her dark stoic face. And I spoke softly not wanting to alarm her: "Minette? Is something wrong?"

Where Minette was staring, I could see nothing. Yet I dreaded seeing something ugly.

She'd shown me slivers of glass, from the shower stall. She'd shown me the defiled towels, toothbrush.

Minette didn't want to report the harassment to our RA, though. And she didn't want me to report it. "You better promise, Gem'a! I can't take no-more people feelin sorry for me, worse yet no-more damn 'investi-gating.' "

If Minette acknowledged me on the stairway landing, she might simply shake her head *no*. Or, more curiously, she might stand irresolute in her heavy down jacket just inside the door breathing hard and frowning lost in thought and not wishing to be interrupted.

I would not provoke Minette needlessly by asking if I should bring her some breakfast back from the dining hall but if I brought back some breakfast for her Minette would accept it from my hand, and Minette would eat it. So long as I didn't linger in the room but left her to her privacy.

Afterward it would be asked if Minette Swift had had "professional" help at Schuyler College. If her psychological condition had been "properly diagnosed."

In fact Minette had been referred by her academic advisor to a tutor (English composition) and a counsellor with an advanced degree in clinical psychology at the Student Health Center. Several times weekly, these appointments. If she could drag herself.

Midwinter, on dark blowy mornings Minette remained in the room.

Minette napped. Minette leafed through the Bible reading passages at random. Minette hummed, sang to herself. Sometimes returning to the room I would hear her muffled voice through the door before I opened it and always as I opened it I rattled the doorknob to warn her of my presence.

" 'Scuseme I'm wondering how do people decide what to *do*? Like, turn left, or right? Which actual minute, to get out of bed? Spose you could not decide, would you just stay *in bed*?"

Minette spoke slowly shaking her head as if she suspected a trick to her own query. She'd been drawing geometric figures for much of the day. Strewn across her desktop were sheets of paper covered in figures of startling precision, beauty: elaborately drawn circles and ovoids, triangles, trapezoids, strangely shaped rectangles of her own invention. Minette had confided in me how in high school she'd loved geometry and math, solid geometry especially using her compass and ruler and it was a comfort to memorize theorems like Bible verse and Minette Swift's homework, quizzes, exams were near-about the best in her class she'd gotten scores of 100% many times and her teacher Mrs. Brownlee had praised her "to the skies."

This semester Minette was enrolled in Math 101—"The Math of Everyday Life"—which was mostly non-math majors. She'd had some trouble with the analytic geometry/calculus course though finally she'd gotten a C in it, or maybe a C– but already in Math 101 on her first quiz she'd gotten A–.

"Just act, Minette. Don't think. Don't even decide. Do *something*."

I spoke with the authority of my father Max Meade though I felt little authority in this overheated room smelling of my roommate's unwashed hair. I hoped that Minette, who appeared to be listening to me with an interest so extreme it might have been mockery, would not hear the quaver in my voice.

Minette laughed. Minette rubbed her nose vigorously with the heel of her hand, you'd think it was a rubber nose that couldn't break. " 'Scuseme! They will only do it back to you, then."

"Do what back to you? Who? What do you mean, Minette?"

Minette gestured toward the tall narrow window above her desk. The cracked windowpane had long ago been replaced but there was, to a discerning eye, a subtle distinction in panes; just possibly, a trace of the original crack still visible in a ghostly spiderweb in the new glass.

On the windowsill where copies of *The Beacon* had once been proudly displayed now there were stacks of books and papers, Spanish language tapes, sweet rolls and crumbling cookies loosely wrapped in paper napkins.

"I'm sorry. Minette isn't here right now."

"I'm sorry. Minette can't come to the phone right now."

"I'm *sorry*. You can leave another message, maybe Minette will call you back but I can't promise."

In mid-winter often I took telephone calls for Minette who refused to speak on the phone with anyone but her parents. For suddenly there were strangers wishing to speak with "Minette Swift" of whom they'd heard. There was an aggressive reporter from the *Schuyler Clarion* who wanted to interview Minette. There was a broadcaster from the People's Radio Network of Philadelphia demanding to speak with "Sister Swift." There were increasingly impatient young women identifying themselves as members of the African-American Student League at Schuyler College demanding to know why Minette Swift had failed to meet with them as she'd promised and had not returned their calls.

I was waiting for "Hendrick Cornish" to call. But no man (except Reverend Swift) ever called Minette.

Minette laughed: "Where'd all these people been, before? Now I'm *niggr go home* guess I am *pop-u-lar* like Sammy Davis, Jr."

A high-level committee had been named by President Belknap to investigate the "racial harassment" of Minette Swift and to look into other, similar incidents at Schuyler that might have gone unreported or unremarked in the past year or two and one by one residents of Haven House were summoned to be interrogated by this committee as we'd been interrogated by Dana Johnson and one by one we denied knowing anything about who had placed NIGGR   GO HOME in Minette's mailbox. We were reminded of the Schuyler College honor code yet still we denied any knowledge. For we knew nothing! Minette herself had met with the committee initially but then failed to show up at subsequent meetings and when the chair of the committee, the provost of the college, personally called to ask to speak with Minette, it fell to me to make excuses for my roommate.

"Minette apologizes, Dr. Schulman. She isn't feeling well. She had to be excused from gym class, she has terrible cramps and she's in bed and I don't want to disturb her . . . I'm sure she will contact the committee, soon."

"A User's Guide to Race Hatred and Harassment at Schuyler 1860–1975" was the provocative title of a series of scandalous articles to appear in the *Schuyler Clarion* in February/March 1975. The undergraduate reporter who'd been denied interviews by college administrators as by Minette Swift was taking her revenge.

Through the decades, most pronounced in the 1920s and the 1950s, there had been numerous episodes of racial harassment: young white women harassing their black classmates, often with the complicity or outright aid of older relatives and alums. Such incidents occurred at many colleges and universities in the United States, of course, and were occurring well into the 1970s, but how was it possible here, at this prestigious liberal arts college whose Quaker founder had intended it to be a model of integration and racial harmony? The most recent scandalous case (which had spilled over into the public press and a jeering "exposé of left-wing hypocrisy" in *Time*) had occurred in 1962: an eighteen-year-old Merit Scholar from Newark, New Jersey, coincidentally a resident of Haven House, had dropped out of Schuyler College for health reasons after being "severely tormented" in a secret sorority hazing involving brooms and field hockey sticks. The administration of Schuyler College had "vigorously denied" the existence of sororities of any kind, secret or otherwise, in 1962.

The *Clarion* series ended:

> Are there "secret sororities" at Schuyler today? Are these white-racist organizations? Do Schuyler alums provide financial support? Are there faculty members sympathetic with racist agendas? The administration "vigorously denies" all knowledge of such sororities and when this reporter dared to ask what truth there is to recent disturbing rumors that an 18-year-old black Merit Scholar living in Haven House has been the victim of continued racist harassment, President Belknap's office issued an icy "No comment."

One blizzardy Sunday morning Minette did not dress for church as usual. She did not dress at all, remaining in her pajamas and navy blue bathrobe for much of the day. I went out, and I returned, and I went out again, and returned, and still Minette had not dressed and seemed content to remain in the room "honoring Jesus" by lighting a half-dozen candles carefully positioned on her windowsill, bureau top and desk.

These were scented candles. Powerful perfumy smells: evergreen, lilac, gardenia. There was something hypnotic about their small quivering flames that seemed to respond to our breathing, Minette Swift's and mine.

Where once Minette's side of our study room was kept orderly and clean as if in subtle rebuke to my more casual housekeeping now it had the look of an eroded beach littered with debris. Clothes, towels, even dirt-stiffed wool socks were scattered on the floor amid books and papers. Some of these books were library books, lying open where they'd been dropped. Even the handsome gold-glinting CHRISTIAN YOUTH FELLOWSHIP poster was slightly torn, fraying at its edges. Minette's closet door was usually ajar, you could see the red coat and purple jersey dress crammed carelessly inside on hangers. Through the doorway of Minette's bedroom you could see a tangle of bedclothes trailing into the floor, soiled underwear, pajamas, the navy blue bathrobe. When Minette was out, I did some furtive housekeeping on her side of the room, emptied her overflowing wastebasket, tossed out stale food and tugged open "my" window. I knelt before it putting my face to the fresh cold air, to breathe.

Thinking *We can live like this. We will be all right.*

I was reminded of the house at Chadds Ford. Those years when strangers came to "crash" with us for a day, a night, a week, six weeks. The boy-men were bearded and gaunt and Christly bristling with nervous energy. There were fewer girl-women but their scattered clothing, their smells, glimpses of their part-naked or naked bodies assailed me in ways that left me stunned, breathless. For the thought paralyzed me *I must be one of them, to make my father love me.*

I was not a young child, I was twelve when one of the girl-women bathed me. Seeing that my homely face was splotched with tears and dried snot. Seeing that I was shy and furtive as a rat (there was a colony of gray rats in the outbuildings at Chadds Ford, Max Meade could not seem to "discourage" them with poisoned bait) and that my parents did not have time for me. "Gem-ma" she called me having misheard my name. Or discounting my name. "Mmmm Gem-ma!" whose small sensitive breasts were just the size of Melanie's cupped hands and whose numbed lips could be made to open, and warmed, by Melanie's practiced fleshy lips.

Everywhere Melanie kissed me there was a "freckle galaxy" she said. Everywhere Melanie kissed me I was "blessed."

Always remember, Gem-ma you are my heart.

Even when you are an old old woman. And I am ashes-to-ashes.

Because, see? We are *here now.*

Now is always and forever and here is everywhere Gem-ma mmmmm-mmmm!

Promise?

Amid the clutter on Minette Swift's desk the white-bound Bible remained prominent. And now there was a black-bound journal beside it.

Minette had gone home for a four-day weekend in late February and after she'd returned this journal suddenly appeared on her desk. I thought *This is for me to read is it?* For though Minette was indifferent to me much of the time yet I had the idea that she wished me to observe her, to take note.

Alone in the room I approached Minette's desk. I listened to hear that no one was on the stairs, no one would enter the room. I opened the journal, which had a stiff black binding and thick parchment pages. I was disappointed, most of the journal's pages were blank. Only the first several pages were filled, with Minette's neat schoolgirl handwriting in blue ink, passages copied from the Bible. And there was a yellowed newspaper clipping from the *Carolina Negro Record*, June 1951:

> I was an eye-witness to the lynching of Nelson Swift in Jasper County, South Carolina. The lynching was in a field near the County Fairground. The victim was a young black man of 29. He had been released from the county jail and was on foot when captured by a mob of Ku Klux Klan and others. There was a conversation between Jasper County sheriff's deputies and the Klan leaders, and the deputies did not remain. The crowd was quite large, maybe 200 individuals including some women and young people. Nelson Swift was screaming as the mob leaders stripped him of his clothes and mutilated him with knives in his lower body. He was then tied with a rope around his neck and dragged from the rear of a truck to the field. By this time the crowd was much larger perhaps 500. Nelson Swift was still alive when tied to a tree in the field, and surrounded with lumber scraps and dried brush. These were soaked in gasoline and a fire lit. Nelson Swift was

screaming Oh God! God help me! but there was no help. He was thrashing and fighting against the rope binding him but could not break free as the fire became hotter. Finally you could not see Nelson Swift's body for the flames.

There had been many cars parked in the field, now these were departing. I was among the final witnesses remaining. The Klan had possession of Nelson Swift's badly burnt remains which were brought back to the Jasper town square where it was on display for several days. Photographers from several states as well as South Carolina have been selling "mementos" of the lynching for $1. Fingers and toes are said to be available as well but the head of Nelson Swift is "missing."

Several times I read this horrific account. My vision blurred with tears. *Nelson Swift!* Twenty-nine years old in 1951, the victim would be Reverend Swift's age if he'd lived. Maybe he was a brother, a cousin. A relative of Minette Swift who'd been murdered before she was born.

"Minette, I . . ."

I, I! Why should Minette care for what *I* felt! I would shrink from her, sick with shame.

For I didn't know what to say to Minette Swift, having looked into her journal. There were no words adequate to what I felt, and what I felt was not adequate to what had happened to a twenty-nine-year-old man named Nelson Swift in 1951 in Jasper County, South Carolina. I didn't even know whether Minette had wanted me to look into her journal. Now it was nearly March I had to concede that I knew my roommate less well than I'd known her, or thought I'd known her, in September.

The black-bound journal would remain on Minette's desk in exactly the same position beside the white-bound Bible but I would never open it again.

"This shit! This has got to stop."

Crystal Odom was furious, eyes shining with tears. Coming at me on the stairs so I had nowhere to escape and I saw her fists, I saw how she'd have liked to hit me except her voice broke, she was begging: "Genna! You have to make her stop, you're her roommate. She's crazy, she's poisoning this house, this shit of hers has got to stop *you tell her*."

On March 7, 1975, Minette Swift claimed to have returned to her locker in the physical education building after gym class, to discover that a sweater of hers had been "defiled" with a black marker pen. Minette did not want the incident formally reported because she didn't want "more hassle" but she'd demanded of the dean of students that she be excused from physical education for the remainder of the term, and the dean had concurred.

Minette celebrated by burning her "boring old" gym clothes. She'd have burnt them in her metal wastebasket in our room except I stopped her, so we went out back of the residence together where in the snow Minette set several matches to the sweat-stained T-shirts, voluminous khaki shorts, pristine-white sneakers before they caught fire and burned with a smoky, smoldering stink that stung our eyes, and made us laugh.

"That smell? That's the stink of the devil. Not just poor old pigs at Gadarene have got to bear the stink of Satan."

I had no idea what Minette Swift was talking about. But she spoke with zest and feeling and was confiding in me as in a sister.

There had been no formal report of the "locker room harassment" but of course there were many rumors.

One afternoon Wendy Yardman climbed the creaky stairs to the third floor of Haven House, to speak with Minette Swift. But Minette had no wish to speak with Wendy Yardman who was "sooo boring" and "full of herself, makes me sick" so Minette hid in her bedroom with the door rudely shut while I faltered trying to explain to the popular senior class officer that my roommate was a devout Christian who believed in forgiving her enemies, turning the other cheek, not stirring up more trouble . . .

Wendy said, exasperated, "But there is trouble. There is plenty of trouble. Damn trouble isn't going to go away, Minette Swift"—Wendy raised her brassy voice to speak through Minette's door—"you can bury your head in the sand all pious and Christian but if there is race hatred on this campus like the Nazis it will only get worse and *we are all involved, sister!*"

I fled the room. I was embarrassed for Wendy Yardman! For I knew that Minette would not open the door to this "sister," very likely Minette was sneering at her through the door, or sitting on her rumpled bed jamming her fingers into her ears.

Minette Swift isn't your sister she is mine.

A few days later I was informed, not by Minette but by another girl in the residence, that Minette had gone to Dana Johnson to say that she could not continue to eat meals in the dining hall. I was disbelieving at first, for Minette had said nothing to me. When I asked her why, what had happened, Minette stared at me as if I was baiting her.

" 'Scuseme! You tryin to say you don't *know*? Sure you do."

Frequently now, Minette spoke in her mock mid-southern-Negro drawl. What had begun as playful had become habitual. It was said that, even to her instructors, Minette spoke this way.

"Know what, Minette?"

But Minette only laughed, turning away. "Go tell 'em why'd I give 'em any more satisfaction. That's why."

It was true, Minette attracted attention in the dining hall. No one was rude exactly. No one stared openly at her, or pointed her out to others. Yet you were aware, if you walked beside Minette Swift, pushed through the cafeteria line with her, sat with her, of the covert awareness of others. And still there were girls who came by our table to speak to Minette, to offer her sympathy, "moral support." After the incident in the locker room, these impromptu interruptions had increased.

"But I'll miss you, Minette . . ."

Minette might have heard this mild protest but she'd drifted away humming and gave no sign.

Following this, Minette ate her meals in Little Hall, a residence for upperclasswomen on the far, hilly side of the quad. Little Hall was a longer hike than our dining hall but Minette was pleased for there she was privileged to eat her meals not in the dining room "with all that pack" but in a pantry off the kitchen, in private.

Strange, the dining hall without Minette Swift! For the first time at Schuyler College I had no roommate with whom to sit. I was hurt, I was angry at Minette, especially I missed Minette at breakfast which was the meal we'd been most likely to eat together. Though now I was free to sit with others. I was free, when I entered the dining hall, to sit at any table I wished.

Separate

. . . the night of March 28, 1975, when I'd been working at my desk writing in longhand a draft of a paper for my art history class not wishing to type and disturb my roommate Minette Swift who'd gone to bed at 10 P.M. and it was 3 A.M. when I gave up, crawled into bed and lay awake unable to sleep as often these nights I could not sleep yet calmly thinking *We can live like this but how long?* as in the house at Chadds Ford in those years even a child might realize *How long? How long? How long like this?* Through the narrow window through my half-shut eyelids I saw what appeared to be shifting planes of light in the sky unless these were shifting planes of light in a color plate of a seascape of Winslow Homer and through the plasterboard wall I heard a familiar creaking of bedsprings, my roommate's sighs and mumbled indecipherable words and what appeared to be a brief but fierce interlude of teeth-grinding followed by silence and after some time the sound of my roommate sitting up in bed, easing her stocky body out of bed, then the sound of Minette making her way out of her bedroom and into the outer room and so by slow painstaking degrees to the door and the thought came to me *Why is Minette so quiet* for nearly every night Minette rose to use the bathroom walking heavily on her heels as she might walk by day. Yet tonight Minette was very quiet. I was fully awake now, listening. I did not mean to listen as I had never meant to listen in the night in the house at Chadds Ford to the mysterious uplifted voices, laughter and occasional cries sweet and piercing as the cries of brightly feathered tropical birds yet I was listening hearing Minette in her measured stealth leave the room and shut the door behind her and after several minutes return and now the thought came to me more curious than suspicious that Minette had not used the bathroom, had she?—for there was no sound of a toilet flushing or a faucet, that annoying and protracted groaning of water rushing through the antiquated pipes of Haven House and now Minette was returning to her bedroom making her unerring way in the dark barefoot slowly and soundlessly as she'd left and only the faint creaking of floorboards gave her away, and the more defined creaking of bedsprings as her stocky body eased back into bed and now the lapse into quiet like a withheld breath and it would occur to me as often it occurred to me in the night in this room that our two beds were exactly parallel and that our two bodies floated together on the surface of sleep as on the surface of water and perhaps we began to sink beneath the surface at exactly the same moment, perhaps sleep drew us down together though we were lying in separate beds a crude plasterboard wall between us to divide us as by day we were divided in two separate skins of necessity for all life must be divided all consciousness must be separate otherwise we could not see each other, we could not love each other otherwise.

Revenge

In the morning it would be discovered that our door had been defaced with the ugly word **NIG** in black ink. **NIG** was blunt and assured, measuring four inches in height and made with a felt-tip pen.

Neither Minette Swift nor I discovered this. We first learned of it when one of our neighbors knocked hesitantly on our door to waken us at about 6:20 A.M. She was a girl who rose early in the dark to work in the dining hall.

Her name was Maria Kubovy. She was a Merit Scholar from Moncton, New Brunswick. Her parents were Russian immigrants, she'd been born in New Brunswick but spoke English with an accent that became more pronounced when she was anxious, excited. Long I would remember how frightened Maria Kubovy was stammering that she had not wanted anyone to think that she, Maria, had defaced our door: "It was only just—it was here when I saw it, now. I never saw it before now, I don't know who put this here. I hope you will believe me I don't know—"

Seeing **NIG** on the outside of our door Minette murmured "Ohhh!" as if she'd been kicked in the stomach, turned away and ran clumsily back into her bedroom.

NIG! It was a jeer, a shout in our faces. Yet it was in fact only marks made by a felt-tip pen in black ink, difficult to scrub off the white door but if I'd been the one to discover these marks how easy for me to have obscured **NIG** by marking over it transforming a "symbol" into a mere mysterious/annoying smudge.

But I had not been the one to discover it. Together, Maria Kubovy and I went downstairs to knock on Dana Johnson's door.

That evening at 7:30 P.M. there was an "emergency required meeting" for all Haven House residents. In Dana Johnson's parlor we sat on sofas, chairs, the floor. Earlier generations of Haven House residents smiled happily if blindly upon us from framed photos on the walls.

This time, unexpectedly, Minette Swift was present. Her presence was intimidating in the way that a totemic carved figure would be intimidating in the midst of ordinary human beings, appearing larger than life if in fact no larger than life, with dark skin stretched tight across her strong-boned face and eyes inside the chunky tortoiseshell glasses that appeared to be unwavering, adamant gazing upon all of us and none of us as in a halting voice Dana Johnson informed us of what at this hour we all knew: another "ugly racist incident" had been perpetrated in the residence.

NIG had been scrubbed off the door by a custodian. But not until **NIG** had been photographed as "evidence." On the stairs to the third floor, in the hallway outside our room, downstairs in Dana Johnson's quarters, Schuyler College adminstrators and staff had been present intermittently through the day. You could see the exhaustion in Dana Johnson's face, eyes ringed in fatigue like soot.

I was shivering. I sat on the floor not far from Dana Johnson's feet, hugging my knees to my chest. I could not bring myself to look at Minette Swift. I thought *She is exacting revenge, she has that right*. I thought *I won't speak. I will not*. I'd been too agitated to go to my classes that day. I'd tried numerous times to call Veronica, in the hope of acquiring Max's number, but there was no answer in the house at Chadds Ford and I was made to realize that I hadn't spoken with my mother in weeks, nor had my mother called to leave a message for me. And yet we'd parted on good terms after the interminable holiday, we'd hugged, kissed unless it was a dream I was remembering in the confusion and strain of this moment.

Dana Johnson was speaking rapidly. Her ungainly hands moved in jerky gestures. Her graying hair was shorn like a martyr's. Since September, she had aged a decade. Where in her classes Professor Johnson spoke with comparative ease and authority and some humor, here, in these cramped quarters, an involuntary audience of girls staring at her in resentful silence, she stammered, lost her way and had to begin again. "There is a madness in this house! Sometime last night one of you, it would have to be one of you, or more than one, defaced the door of room 303. We know that it can only be someone from this residence, all the doors were locked from the inside. It is a very blatant and crude and cruel gesture of hatred that flies in the face of common sense as of common decency. An ugly, obscene word scrawled on a door by a cowardly individual. We will not leave this room, any of us, until . . ."

There was an excruciating pause. Such strained emotion, the girls of Haven House were feeling the danger of bursting into hysterical laughter. Minette's fleshy lips twitched, I wondered if she was trying not to smile, or sneer; though possibly it was a prayer her lips were forming, unconsciously. I understood that prayers, snatches of Bible passages and Christian hymns streamed through Minette's mind at all times waking and sleeping and that these words were a comfort to her.

Shyly my eyes had lifted to my roommate's face. I was reminded of the first time I'd seen Minette Swift in the college chapel, and afterward outside the chapel, and after that in Elias Meade House, and felt so powerful an attraction to her, impossible to comprehend as to rebuke. Since that day Minette Swift had gained perhaps forty pounds. The shell-pink glasses were long gone as if they had never been. The eyes that had been beautiful, thick-lashed and alertly wary were duller. *You can't make her like you. You can't change her. You can't even change yourself.* I knew that I was obliged by the honor code of Schuyler College to inform on Minette Swift and to expose and betray her but I could not determine the words I must use, I could not "hear" the words in my voice. For Minette was sitting very still beside Dana Johnson, shoulders back, head uplifted, her expression abstracted, inward. She looked like one whose pain is wholly inward, unacknowledged. So deep, it might be transformed into radiance. I feared her gaze suddenly meeting mine but there was no glimmer of recognition. Minette listened unperturbed as Dana Johnson stumbled, faltered, persevered. Minette was wearing her winter outfit: wool slacks, shirt and sweater and wedge-toed boots. The front of the sweater was dribbled with what might have been congealed gravy. Her hair was so stiff with grease it resembled a hat set rakishly askew on her head. An aura of unwashed underarms, long-soiled clothes emanated from her permeating every corner of the airless room. Her expression remained aloof, ironic as Dana Johnson stammered, "How can this be happening, you young women are the 'cream of the' "—unable to remember what she was saying—" 'the crop, the cream'—the very best and brightest and yet—a nightmare has been perpetrated upon us, I ask you to tell us *why?*"

I was frightened that this woman, the only adult in the room, would break down and begin to cry and none of us would know what to do, whether to dare touch her, comfort her, even to acknowledge her tears. In the painful silence I began to speak in the way of one with impaired vision groping in semi-darkness: "I don't know who defaced our door last night. But I heard someone. It was about three-thirty in the morning and I heard someone outside the door. I'd been working at my desk. I wasn't paying much attention but definitely I heard someone outside in the hall, close outside our door I think, I would not have had any suspicion thinking it was just someone on the way to the bathroom, people are always coming and going into the bathroom, and our room is by the stairs, and later I would think that maybe someone had come up the stairs, I'm not sure. Because at the time I wasn't suspicious, I was concentrating on my work. Minette was in bed, her light was out. She'd gone to bed before midnight. I don't think I went to bed until about four." I was speaking more rapidly now. My heart had begun to leap and kick in that erratic way it had one day the previous year in the frantic exertion of a basketball game at the Cornwall Academy when I'd had to be carried off the court. "Now I wish that I'd gone to the door to open it, to see if anyone was there. To see who was there. Because it might even have been someone from outside Haven House, it would have been easy for someone to hide in the house until the doors were locked, and sometimes the doors aren't really locked, we know this, we know that the rear door is sometimes left open with a wedge, anyone could get in, any number of people have access to Haven House. If I'd been suspicious—" My voice hovered in the air, like a bird beating its wings against the wind.

As I spoke, everyone looked at me. It must have been a revelation that Genna Meade would speak like this, for I had the reputation of being quiet, self-effacing. Yet I was aware only of Minette Swift looking at me as I spoke, seeing me. For the first time seeing me. Her expression was astonished, disbelieving. *Now she knows. She knows that I know. Now it will end.*

Questions were put to me by Dana Johnson and some others. Earnestly I repeated what I'd said. I would not vary what I'd said. Like one who has made her way across an abyss on a very narrow plank I would not vary my strategy. Minette Swift continued to stare at me and now her lips had parted, audibly she was breathing through her mouth. As if her heart, too, was beating erratically. In the midst of a question from one of the other residents Minette suddenly stirred, heaved herself to her feet, mumbled " 'Scuseme!" and walked out of Ms. Johnson's parlor without a backward glance.

We heard her heavy footsteps on the stairs, ascending.

Next morning Minette Swift demanded to be moved from Haven House to another residence, and a single room. By early afternoon new quarters had been found for her and by late afternoon she and her possessions had been cleared from Haven House.

This was a shock! Naively I'd anticipated a very different reaction to my testimony. "Minette? Why . . ." Several times I tried to speak with Minette but she shrank from me. As if I inhabited a blazing blinding light she could not bear to face, she turned away not meeting my eye. After college porters carried her things downstairs to a van to be hauled to her new residence, I was stunned to see that she had left the Italian shoulder bag behind, on her bureau.

The bag was still stuffed with tissue paper from the store. There was no accompanying note.

No single rooms were available in Little Hall, or in any undergraduate residence, so "emergency arrangements" were made for Minette to live in Stone Cottage, Schuyler's alumni house. Here, Minette had a sitting room with a fireplace, a spacious bedroom and a full bath. Stone Cottage was one of the college's historic landmarks close by the Elias Meade House and most of the time only one or two rooms were occupied, and these rarely more than overnight.

Next day, Reverend and Mrs. Swift drove up from Washington. They met with President Belknap and other college administrators as well as Minette's academic advisor and her "counsellor" from the Student Health Center. It was said that they'd been approached by the zealous reporter for the *Schuyler Clarion* but had "politely declined" being interviewed, as their daughter had declined several times. At a distance I saw them walking with Minette in her red coat and white angora scarf, leaving the administration building and crossing the snowy quad in the direction of Stone Cottage. It was mid-afternoon, classes were in session and so relatively few people were walking on the quad. I hoped that Minette might glance in my direction, smile and beckon for me to come meet her parents, in one of those abrupt switches of mood and temper typical of Minette Swift, for now my roommate had repudiated me, and wounded me, and left my gift to her behind, perhaps she might feel some measure of sympathy? guilt? affection? She had saved my life, after all.

At the same time, I didn't seriously expect Minette to acknowledge me, for this was hardly an opportune time.

Unobtrusively I followed them. I was headed for the library in any case. I was sorry that Jewel wasn't with them, I had gotten along better with Jewel than her older sister, from the start. I saw that Mrs. Swift was shorter than Minette, which I hadn't remembered, and that she was heavyset as Minette had become; she appeared older, tired, not so attractive as she'd appeared on Orientation Day. But Reverend Swift was a handsome man, you could see heads turning as he passed. His walk was springy, aggressive. He had the air of an ex-athlete. On this chilly overcast March day he was wearing a long dark overcoat that looked like cashmere, over his shoulders, unbuttoned, and a very dark blue suit with a red vest. His expression was fierce, undaunted. The strain of meeting with President Belknap and other Schuyler officials seemed to have energized him even as it had exhausted

Minette and her mother who struggled to keep pace with him. As to an admiring audience, he was talking and gesturing animatedly. Reverend Swift's breath steamed, his hands moved in quick compelling gestures.

At a V-juncture of two sidewalks we passed within twenty feet of one another. None of the Swifts noticed.

Not just poor old pigs at Gadarene have got to bear the stink of Satan.

Rumor!

He'd killed himself at last. Five years to the day after the death of the black security guard.

The death of the forty-three-year-old guard in the Dow Chemical bombing had not been calculated, the death of Ansel Trimmer was calculated.

Except Ansel had killed himself playing Russian roulette with a handgun. Is a bullet in the brain fired in a "game" of Russian roulette calculated?

Though maybe, Ansel Trimmer wasn't dead. Maybe he'd only just fled the United States on a new passport.

Or maybe he was planning to flee the United States, his associates were spreading the death rumor to obfuscate and confuse their enemies.

His associates, and/or his legal counsel.

A very loyal legal counsel. Pro bono for nearly ten years.

Trimmer had lived a fugitive life in the area of Altoona, Pennsylvania. Unless it was Wilkes-Barre. Port Alleghany? It was a fixed-fugitive life not wholly different from imprisonment. Working as an auto mechanic under an "assumed name." He whose political heroes had been Che Guevara, John Brown, Mao Tse-tung. He whose poet-heroes had been Walt Whitman, Pablo Neruda, Gary Snyder, Allen Ginsberg.

He'd never lost his faith in the Revolution/he'd been depressed, suicidal for some time. "Devoured" by guilt unless it was envy, rage. His "unlived" life as a poet-revolutionary. His "unrealized" political vision. He'd lived through the Vietnam Era and now by 1975 the war had long since ended and Nixon had been vanquished and yet little had changed in the essential American soul. And he was thirty, his youth was gone. And most of his teeth.

He'd become a junkie. He'd become an alcoholic. He'd gone into rehab and was clean. Or, he'd been "detoxed" and was clean.

He'd been demanding that Max Meade make a pilgrimage to see him in the gone-to-seed countryside of Altoona, or Wilkes-Barre, wherever this exile was. Max Meade had made a "martyr" of Ansel Trimmer now Max Meade must make a pilgrimage to see Ansel Trimmer.

Close as father/son. In fact closer: Max Meade's son had fled his influence aged sixteen; Ansel Trimmer's millionaire father had kicked him out of the house aged eighteen.

For years Ansel Trimmer and Max Meade had been estranged, they'd quarreled over "ideological" differences. Possibly there'd been a young blond woman involved. Possibly, women.

In exile, Ansel Trimmer was yet armed. His cache of handguns, rifles, a twelve-gauge double-barreled shotgun was impressive. He'd showed Max Meade the handgun he carried often with him, on his person or in his pickup truck, a .38-caliber Colt revolver.

Most of these weapons, though not all, Ansel Trimmer and his (ex-) comrades had been provided by Max Meade and associates. Or, funds to purchase the weapons had been provided from myriad sources.

He'd shown the revolver to Max Meade. In one variant of the rumor, Max had tried to disarm Ansel. In another variant, Max had been terrified and Ansel had laughed at the older man for his "moral cowardice."

Eventually, Ansel held the barrel of the .38-caliber revolver to his forehead and pulled the trigger not once not twice but three times in rapid succession and on the third try he'd died instantaneously, a bullet in the brain. He died in the kitchen of a farmhouse in the countryside near Altoona, or Port Alleghany, or Wilkes-Barre, or across the state line in Maysville, West Virginia . . .

With others in the house, Max had had to drag Ansel Trimmer's body out in the woods to bury it.

Shaken and terrified, they were amateurs at death. Often they had spoken of death but they had never touched nor even seen death at such close quarters.

Bullshit I don't believe this! Max would not be involved in anything like this.

If you need to believe that, fine.

The ground would be frozen! No one could dig a grave. Not by hand. This never happened!

Fine, Genna. I'm just passing the rumor on to you.

It's a ridiculous rumor. It could never have happened. You know that our father has never violated the law.

Genna, fine.

I just don't think this could be. It's ridiculous. The ground is still frozen solid, the Schuylkill is frozen.

Possibly it didn't happen in quite this way. They didn't bury him in the earth but in another way.

Oh Rickie, bullshit! How?

I told you, I'm not "Rickie." I'm "Richard."

Tell me how?

In a gravel pit for instance. If the ice was beginning to crack, in a lake or river. In a quarry.

This is purely invented. I don't believe it.

Or maybe Trimmer isn't dead. The rumor was fabricated. To mislead.

Mislead who?

Authorities, undercover agents. Max's family. Us.

I don't believe that, either. Bullshit!

Genna, I just thought you would want to know. You should know. In case you need to know. If anyone asks you about our father, as they've asked me.

Who? Who has asked you? When . . . ?

Say you know nothing. Which is what I know too.

Loss

Now Minette Swift had departed from Haven House and from my life. Entering the room I stepped into a stunned silence as in the aftermath of a thunderclap.

In such emptiness I felt self-conscious, uneasy. I knew myself guilty yet of a crime, or a sin, I could not clearly recall.

The third-floor room had become a "single" and was therefore perceived as desirable. Nearly as much space as in my old room in the house at Chadds Ford.

I wasn't comfortable taking over Minette's closet. I would not need her bedroom, I kept the door closed. (The mattress was soiled, stained. I kept it covered with a loosely flung sheet.) I might reasonably have taken over Minette's desk by the larger of the windows but for some reason I did not.

Waiting for Minette to return. Maybe.

On the wall where Minette's CHRISTIAN YOUTH FELLOWSHIP poster had been, a ghostly rectangular shadow.

In late March, an unexpected call.

"Genna? Some guy."

It was an obscure fact, there were *some guys* in my life. They were not boyfriends exactly. None was a lover.

One of them, the most unlikely, was Dr. Ferris, my (former) sociology professor.

Several times since the end of the fall/winter term we'd encountered each other by chance, he'd invited me to have coffee with him on Pierpont

Avenue. I was not at ease with Dr. Ferris, I lacked the daughterly/seductive manner required for such relationships. I knew that the man was married, he was of my father's generation. Our conversations were theoretical, never personal. He had not evoked Maximilian Meade even obliquely. He had not asked about my family. Still I thought *I can't trust him, he knows who I am.*

Dr. Ferris hadn't called, though. *Some guy* turned out to be yet more unlikely: my brother Rickie from whom I hadn't heard in a very long time.

Stiffly it was said of Rickie by my parents that he'd "gone his own way." You were meant to envision a headstrong, foolish boy hacking his solitary way through underbrush, you were not meant to envision a canny young man fleeing the glamorous squalor of the house at Chadds Ford for a more orderly life in Philadelphia, a calculatedly brilliant undergraduate career at Penn and post-graduate studies at the Wharton School of Business.

Except he wasn't "Rickie Meade" any longer. Nor even "Rick." He was "Richard"—"Richard H. Meade."

Out of nowhere calling me to ask if I'd go to a pay phone, and call a number he would give me, and I did this, and informing me then that he wanted to drive out to Schuylersville to see me, we could meet as if by accident in the college bookstore, and walk somewhere, vaguely he recalled Pierpont Avenue, and the Schuyler campus, we could avoid the campus and walk along the river beyond the business section of town, and so I followed my brother's matter-of-fact instructions, and we met in this way, and it was then he told me about the "rumor circulating in Philadelphia" about the terrorist-fugitive Ansel Trimmer and our father Max Meade.

It was not a pleasant meeting. I resented my brother upsetting me in this way. Intruding in my life. He was nothing to me now, an ambitious young investment banker! My old love for Rickie, and the anguish that had accompanied it, had faded from my memory like the Polaroid snapshots of the two of us thumbtacked on the cork board in the kitchen at home, exposed to the sun. Years of estrangement and indifference and now: "I just thought you would want to know, Genna. You should know."

"Bullshit."

"*Genna.*" He was mildly shocked, his young sister using such language. It had not occurred to him that he no longer knew me.

I did not want to collude with my brother in any way that might constitute a betrayal of our father. Even if I was furious with Max, and had been hurt by him.

"It's just a rumor, as I've said. But you should know. In case someone approaches you. He's been playing with fire, much of his 'adult' life. He'll have to expect to get burnt."

Rickie, that's to say Richard, was twenty-four. He might have been thirty-four, he carried himself with such stiff dignity, wariness. There was a crease of a frown between his heavy eyebrows, a combative set to his mouth. As we walked together beside the river, no one else in sight, Rickie glanced repeatedly about.

We passed the scruffy park bench where Minette Swift had sat, back to the street. Almost, I could hear the wind-borne voices of the church choir.

"Both of them. It will happen, eventually."

I did not want to hear this. I'd lapsed into a kind of trance of resistance. My brother's malevolent will. His wish to upset, intrude. His account of Ansel Trimmer, Max Meade, "Russian roulette" had been delivered in a way to suggest sorrow and urgency yet you could see that he was suffused with satisfaction. He was glad that Trimmer was dead and dumped in the woods, if only in fantasy; he was glad that Max Meade had been terrified, humiliated and made desperate, if only in fantasy. He'd loved to spread such a rumor as one might love to spread disease.

Rickie lived now in a five-room apartment in one of the "old, beautiful" brownstones in Society Hill, Philadelphia. He'd been hired out of the Wharton School by one of the "top, prestigious" investment firms in Philadelphia. Glancing about as he spoke, squinting, expecting to see— what? Who? Max Meade observing us at a distance, impressed.

We turned back, headed for Pierpont Avenue. We had met in the bookstore "by accident." On the street, girls I knew smiled at me hoping to be introduced. Girls I'd become friendly with, or seeming-so, who'd had no idea that I had an older brother. Vaguely I said, "This is my brother Rickie—Richard. This is my brother Richard H. Meade who lives in Philadelphia and works as an investment banker." The words came mechanically as if I'd uttered them many times.

Through the eyes of these admiring others I saw my brother: tall, lanky, restless as if his clothes fitted too tightly, attractive as Richard Meade was attractive though lacking any single attractive feature. His face was asymmetrical, his eyes rather close-set. You could see how one day his bald dome of a head would protrude, though at the moment his hair was thick, stirring in the wind. Hair very similar to my own.

As his splotched-freckled face was similar to my own.

We walked on. The admiring girls looked after us. I had risen in their esteem, now. As, in the disastrous matter of my roommate Minette Swift, I had occupied a very dubious position in their esteem.

" 'Elias Meade House.' It's on campus, right? I haven't seen it in years."

Rickie had asked very few questions about Schuyler College, or about me. I understood, it was difficult for a brother to take his younger sister seriously. Only Max merited his interest, and to a lesser degree Veronica. He'd allowed me to know that he wasn't in contact with Max in any way; he heard from Veronica often, she was "always" inviting him to visit Chadds Ford but he kept his distance of course.

We passed through the front archway of Schuyler College. The scrolled letters in elegantly fashioned wrought iron. Beyond, the hilly campus sculpted in white like flawless Styrofoam. In the bell tower of the chapel the hour was being chimed: five.

"It seems so remote here. Another world. You should have gone to Penn. And you must be known here, right? The great-granddaughter of the Quaker founder."

I told him no. I didn't think so.

"What about Maximilian? It must be known he's your father."

No. I didn't think so.

"Remember, Max wanted to 'radicalize' this place? His Utopian vision was Mao's Red Guard. That thug!"

Rickie's laughter was excited, breathless. I didn't know who the thug was: Mao, or Max.

Max had said once, joking, that the difference between him and Mao Tse-tung was: Max Meade wouldn't have killed nearly so many people.

This was a joke, you were meant to laugh. Told in Max Meade's hoarse throaty voice like dried reeds cracking.

Rickie said, suddenly embittered, "I'll never forgive them, Genna. Those 'adults,' our parents. Exposing us to that life. You, at that age."

"Rickie, I'm fine. I lost my capacity for surprise, that's all."

"You don't know what you lost, Genna. It's in the nature of loss, you never know."

"Bullshit."

I didn't want to hear this, my heart clutched in panic. I was laughing to show that I took very little of this seriously. We tried the front door of Elias Meade House, but it was locked and darkened within.

Research

Now Minette Swift had departed from Haven House and from my life the sly stinging thought often assailed me *Your punishment is just.*

It wasn't true, what I'd told my brother: I had not lost my capacity for surprise. I was like one who has been anesthetized, who has no knowledge of how she has been "wounded," or even, with certainty, that she has been "wounded."

Easier to laugh in contempt. *'Scuseme!*

It had been an utter surprise to me, the reaction of my roommate Minette Swift when I'd borne false witness on her behalf.

It had been an utter surprise, you could say, yes, a wound, when Minette moved out.

And the Italian shoulder bag left behind.

I don't need your lies. I don't need you. I loathe you.

In the days, weeks that followed often with a pang of emotion I sighted my former roommate crossing the quad, descending the steps of a building amid clusters of anonymous others this solitary, indomitable and unmistakable figure: Minette Swift. As always she walked with punishing deliberateness, eyes fixed and unwavering glancing to neither the right nor the left not so much disdainful of her surroundings as oblivious, indifferent.

Like, in a cascading stream, a rock with its own mysterious motion. Wholly unrelated to the motion of the stream, or of the observing witness.

I knew Minette's schedule: ten o'clock Spanish (Minette had had two years of Spanish in high school, now at Schuyler she was taking second-year Spanish Conversation to fulfill her language requirement for what she hoped would be an easy A) in the Romance Languages Building and from this, Mondays/Wednesdays she would cross to her lecture in American lit. in Woburn Hall and on Fridays she would cross to her American lit. precept in the library. Afternoons, Minette had botany lecture and lab in the New Science Building: I was in the lecture, one of seventy-five students, but not in Minette's lab. (I was in the American lit. lecture, too. In neither large class did I make any attempt to sit near Minette. Usually I sat a few rows behind her. She took little notice of others and had not once noticed me though, before her departure from Haven Hall, we'd frequently sat together in these classes. Unobtrusively I could observe Minette's scrupulous note-taking, her frowning interest in the lecture that inevitably shifted, over the course of the fifty-minute session, to restlessness; sometimes I could even make out Minette's intricate doodling in the margins of her notebooks, elaborate geometric figures you might mistake for exploding suns.) Minette had Math 101 in the math building, Tues/Thurs at one o'clock: a weather-worn granite-Gothic building I had no reason to enter.

Freed of phys. ed. she'd so despised, Minette no longer had to hike across campus to the gym and the playing fields, and would not be sighted at that edge of the campus though once or twice I saw her there, seemed to see her, followed after her figure in the bulky down jacket, hood drawn over her head, until I discovered no, this wasn't Minette Swift after all but another girl walking swiftly and alone with a book bag slung over her shoulder.

In the vicinity of Little Hall at mealtimes, Minette was more reliably sighted of course. And in the vicinity of Stone Cottage. These were familiar buildings on the central campus which, in the course of a day, I might pass several times.

"Minette? Hello!"

Casually I would call to her. My voice high, bright, soaring and weightless and without reproach as a kite. Sometimes Minette heard, glanced around with a frowning smile, taken in polite surprise: for Minette Swift had been trained in politeness, this was her immediate response to any intrusion. Seeing who I was, or, with a flutter of her eyelids behind the thick lenses of her glasses, not-seeing, inaudably she would murmur what might have been "H'lo" and continue on her way.

Sometimes, Minette continued on her way not-hearing.

There were days, nasty-weather days in March and early April, when Minette did not appear at these expected times. She'd cut our large lecture classes several times. At least, I failed to see her.

(I did not wish to linger, to watch for Minette Swift. I did not wish to be perceived by others lingering and watching, lovelorn, for my former roommate Minette Swift who'd repudiated me in the most public of ways.)

In the college library I looked up *Hottentot Venus*. I found three books containing the exact caricatured drawing that had been photocopied and shoved beneath our door. Through a friend who worked in the circulation department I was able to determine that no one had checked out these books, not one of them, since spring 1974.

Still, there were photocopiers in the library. On every floor. Very easily Minette might have copied the drawing in the library without needing to check out the book. My investigation proved nothing.

Yet: if Minette had written **NIG** on our door, it did not follow that Minette had also staged the previous acts of "harassment." In Intro to Phil we were being trained to resist false causality, imprecise terms, illogical syllogisms.

Nothing.

Also in the library I'd tried to research "Nelson Swift" who had been lynched in Jasper County, South Carolina, in June 1951. Even in books and articles dealing with lynchings in the American South, the Ku Klux Klan, "race discrimination," not a trace.

It isn't true that Minette Swift was always alone. Occasionally I did see her with others. Once, in the student center, at a cafeteria table with Wendy Yardman and another senior, a husky dark-skinned girl-woman who wore her hair in bristling cornrows, a sub-editor of the *Schuyler Clarion* named

Hannah Steele who'd written controversial editorials in defense of the Black Marxist Angela Davis, the Black Panthers, even, to an ambiguous degree, the Symbionese Liberation Army. Between these two high-powered individuals Minette Swift sat unyielding, her stoic patience put to the test. Passing by their table at a little distance, I did not intrude; I did not call out a greeting to Minette; in my heart I rejoiced, that Minette's face was a mask of mere courtesy, I knew that in a few minutes she would murmur " 'Scuseme!" and escape and Wendy Yardman and Hannah Steele would stare after her in dismay.

Can't catch me! Can't come close.

Yes it had occurred to me: to vindicate Minette Swift's charge of racist harassment, to absolve her finally and irrefutably from (unofficial, unvoiced) counter-charges of fabricating the harassment herself, I might address to MIN SWIFT STONE COTTAGE another message NIGGR GO HOME. I might enter Stone Cottage by stealth, and scrawl in black felt-tip pen **NIG**.

Sometimes I thought yes, I will do this. And Minette will understand.

At other times I thought, no! This is madness. No one will understand.

The great-granddaughter of Elias and Generva Meade. Granddaughter of Alden Meade, daughter of Maximilian Meade. Revealed as a white racist. Publicly exposed as one who has sent racist hate mail to an eighteen-year-old black Merit Scholar, a minister's daughter and her (former) roommate.

My heart beat in panicked shame, hearing such accusations.

Oh but I wanted to laugh: Max Meade's face!

In late March, I bought a black felt-tip pen at the bookstore. The pen with the widest tip. Practically a paintbrush. I liked the smell of the ink. I liked the broad confident smear of black on a sheet of white paper. I recalled the felt-tip pens Minette had had, neatly arranged on her desk.

I'd tried to write to Minette. Sometimes even as girls drifted into the room that was now "my" room—"Genna's" room—to blink and stare and make inane, awkward comments ("Can't believe she's gone! You must be so relieved") to mask their discomfort, their confused shame/defiance ("Whoever did it, if anybody did it, at least it's over now no matter what people are saying about us.") and prurient curiosity ("Is her mattress really so filthy? Is it still in that room?"). I would not indulge by allowing them to open the door to Minette's former bedroom which I kept closed at all times as if uneasily aware of the possibility that yes, Minette Swift was inside, my roommate's privacy could not be violated.

"Of course I miss her. I was Minette's friend. We can't understand the pressure she's under, it isn't for us to judge . . ."

They laughed at me, I think. Max'milian Meade's daughter so pious! Yet they liked me and perhaps to a degree admired me as a "character" in the narrative of their freshman year at Schuyler College that had turned out to be so much more tumultuous than anyone might have anticipated: a narrative that had unfolded in lurching and careening skids until the abrupt departure of Minette Swift from the residence, but had not yet played itself out.

April 11 was Minette Swift's birthday. April 13 was my birthday.

I wondered if Minette would remember?

Stradegy

From *Richard H. Meade* in Philadelphia to *Generva Meade* in Haven House, Schuyler College came a typed, curtly brief letter dated April 8, 1975.

> **Why don't you simply forget, Genna, our conversation of the other day. Since you can't handle certain facts staring you in the face I think that is the wisest stradegy for both of us as children of M.M. Thank yoiu.**
>
>

Richard

Stradegy, yoiu were mistypings that would have been detected if my brother had reread what he'd written. He had typed it out in haste, then. Also jarring, like a nudge in the ribs, was the placement of *Genna* in the first sentence.

Yes, I thought: I will forget.

And what our mother spilled out to me, too, as in an act of vomiting, in the Valley Forge Mall.

Black Girl/White Girl

In early April 1975 Minette Swift would apply for, and be granted, a leave of absence for medical reasons from Schuyler College for the remainder of the semester with the proviso that she be allowed to return, as a Merit Scholar, in the fall.

Abruptly in late April 1975 Generva Meade would withdraw from Schuyler College for medical reasons. She would not return.

Stone Cottage

Uninvited I went to visit Minette Swift in her "suite of rooms" in Stone Cottage on April 10, 1975, which was the eve of Minette's nineteenth birthday. Unknowing, I would be the last person to see Minette Swift alive.

It was a whim! Bringing Minette a bouquet of one dozen white roses from a florist on Pierpont Avenue. For the following day was her birthday, and I'd been hearing that Minette had not been well.

I knew, Minette had been absent from our lecture classes. She was behind in her botany lab work. There were rumors she'd failed to take her makeup exams (American lit., biology), and that she'd applied for a leave of absence from school allowing her to withdraw from her current courses without failing them, to return to Schulyer in the fall.

The most troubling rumor was that Minette had "slipped"—"fallen"—"been pushed"—on the library steps, at that time slick with ice from a sleet storm, she'd turned her ankle, badly sprained it and was on crutches. Yet Minette refused to formally report having been "pushed" to any college official and there had been nothing about the incident in the *Schuyler Clarion*.

By early April *l'affaire Swift*, in Crystal Odom's coolly coined phrase, had gradually subsided, after the initial flurry of excited and scandalized interest on campus. The seventeen remaining residents of Haven House inhabited a kind of poisonous mist: vaguely we were known, not as individuals but in the collective, as racist, treacherous, mean-spirited, catty.

In Haven House, the collective wish was to forget. It was becoming increasingly rare for anyone to allude to Minette Swift. Visitors to my room ceased to speak of her. Some mornings, I woke without thinking of my (absent) roommate. Only when Maria Kubovy and I met our greetings were awkward, embarrassed. It was as if we'd committed an act of desecration together, obscurely but painfully recalled.

This is a mistake. She doesn't want you. You will only remind her. Have you no shame!

It was Max Meade's voice warning me. One of his catchphrases, a comic scolding with an edge of paternal severity, was *Have you no shame!* The reproach was an allusion to the notorious Republican Senator Joseph McCarthy.

Nonetheless I brought one dozen white roses, beautiful soft-skinned/subtly fragrant white roses amid ferns delicate as lace, to my ex-roommate Minette Swift in the knowledge that she would probably disdain the roses, as she would disdain me.

When my wealthy Meade relatives visited Schuyler College for trustees' meetings, they stayed in Stone Cottage. So I'd been told. I had never been inside before. Where Haven House was a hive of activity, Stone Cottage was a sepulchre. I had noticed that most of its windows were darkened. A lone housekeeper lived on the first floor. Built in an era predating even Elias Meade House, the "cottage" was made of massive ugly rocks that looked to have been jammed together by force; it appeared squat, dwarfish. Of course it had been furnished to be "quaint"—"charming." In the front parlor there was a spinet piano with a covered keyboard, there were velvet settees and chairs with sashes tied about them forbidding use. There were (unlighted, dust-dimmed) crystal chandeliers. There were ceiling-high shelves of drearily matched leather-bound books— Shakespeare, *The Federalist Papers,* Sir Walter Scott, James Fenimore Cooper—and there were walls of framed photos of Schuyler College history. Much of this was semi-darkened and exuded a stony damp. As soon as I entered the foyer I began coughing.

The wild thought came to me, how outrageous **NIG** would be in Stone Cottage. Black felt-tip pen on one of the pristine-white doors, or on a frayed-silk-wallpaper wall.

The Irish-looking housekeeper curtly informed me, Minette Swift's "suite" was 2B, on the second floor.

I thanked her. I climbed the twilit carpeted stairs. I felt how, behind me, the housekeeper stared at my back. *White girl/black girl. Something not-right.* The housekeeper was a woman of stout middle age whose expression, when I'd uttered Minette's name, had told me all I needed to know of her fury at the black girl's presence in this "historic" house.

My heart was beating hard. I knocked at the door of 2B. I knew that Minette was in, I could see a glimmer of light beneath the door. "Minette? It's . . ." My throat was dry, I could not utter my name. A terrible shame came over me, that Minette would not remember my name.

There was silence inside the room. I felt the tension in this silence. I knew that Minette was staring at the door, suspicious and hostile. Again I knocked and this time spoke my name shyly, as a kind of question: ". . . Genna Meade?"

I could hear Minette hobbling on crutches to the door, and with sudden violence the door was yanked partway open. Minette's face loomed in the crack like a dark angry moon. " 'Scuseme it's late! I get up early, I don't stay up late."

It wasn't really late: the illuminated clock in the chapel bell tower had indicated only nine-ten. Most Schuyler girls stayed up past midnight. Minette had changed into her navy blue bathrobe and pajamas, wool socks on both her feet. It was the right ankle she'd sprained, thickened by gauze inside the sock. Leaning on her crutches, panting, Minette glared at me. Through the smudged lenses of her glasses her eyes exuded fury, resignation.

You, girl! Why you!

Blindly I held out the roses to Minette, who hadn't a free hand to take them. I heard myself explain that I'd heard that she had sprained her ankle, and I knew that her birthday was the next day . . .

Without a word Minette turned aside, as if to allow me entry. This gesture would have to be sufficient, to invite me inside. Hobbling on her crutches Minette was brusque, careless. She seemed hardly to notice or to care that, wielding the crutches so clumsily, she was coming down hard on the injured ankle.

Minette had been lighting scented candles: candles of all sizes, shapes, hues set in small glass holders on the surfaces of tables, Minette's desk and windowsills, and, in the form of a cross, on the carpeted floor. The smell was overwhelming. Many of the candles were dripping onto the carpet. I could imagine the appalled dismay of the housekeeper downstairs.

". . . how beautiful, Minette. This is . . ."

I felt shy, self-conscious. As if, unknowing, I'd stepped into a shrine.

Into a private madness. "Honoring Jesus."

The candle flames were dazzling. Flickering, winking. So many, and the smell so strong! The effect of these myriad flames was dreamy, hypnotic. The cross, which was at the center of the candle display, measured about three feet by seven. There was a geometric pattern to the arrangement of candles around the cross, an octagon perhaps. *To keep out evil spirits. Demons.* I saw that several tall tapering green candles were dangerously near ruffled organdy curtains.

Minette was both embarrassed of being discovered, and proud. She was presenting her god to me, in his mysterious fiery form.

I'd interrupted the ritual, not all the candles had been lighted. I saw my opportunity, I would light those that remained for it was difficult for Minette to maneuver herself, and to stoop over, on her crutches.

Minette sat heavily on a sofa that creaked beneath her weight, and let her crutches fall carelessly to the carpet. Every gesture of hers seemed intended to suggest how indifferent Minette Swift was to this "historic" place in which she'd been housed.

The campus rumor was, Minette Swift was living in a spacious suite of "antiques" but the furnishings in this room did not appear to be genuine antiques, only just old, graceless American Colonial pieces. The hand-loom carpet was of good quality but threadbare in places. The dove-gray silk wallpaper, imprinted with a vertiginous, infinitely repeating floral pattern, was also of good quality but discolored. On the walls were portraits of dour-looking forebears, mostly male with curdled-milk white skins. (Amid the portraits was a single woman with a jutting jaw and hawk eyes: Generva Meade? The woman wore a frilly white cap like a nightcap. I could not believe that this plain-featured woman was my great-grandmother.) Above Minette's desk was the frayed poster CHRISTIAN YOUTH FELLOWSHIP she'd crudely taped to the wallpaper, and close by, also taped in place, was a calendar turned to the month of April.

The first ten days of April had been pointedly X'd out in black felt-tip pen. I wanted to protest to Minette, April 10 wasn't yet over.

Books, papers, articles of clothing had been strewn about the room like a kind of pillage. For here was a space twice the size of our study room in Haven House, needing to be claimed. On Minette's desk, which was an impracticably fussy "writing desk," was her typewriter, beside it a battered-looking botany lab book, sheets of yellow paper covered in the compulsively intricate geometrical figures, the ravaged Norton anthology with the cover I'd fashioned for it. And there was the black-bound journal.

Beside Minette on the sofa were her Bible and one of Mrs. Swift's baked-goods tins, out of which Minette had been eating. On the floor at Minette's feet was a liter-sized bottle of Hires root beer, two-thirds empty.

I had interrupted not only the honoring of Jesus, but a bedtime feast. Minette would feel obliged to share her food with me, out of politeness. She hadn't invited me to stay, still less to remove my jacket, but I removed the jacket and laid it across the back of a chair. I asked if there was a vase I could use, for the roses, reluctantly Minette pointed to a breakfront in a corner of the room. I located a vase inside. It was made of milk glass, but chipped. I heard my voice lifting light as a kite in the breeze asking Minette how she was, how long would she be on crutches, how were her classes going this semester . . . I did not think that these were questions Minette would wish to answer but I had no others.

I hadn't seen my former roommate in such close quarters for weeks and was shaken by her appearance. Not just that Minette hadn't been grooming herself as before but she was looking ill, depressed. Her face seemed swollen and glistened with an unwholesome oily perspiration, her eyelids were puffy and her eyes bloodshot. *Minette is sick. This is sickness I am smelling.* Beneath the cloying incense smells, I'd detected the burnt-orange odor of Minette's skin or breath that meant drugs, in my experience. In Minette's bathroom where I went to fill the vase with water, I saw an opened container of chunky white pills on the sink, on the label the typed word CODEINE.

A powerful painkiller. Veronica had loved CODEINE.

The mirror above the sink was splotched with waterstains. There were black hairs and a patina of grime in the sink. I didn't want to look too closely at the soiled towels on the racks, soiled socks and underwear on the floor and in the brimming wastebasket a sanitary pad stiffened with dried blood. I felt faint, I held my breath against the odor.

Happily I carried the vase of roses in the milk-glass vase to Minette, to present to her: "Well! Happy birthday, Minette."

(White roses! Why had I brought Minette creamy-white roses! Not until this moment, seeing them in Minette's eyes, did I realize.)

(But crimson had seemed too romantic/lurid. Crimson had seemed, in the florist's shop, too much the cliché.)

Minette appeared moved. She swiped at her eyes, muttered thanks. Her smile was pained but it was a smile. In her sulky-girl voice she said, "How'd anybody know it was my birthday!"

I told Minette of course I knew it was her birthday. My own was two days later: April 13.

Minette peered at me over the roses she was sniffing. "*You?* How old?"

"Nineteen, like you."

"Nineteen."

Minette frowned, considering this. It wasn't clear if nineteen was too old, or too young.

I said, with awkward humor, "It makes us almost twins, under the same astrological sign."

" 'Twins'!" Minette's laughter was both scornful and startled, like the laughter of Jewel in the secret attic of Elias Meade House.

It was funny. I laughed. My laughter was high-pitched, flamey. Tears stung my eyes, there was a joke here cruelly funny as it was unsayable.

It was clear that Minette wasn't well. She seemed tired, exhausted. A heavy sadness weighed upon her, giving a middle-aged downward droop to her mouth. Her eyes that had seemed beautiful to me had lost their lustre, the whites were sallow, bloodshot. Within a few years Minette Swift would be heavyset, short of breath. Gone forever the brash schoolgirl in the shell-pink plastic glasses challenging *'Scuseme?* Across an abyss I stared at Minette, transfixed. Why was I here? Why had I come, where I wasn't wanted? (And yet, Minette hadn't been surprised to see me.) What did I want from Minette Swift, and what did I have to give Minette Swift that might be of any value? In my nervousness I'd taken up a box of matches to light the remainder of the candles. I should have blown the candles out, this was madness, this was dangerous, so many candles burning, some of them teetering as if about to topple over . . . "You are 'honoring Jesus,' Minette. I remember." The candle flames were mesmerizing. How like human souls tremulous, transparent and fleeting, this continuous burning-away, expiation and extinction. Reverently I stooped over the un-lighted candles, putting a match to their wicks. I saw how Minette was watching me, intently. I would never betray her, I had borne false witness on her behalf. I had violated my own honor for her surely this was good? this was generous? this was sisterly? *Be here now! Be here now! God is here, everywhere, now!* My pulse quickened in the sudden knowledge that this was so, all that Max Meade denounced as bullshit was so, the very core of the living god that binds those who believe together yet it was not a truth that one could bear for very long, like a passionate inheld breath.

Minette said quietly: "We are weak. Jesus is strong. In us, Jesus is strong."

There were five candles perpendicular to eleven candles. The cross, the stave. The incense smell was making me light-headed.

"It wasn't Jesus but you who saved my life, Minette!"

In the way of sudden drunkenness I spoke. Minette laughed, startled and subtly offended. " 'Scuseme when was this?"

"In December. On Pierpont Avenue. We bought candles."

Minette shook her head, bemused. "Nah."

"Minette, you did! Or maybe it was Jesus, in you. You acted without thinking. It was your instinct, like a fool I'd stepped out blind into traffic."

Minette frowned, shaking her head. Nah!

". . . I wish, now"—pulses at my temples throbbed with the enormity of what I was saying, dared to say as Minette Swift stared at me from beneath drooping eyelids—"that I could pray for you. I know that you can pray for me, but I wish that I could pray for you. That my prayers had any power. 'A long and a happy life' I would pray for Minette Swift."

Minette laughed, irritably. " 'Scuseme, girl, I can pray for myself."

". . . that your ankle will heal, and—"

"My ankle is healing! It's a sprain not a break." Suddenly Minette began speaking in a rush of words, protesting. "See, those girls pushed me coming out of the library, it's past dark and slippery from the ice and they're laughing pretending not to see me where I'm trying to fix my damn book bag over my shoulder and they run into me then act all surprised, 'Ohhh we didn't see you!'—'Ohhh can you get *up*? Can you *walk*?'—like devils I could see the wickedness in their eyes like hot coals, I could smell Satan's stink in their breaths like those bitch-devils in the other place. Jesus was testing me I think, how far can my forgiveness go, 'turn the other cheek' see you get kicked in the ass-cheeks you're some old *Niggr* they can kick knowin' they will get away with it. Even the ones who 'like' you they will kick you for sure! So I'm telling those devils don't touch me don't any of you lay a hand on me *I will kill you*. Ran off limping wouldn't let any of 'em have the satisfaction. Didn't report it to any proctor. Why'd I do that! Give 'em the satisfaction. Back here, and my ankle is starting to swell, soaked it in hot water and near-about fainted with the pain and next thing one of the proctors is driving me over to the infirmary and the nurse looks at my ankle and calls an ambulance!—next thing I know, I'm in the ER being X-rayed. And they got to call my parents. And all the rest of it."

Minette seemed suddenly tired. She'd shoved her glasses up, rubbing her eyes so hard I wanted to seize her hands, to stop her.

"You didn't report being pushed, Minette."

"See why'd I give 'em the satisfaction! Everybody knows what they are doing."

"But, if you were pushed . . ."

"It's like the other times! What is done to you, you have to bear. 'I am weak, but He is strong.' It was my weakness, to report any of it. Jesus doesn't give you more than you can bear. He can give you pain, he can give you hurt, he can give you shame, he can give you sorrow, he can give you a broke-heart but he will not give you more than you can bear. Not ever."

"Not more than you can bear, Minette, but you can become very tired. Your health . . ."

" 'Scuseme this is not 'my' health! This is not 'your' health. This is Jesus' health, he provides."

Minette's logic was so vehement, I could not withstand it. I felt the powerful undertow of her madness, I wanted to inhale deeply, to succumb. Faintly I protested: "But your ankle is sprained, that is 'real.' Pain is 'real.' If—"

"See, tomorrow's my birthday. It happened that way, they're coming for me. To take me back home."

"Home? You're going home tomorrow?"

" 'Leave of absence.' My father was on the phone with who's it—the dean. It's agreed I can come back, I will have my scholarship."

Minette spoke slowly. Her mouth twisted around *scholarship* as if it tasted like acid.

"Oh Minette, I'm sorry. That you're going home, I mean . . ."

" 'Scuseme, *I am not sorry*."

Minette was still breathless from her outburst, but not so agitated now. She was fumbling to break off a piece of muffin, to eat; the sofa was littered with crumbs.

"When will your parents be here, Minette? Maybe I should stay with you, until . . ."

Minette shrugged. She didn't seem to have heard me though she repeated, more emphatically, "*I am not sorry* like my Daddy is, and *I am not ashamed* like Daddy. Jesus will help me, Daddy will learn to forgive me. I have that faith."

Minette shoved the muffin tin toward me. The muffins were made of a dark chewy grain with a small, slightly bitter fruit or berry inside— cranberries? So delicious, saliva rushed into my mouth. I had not known I was so hungry.

Quietly we sat eating muffins. Minette drank from the bottle of root beer, and passed it to me. The dark liquid was lukewarm, gaseous.

Sickening-sweet. Still I drank, I was terribly thirsty. My mouth was dry as if in panic, or the memory of panic.

I wondered what Minette had been reading in her Bible. If she'd been reading aloud. The heavy white-leather-bound Bible was open, strewn with muffin crumbs. I could not see which book it was open to. She had never read to me from her Bible, she'd never invited me to come with her to church. Yet I had not asked her, maybe she'd been waiting?

Between us, we devoured all the muffins in the tin.

The chapel bell tolled 10 P.M. It was time for me to leave. Minette was yawning. I was exhausted as if I'd been awake for days. I was no longer so aware of the burning candles, my eyes had adjusted to the flickering light. The smell of incense wasn't so powerful. Only when I left Stone Cottage would the fresh air revive me, like a slap in the face.

"Minette, good night."

As if I could not bring myself to say *good-bye*.

In the Night

In the night, shortly after midnight, a sudden eruption of sirens.

In my third-floor room in Haven House I stood at my ex-roommate's window staring out into the night not able to see the fire, for buildings and trees intervened, and the sooty density of smoke that began to seep into the room like paralysis, I could not move, or breathe.

Unexpected!

"Genna. I'm so sorry."

This was unexpected: Veronica in my room in Haven House.

Her dyed-black hair not piled and teetering on her head or wild-mane tumbling to her shoulders in middle-aged hippie abandon but pulled back from her face in a sleek French twist, austere and elegant.

Veronica's head looked smaller: no longer a cartoon head. On her face, fine white lines.

Veronica fumbled for my hand, that was limp and unresponsive.

"You've lost your closest friend, Genna. I know what that can be."

I wondered if Veronica meant Max. I wanted to protest *He was never your friend, he was your husband.*

I had not expected my mother here. Yet she'd climbed the stairs, she had entered my room and stood before me. And she was wearing black: a fitted Chanel jacket, trousers. The fabric was softly nubby in light wool.

Sympathy shone in her eyes like tears.

When Veronica moved to embrace me, my body stiffened. In an animal way it knew to resist. I was not ill but my skin was fevered and painful when touched. I did not want my mother's sympathy to diffuse my grief. I did not want my loss of Minette Swift, and my guilt for that loss, to be soothed.

"And so near your birthday, Genna! This is very hard."

Lost Gift

"I'd brought her roses for her birthday. What she was going to give me, she'd hinted, but I had no idea what the lost gift might have been."

"Remains"

Here was a bitter irony: Minette Swift's parents had been scheduled to drive from Washington, D.C., to Schuylersville on the morning of April 11, Minette's nineteenth birthday, to bring her back home with them; in the very early morning of that day, they received a call from the college provost informing them of Minette's death.

Reverend and Mrs. Swift would make the trip to Schuylersville, but it was their daughter's remains they would arrange to bring back with them for burial.

Funeral services were held at the Temple Vale of the World Tabernacle of Jesus Christ where Reverend Swift was minister. The ceremony was private. The casket was closed. No one from Schuyler College was invited.

No Shadow

I can live like this. Fast-moving, casting no shadow.

Do Not Enter Do Not Enter

Most of Stone Cottage was destroyed in the fire but adjacent "historic" buildings, one of them Elias Meade House, were spared by emergency measures of the Schuylersville fire company.

The fire, the death of Minette Swift on the eve of her nineteenth birthday would be ruled "accidental" by the coroner of Montgomery County, Pennsylvania.

Minette Swift was the sole victim of the fire. There were no guests in Stone Cottage that night. Overcome with smoke inhalation in her first-floor quarters at the rear of the residence, the housekeeper had been rescued by fire workers.

For a long time a pall of acrid smoke would hang over the campus stinging our eyes in rebuke. For weeks we would pass in an appalled silence around the smoke-blackened part-gutted ruin of Stone Cottage blocked off by sawhorses and yellow police tape warning DO NOT ENTER DO NOT ENTER DO NOT ENTER manic and fierce in repetition as the barking of a deranged dog.

Borne by the tainted air there were campus rumors of a "voodoo" ritual involving lighted candles and there were campus rumors of "suicide" but none of these rumors were ever substantiated.

In the public press, in certain quarters, there were reported rumors of "arson"—"homicide"—"racist murder." These were never substantiated.

There would be two, independent investigators into the fire that caused Minette Swift's death: one from the Montgomery County fire inspector's office, the other representing Schuyler College's insurer. As the last person to have seen Minette Swift alive, I was questioned by each.

Some truths are lies was not a principle in which I wished to believe and yet: to have told the "truth" about Minette Swift would have been to defame and distort her, therefore to lie. I would not do this.

I would not speak of Minette Swift after her terrible death as in any way "distraught"—"irrational"—"paranoid" as others seemed to wish to believe she'd been. I would not portray Minette as a pitiable object in the way of the *Hottentot Venus* to be dissected, examined, analyzed, "judged." Each of my interrogators was a white man, I did not want to be seduced into aligning myself with his whiteness in the most subtle and unconscious of ways. I spoke of Minette looking forward to her parents arriving the next day for her birthday. I spoke of Minette happy about her leave of absence from school and her planned return in the fall. She had not been depressed, "suicidal." She had not. For she'd been a devout Christian, she had enormous faith in Jesus Christ. It was so, Minette sometimes lighted candles to "honor" Jesus as she had lighted candles that night. But not many. And not recklessly.

I had already answered many times questions about the "alleged racist harassment" of Minette Swift. I had nothing more to add to what I'd already said.

Minette had loved her parents very much. Her younger sister Jewel.

Minette had had a beautiful singing voice.

Minette's last words that I could recall were *I have faith*.

Too Late

And then, as in a cruel fairy tale in which your wishes come true, but too late to matter, to assuage my grief Max came to see me. Now it was too late to meet my roommate Minette Swift.

I think it was to assuage my grief, Max came to see me in Schuylersville. I was never certain of my father's motives.

Like Veronica, Max embraced me and in animal cunning I knew to stiffen against him.

I was not ill (I was certain!) but my skin hurt like sunburn. I could not bear to be touched. The touch of another person was repulsive but even the touch of clothing, its abrasion against the skin seemed to wound.

Outside, even a sudden gust of wind against my face. I swallowed hard, the burning shock of it. That air acrid and tainted with the smell of Stone Cottage.

As always Max Meade was urgently wanted elsewhere. He'd been urgently wanted in Los Angeles where he'd been (intermittently) for months and now he was urgently wanted in D.C. He had only flown to Philadelphia Airport to rent a car to drive out to Schuylersville to see me, he would drive then to D.C., a trip of approximately three and a half hours, after our dinner. Max Meade's travel plans, calculations! You were caught up in the fever of his accelerated time, glancing frequently at your watch.

We would be together for ninety minutes. Max arrived in Schuylersville in the late afternoon of April 17, he would depart Schuylersville (he took care to tell me) by no later than 9 P.M. of April 17.

The situation was very urgent. For Max was consulting with an attorney, unless he was himself the consulting attorney, in a complicated case in federal court involving a lawsuit filed against the FBI on numerous charges of illegal wiretapping of private citizens.

We ordered our dinners, we ate. Especially, Max Meade ate. For Max was a man of vigorous middle age, hearty appetites. He ate, he drank. He smoked cigarettes between courses, not in Veronica's luxuriant languorous way but briskly and deeply as one might suck oxygen. I was fascinated by Max's head. Hairless gleaming head. The glazed-cracked look of the head, rippling nervy veins like forbidden thoughts. It was a Roman bust of a head. It was a head to be toppled, broken. I had not seen my father in so long, I would fall in love with a stranger. Unless I would not fall in love. Unless he was not a stranger. But Max was very kind, remembering to ask about "your roommate, the minister's daughter." Leaning on his elbows on the table facing me in the candlelit dining room stooping patiently to hear my murmured replies that were so brief. Max knew a few details about Minette's death of course. At this time, the cause of the fire was still being investigated. I understood that Veronica had spoken with him. He would have seen the news in the media for Minette Swift's death had been taken up by national print and TV. The Associated Press had carried a column of print headlined

COLLEGE STUDENT, 19
ALLEGED RACIST TARGET
DIES IN SUSPICIOUS CAMPUS FIRE

There were more detailed articles, with Minette's high school graduation photo, Minette in white cap and gown and schoolgirl plastic eyeglasses smiling so hard her cheeks must have hurt, in the *Washington Post*, *Philadelphia Inquirer*, *New York Times*.

When my voice ran down, Max reached over to squeeze my hand. I flinched at his scalding touch.

Max was warmly sympathetic if perhaps distracted. I thought it was the time: time careening by: Max's impulse to check his wristwatch which he meant to resist, not to offend me. For this was a serious conversation we were having.

I was not crying. I had not cried in public. It was only just my skin. My face was numb, I was having difficulty swallowing food and so I managed to eat little, hoping Max wouldn't notice. My hair seemed to hurt my scalp. I was frightened that my scalp was covered in hot flamey rashes but did not dare to touch it with my fingertips.

In his warm vague way of enthusiasm Max spoke of Veronica and the house at Chadds Ford. He did not inquire after Rickie as if he'd temporarily forgotten he had a son.

He told me of the case in D.C. A longtime critic of U.S. foreign policy who'd been staunchly anti-war, anti-Nixon/Kissinger, whose name I would know, suspecting his telephones tapped, himself and his family under FBI surveillance, had, with the help of friends, broken into unmarked FBI headquarters in Meridian Park, Maryland. They had photocopied documents on FBI office machines. They had departed without a trace, undetected. It was an astonishing coup! For the past ten months they had been leaking these documents to the media, proof that the FBI was operating illegal wiretapping, and only just recently . . . "Am I boring you, Genna?" Max broke off, annoyed.

I'd been watching a young blond woman who was seated alone on the far side of the dining room. She was reading a book propped up against a candlestick holder; from time to time, she paused to underline a passage. Her hair was stylishly short at the sides, a swath falling across her forehead at a slant. The hair appeared lacquered, very pale blond. She was beautiful, in profile at least. Occasionally she glanced around to signal a waiter, or to see who else had entered the restaurant. Several times, thinking that I couldn't see her, but perhaps Max would, she glanced in our direction.

His assistant. One of his assistants.

I hadn't heard my father's question. Or maybe I'd heard but I couldn't remember what he'd asked. Suddenly I was very tired. The flickering candle flames hurt my eyes. My head was so heavy, I had to fight the impulse to lower it onto my crossed arms on the table, and sleep.

Somehow I'd done this. My head was so heavy. Hesitantly Max

touched my shoulder. For a moment his husky broken voice sounded alarmed. "Genna. C'mon, sweetie. Don't."

I would excuse myself, and go to the women's room. Discreetly I would allow a few minutes for my father and his assistant to confer, before he walked me back to campus.

It was a misty April evening after a day of rain. Only a ten-minute walk back to Haven House but Max offered to drive me in his rented car. I preferred to walk. I was feeling stronger now. I did not want to further disappoint my father whom any visible symptom of weakness offended and dismayed. He would be bluff and hearty saying good night at my residence. If other girls were there, he would wish to be introduced. He would embrace me, brush his lips against my cheek. I would stiffen in that brief embrace, but I would betray no sign of pain. As we crossed campus, the smell of Stone Cottage seemed to lift perversely from the wet grass. We would avoid that corner of the quadrangle of course. Max had become quiet. Max was thinking perhaps of Elias Meade House: probably he had not seen it in some time, he'd avoided Schuyler College. Probably Max had his reasons for he, too, had been a son estranged from his father. Above a row of budding trees, the chapel bell tower was swathed in light. A clock face floating in light. A soft sonorous tolling: eight-thirty.

Eight-thirty! Possible to think, it had not happened yet.

I'd been waiting for Max to ask in his offhand way why my roommate Minette Swift had moved to the alumni house. But he never asked.

Confidential

I was dragging myself along the floor. It had come over me suddenly *My legs are so weak* and in that instant the panicked realization *My legs are gone.* In the terrible blast my legs became shreds of bone, gristle, tissue but I had no knowledge of it because the explosion had obliterated all knowledge. And it is not so difficult as you might think, dragging yourself along a hardwood floor, not carpeted. And in dream logic I knew this. To avoid falling when my knees went weak on the stairs, it began on the stairs, on the landing just below the third floor when my knees went weak and I was alone, no one to observe I crawled up the remainder of the stairs, and made my way into my room, and I was safe, for crawling when you are suddenly weak is more sensible than trying gamely to walk. In the middle of the night able to make my way on foot to the bathroom but returning I was light-headed, so weak, there was not Max Meade to observe me in pity, distress, distaste. I knew this and then I realized as I was pulling myself *She didn't lose her legs, she did not die in the explosion but in a fire* and for a moment I was confused as in a fever dream though thinking: possibly she'd dragged herself, too. Amid the flames she'd dragged herself. Dying, she'd dragged herself. I had to concede, I wasn't dreaming but was in fact dragging myself from the third-floor bathroom to my room in Haven House. You wish you might be dreaming but you are not. You wish the dream might dissolve in the magical way of dreams but it will not. A girl from the room next to mine saw me. By chance, it was 2 A.M. and most of Haven House was darkened, by chance this girl was on her way to the bathroom and she saw me. And she stooped over me frightened. "Oh, Genna. My God." She helped me up, onto my feet, my legs that were so weak, she helped me back into my room and into my sweat-soaked bed and soon after there was Dana Johnson stooping over me white-faced, appalled. Dana Johnson summoned in the middle of the night in a terry cloth robe hastily thrown over her flannel nightgown, crouching beside my bed, hesitantly she laid her hand on my forehead, she was speaking to me words of comfort, concern such as you might speak to a small frightened child, she was not by temperament a woman for whom words of comfort and concern came easily yet in my room that smelled of fever, sickness, desperation Dana Johnson summoned all her strength, she too was trembling but she became strong, gripping my hands that flailed like small wounded birds she became strong, and she became kind, and her kindness made me cry. I had not cried that anyone might observe for a very long time. For I was not weak—was I? And yet I was crying now, I would make my confession to Dana Johnson. Suddenly, this was so. This was the logic of my sickness. For I could not bear it any longer, all that I knew, or half-knew, that had been given to me, to bear in secret not knowing what was true, what was imagined and hallucinatory. I could not bear it after Max Meade left me. He had not abandoned me, he had only just left me temporarily. I knew this. I understood this. All of Max's leave-takings were temporary and not permanent, I knew this. I was an adult, I was a daughter but also an adult, I could take responsibility. Still, I could not bear it. I would make my confession to this woman of strength and kindness who was leaning over me, ice pick eyes dilated, very dark and attentive. She must have thought it would be Minette Swift of whom I would speak in my distress. She must have thought that the truths I knew, and no one else knew, that were making me sick, were about Minette Swift's life and death. Yet—so suddenly!—it was of a very different subject I began to speak. It was of Ansel Trimmer I began to speak. Telling Dana Johnson in my choked voice what I knew of the Dow Chemical bombing, Niagara Falls, March 1970, and "John David Donovan" living in secret in Altoona, or Port Alleghany, or Wilkes-Barre, or Maysville, West Virginia, since the bombing, since a night watchman was killed in the bombing, though possibly Ansel Trimmer was himself dead, or had fled the United States, unless Ansel

Trimmer was still alive as "John David Donovan" living in Altoona, or Port Alleghany, or . . .

I was becoming hysterical. My voice broke off. Dana Johnson stared at me astonished. Her hands gripped both my hands tight. She would comfort me, she would urge me to tell all I knew: "This is confidential, Genna. I promise."

Epilogue

[SEPTEMBER 1990]

Some Truths

Maybe some truths are lies. But no lies are truths.

I've never told him, I was the one who informed. Never told anyone.

What I've acknowledged here in my text without a title, I could not acknowledge in my life.

My identity was obscured at the time. My identity was never an issue. I was not served with a subpoena to testify for the prosecution, I was never involved with any investigation. Except as an anonymous informer, I did not exist. Except that information provided by me was (evidently) passed along to federal authorities by a private citizen herself uninvolved in the investigation. In this circuitous way my father Max Meade was trapped.

Out of my sickness. My hysteria. The fever-dream of no legs. Crawling on the floor in Haven House that night too weak to walk and out of that weakness a few weeks later in May 1975 as he was preparing to board a TWA aircraft bound for Frankfurt, Germany, in the company of a young woman legal assistant, Maximilian Elliott Meade was arrested by FBI agents on multiple charges including malicious destruction of property and conspiracy to commit malicious destruction of property, aiding and abetting fugitives, accessory before and after the fact involving crimes of theft, arson, second-degree murder.

Thirty-five years to life in a maximum security federal prison.

I hadn't known. How could I have known!

For always I'd been told *Max Meade has never violated any law.*

Always I'd believed. I'd wished to believe.

Here was the abiding shame: he'd been publicly broken.

Forced to plead guilty and the act of Maximilian Meade's capitulation to his enemies in federal court was televised on network TV news. For there was the likelihood of a death sentence otherwise. And Max's former disciples had informed on him, desperate to escape death sentences of their own.

When "John David Donovan" was arrested in April 1975 in Maysville, West Virginia, and charged with, among other felonies, second-degree murder, it was not immediately understood that his former defense attorney Max Meade would be criminally involved. For it wasn't at that time known by federal agents that Max Meade had provided not only legal counsel to a cadre of anti-war protestors suspected of several bombings in 1968, 1969, 1970 in a half-dozen states as well as Washington, D.C., but cash for the purchase of firearms, ammunition, and explosives; it wasn't yet known that Max had arranged to secure safe houses and counterfeit I.D.s for the cadre, that he'd been a co-conspirator and an accessory before and after those actions for which Ansel Trimmer was arrested and charged. That Ansel Trimmer, at that time thirty-one years old, would name the man he'd once so revered.

Many times in fact, Maximilian Meade would be "named." By Trimmer, and others. Initially Max denied all involvement in any illegal activities but finally he would have no choice except to capitulate, for his enemies had him trapped.

He would not be a martyr for his beliefs after all. Put to the test, he would capitulate.

Not for Maximilian Meade, the fate of the Rosenbergs.

In this way, Max was broken. All that remained of his dignity was his refusal to name other names.

Thirty-five years to life. Which means the possibility of parole as early as fall 1993. By which time my father will be seventy-one years old.

"Not old! Not old at all."

In this, Max's enemies were most cruel. Giving him the "possibility" of parole—as if, for Max Meade, afflicted with notoriety as with leprosy, there could be any possibility of parole!—his enemies gave him hope. In giving him hope, they took away his rationality, his capacity for stoic resignation. In giving him hope they gave him chronic insomnia, stomach ulcers, cardiac seizures, blinding headaches and bouts of mania, paranoia, depression. They took away his sanity.

These fourteen years my father has been incarcerated in the maximum security federal prison for men at Follette, New York, behind twelve-foot stone walls topped with coils of razor wire that glint in the sun like smiling teeth, he has had no rest. In a fever of activity he is forever drafting new appeals, new motions, memos, letters, op-ed pieces for newspapers; like an actor rehearsing a script in continual revision he has been preparing for the parole hearing shimmering before him like a mirage. Fourteen years, he has become deranged. For one doomed to die in prison, hope is the most insidious of poisons.

"You have to have faith, Genna. I have faith!"

Follette is one of the older prison facilities in New York State. It's located twelve miles north of Watertown in the desolate foothills west of the Adirondacks. Nearby is the enormous restricted U.S. military reservation Camp Drum whose deafening aircraft fly low over the prison. When Max began his sentence at Follette, already at fifty-five he was one of the older prisoners in the general population; now, sixty-eight, he is the oldest prisoner in the segregated unit.

Oldest, most infirm. Yet most energetic.

Within a week of Max Meade's incarceration at Follette he was savagely beaten by inmates one of whom pierced his left eye with a sharpened piece of metal, he was kicked, stomped, left bleeding and helpless in a mysterious midday interregnum when no guards seemed to be close by, for in the facility it was known, presumably the information had been leaked, that this middle-aged white man serving a life sentence had acted as legal counsel for anti-war protestors, mockers of the U.S. flag and Vietnam veterans; he was the son of a wealthy Philadelphia family; a criminal defense lawyer who'd crossed the line to aid and abet bombings culminating with the murder of the black security guard at the Dow Chemical plant in Niagara Falls in 1970. Max's left eye had had to be surgically removed. He'd suffered multiple contusions in the beating, cracked bones and lacerations, teeth broken in his jaws, a perforated eardrum, could afterward walk only with a cane, yet refused to identify his attackers, even the color of their skin.

It had happened too fast, Max insisted.

"They left me my life. I am grateful."

Since the beating Max has been housed in Segregation: child molesters and rapists, psychotic killers, older men unable to protect themselves, Caucasians.

Mad Max! Some days at Follette, after my eight-hour drive into the desolation of upstate New York, the strain of queueing up to be I.D.'d and admitted into the coldly lighted visitors' area with its smudged cinder block walls, sticky floor tile, grimy Formica-topped tables and counters, there he is, a snarl of tissue where his left eye had been, smiling at me.

Sixty-eight and tremors in both hands, half-blind, half-deaf, wattles at his throat, chronic cough, fingernails split and discolored, face sickly-pale and creased, broken teeth and broke-back posture, hobbling on a cane and yet—Mad Max! The bald head no longer requires shaving, it's just a bald head, exposing too much. Veins quiver in the scalp that's mottled with an ugly rash Max knows better than to scratch but can't seem to resist. Still this is a Roman bust of a head, buzzing with plots. Max has photocopied documents to show me, he has written yet another draft of his lengthy appeal to federal court, an op-ed piece for the *New York Times*, a personal letter to the notoriously conservative Supreme Court justice who'd been, in 1939–41, a fellow resident of Max Meade's in Lowell House, Harvard. Mad Max never forgets a name, a face, a contact!

This Max, Mad Max, always has tasks for me to "expedite." Much photocopying, stamping and mailing of envelopes. A list of telephone calls to make. Library research. Everything that Max wants to give me must be vetted by security officers, as everything I bring for him, mostly printed materials, is vetted. A Plexiglas barrier separates us, inmates and visitors don't exchange so much as a handshake. There is nothing remotely confidential/classified in any of our transactions and yet there's Mad Max's gloating good eye fixed upon me, a co-conspirator.

"It's a game. The system. 'Justice' is the jackpot. If you can master the game, you have a chance of winning."

And: "A straw in the wind, a single chance!—that's all we need."

Yet, another time: "I don't want to die in this place. Oh God."

Visiting Max Meade at Follette is no easy matter. It's a joke at the facility that the place is eight hours from anywhere.

Usually, I try to make the trip in a single day not liking to stay in a motel in the area. Sometimes, on the way back, I will have a passenger or two, sister-visitors who live downstate and who have come to Follette by bus.

The majority of Follette prisoners are from downstate. It's commonly believed that part of their punishment, exacted upon their families, is their exile in the north.

Over the years I have become Max Meade's sole visitor, I think. I would not ask since Mad Max wouldn't give me a truthful answer and the other Max, the one who doesn't want to die in this place, has to be spared the question.

Max's relatives have never visited him at Follette. He'd long been estranged from most of them, now they were estranged from him. Veronica divorced him at about the time of his sentencing, in 1976. Long abandoned by Max, now it was Veronica's turn to abandon him. But Veronica waited until Max's case was adjudicated before filing for divorce: that way, prosecutors couldn't serve her with a subpoena to force her to testify against her husband.

Rickie—"Richard H. Meade"—has never visited Max, of course. Rickie has had very little communication with his father since he'd moved out of the house at Chadds Ford to live with relatives in Philadelphia, aged sixteen.

Since Rickie moved out, and Max hadn't gone after him.

Once, Max was at the center of a bright peopled world, now that world has shifted from him. Mad Max confidently awaits its return—"The future will vindicate us, Genna! We were never wrong and we will have justice someday." As the other Max his expectations are not so extravagant.

". . . your mother, Genna? Does she ever . . . ?"

Yes of course, Max. Every time we speak.

What relief, the smudged Plexiglas barrier is between us. If my father fumbled to squeeze my hand, I could not bear it.

Strange to be called "Genna." When I am no longer "Genna."

Strange to hear Max Meade speak of justice. To realize that he has never taken responsibility for the death of the night watchman, no more than his young comrades have taken responsibility. To realize *He has pleaded guilty as a legal stratagem but he has never acknowledged guilt. He is one of the righteous who can't acknowledge guilt because he knows (he knows!) he is incapable of behaving in any way to justify guilt.*

Visiting a doomed man, even a man only sporadically aware that he is doomed, you find yourself subtly altered. In the AUTHORIZED VISITORS AREA chill-clinical in fluorescent lighting as a morgue you become the person visiting a doomed man in the AUTHORIZED VISITORS AREA chill-clinical in fluorescent lighting as a morgue.

This becomes your identity as soon as you step inside the prison. As soon as you present I.D., pass through the metal detector, are admitted into AUTHORIZED VISITORS AREA where you will perform that role with all the strength you can summon.

Father, I am the one who betrayed you. If you knew would you forgive me?

He volunteers to teach in the prison literacy program.

Provides legal counsel to other prisoners.

With his cane, half-blind/half-deaf yet he helps out in the infirmary.

If only Max Meade were strong enough, think what a valuable inmate trustee he'd make! In Segregation, he's the only prisoner the guards can trust.

These are truths you could dismiss. You could say that Max is a shrewd operator. He's amassing "good behavior" points. In his file will be a number of "strong, positive" letters of recommendation from prison guards, administrators, the warden himself to impress the parole board in fall 1993.

I have never seen my father's prison cell. But I know that it is smudged cinder block walls enclosing an open space of a few square feet, narrow bed, stainless steel sink and toilet. In the smudged cinder block wall no window. The stale air reverberates with the noises of other inmates. The rank smells of other inmates and a pervasive odor of disinfectant. I know this, vividly I seem to have seen this as if Max's "good" eye were my own.

"Genna. How changed we are, aren't we?"

Cupping my hand to my ear, smiling uncertainly to signal that I haven't quite heard this.

"Genna. I am not going to die in this place am I?"

This isn't Mad Max but the other. My broken-backed father squinting at me through the smeared Plexiglas with his single "good" eye.

My smile begins to break. Trying to hear but having trouble.

This noisy place. Humming, buzzing. Strangers on both sides of us talking loudly to one another. Often I truly can't hear what Max is trying to say, his voice is weakened, hoarse. In the beating, his throat was injured again. Prison is not a place for an aging man.

"Genna? Are you really her, my daughter?"

When I first visited Max in this place, when we were both younger I heard Max's every word clearly and such words made me cry. We cried together. A broken-backed bald man with a missing eye, a distraught young woman. We cried, we were exposed in the chill fluorescent lighting, we were exhausted. Now I am no longer a young woman and grateful for that. I am not distraught. I have learned the futility of crying, especially in a public place and with the prospect of an eight-hour drive awaiting me. Instead I have learned to smile convincingly with the lower part of my face, my hinged mouth.

"Genna? Are you taking me home today?"

Fourteen years. And Minette Swift has been dead for fifteen years, six months, eleven days.

Since April I have been composing my text without a title. I wake at 5 A.M. each morning to work for at least two hours before I must begin to think of my work, my public life. What an exhausting experience it has been, this text! I think, because I have wanted it to be utterly truthful. Because I have wanted not to spare myself. Unlike Max Meade who knows he is not guilty, I know that I am riddled with guilt like rot or cancer but like an afflicted person I seem not always to know where my affliction lies.

I think of Ansel Trimmer fumbling to sink a paring knife into his belly, to stab and twist his guts.

Self-evisceration: "spilling your guts."

These are crude words, I'd never realized how insightful.

Initially I'd thought of writing my text without a title for my father to read. Max in a lucid state, not in the other. As the months passed, and the text became longer and more complicated, I came to doubt the wisdom of giving it to Max. For, unwittingly, as I composed my text about Minette Swift, I was composing a shadow-text that had little to do with her. I'd intended to compose an inquiry into Minette Swift's life/death exclusively, but like an eclipse of the sun the shadow-text began to intrude. I could not seem to prevent it! The shadow-text is an inquiry into Max Meade and a portrait of the daughter who betrayed him.

Now in September 1990 I have finished most of my text. Still it is without a title. It has become longer than I'd expected, nearly three hundred handwritten pages! I have been writing in black-bound journals of about seventy-five pages each.

I've written past Minette's death, which hadn't been my intention. There was a kind of spillage of my guts. I think of myself as a mature woman inured to emotion yet the other morning I woke agitated, anxious. I'd had again the nightmare of dragging myself along a floor, pulling my weight with my arms, my elbows, because my legs were paralyzed, or had been amputated or pulverized at the knees. And the knowledge came to me *This is a dream but a dream recollecting what was once actual* forgotten for fifteen years when I'd been mysteriously weakened by flu, or grief, stumbling when I walked, the strength draining out of my legs, I was forced to crawl for it was safer than trying to walk normally and falling. And so, I had no choice that morning except to write beyond Minette's death: my father's visit to Schuyler that was so cruelly belated, for he never met Minette; our exhausting dinner at the Schuylersville Inn when Max's blond mistress-assistant sucked up all the oxygen in the room and left me breathless; and the dream-like walk back to campus, the shock of the chapel bell tower so beautifully illuminated by lights seeming to float above the trees. And how vividly I saw the clock's hands at eight-thirty which was at least four hours before Minette Swift's death so that it seemed to me in my confused state *It hasn't happened yet, this time I will prevent it.*

Nor had I known that I would write about Dana Johnson in my bedroom.

For I'd opened my eyes, and there she was: feverish as I was, her eyes ardent, excited. Gripping my hands in her strong hands and not letting go urging me to confide in her, it would remain a secret between us.

That woman I hadn't trusted previously, why did I trust her then!

For now it seems clear to me, in retrospect, as a woman of thirty-four with some knowledge of institutions like Schuyler College, and far more knowledge of human nature than I'd had as a girl of eighteen, that Dana Johnson had certainly known who my family was. She would have been told about my background, and my father Max Meade. She would have been one of those approached by FBI agents: one of those who would have responded coldly to the agents' initial overtures, yet, as events unfolded, shaken by Minette Swift's behavior in our residence and by her death, when I suddenly confessed to her, spilling information of value to authorities, Dana Johnson had called the number the agents had left with her, Dana Johnson had behaved as most Americans would behave in such a situation, and who is to say that she behaved wrongly? For Ansel Trimmer and his comrades were responsible for an innocent man's death, and who could have known that Max Meade was also involved?

In retrospect it seems clear to me. At the time, I had not a clue.

Next morning I called my mother. I was sick, I said. Sick to death please come and take me home.

I never returned to Schuyler College. Never saw or spoke with Dana Johnson again. With less than four weeks remaining in the second semester of my freshman year, with an A average in my courses I dropped out of college and would not return. Through much of the summer I was sick in the house at Chadds Ford, so tired, exhausted, no appetite, diagnosed with anemia, a kind of mononucleosis nearly as lethal as hepatitis C. By August my weight had dropped to eighty-five pounds, Veronica overcame my objections and had me hospitalized at the University of Pennsylvania Hospital where I was fed intravenously and made to survive.

By the time I was discharged it was another season. My father hadn't yet capitulated to his enemies but his attorneys were advising him, Max you have no choice.

I've become a stout girl. You'd be surprised.

In my twenties I gained weight. Steadily. Hips, thighs, shoulders and breasts. The calves of my legs are hard-muscled as a man's. My skin is still smooth and creamy-pale splotched with freckles, but my face has thickened. My hair has darkened, I wear it trimmed close like a tight-fitting cap. I like the sensation, wearing my body like armor. Knowing, as I move into your vision, that you "see" me as I wish to be seen, not as you wish to see me.

At first, in a kind of frenzy I ate to regain the weight I'd lost. I was a starved animal, always hungry. But I continued to put on weight until by my mid-twenties I weighed over one hundred forty pounds.

No one in the family has commented on my weight. In Veronica's eyes I see an appalled fascination. I wonder if she envies me, in a way. That I've had the courage to make a claim she has never been strong enough to make.

What does Max think? Sometimes through the Plexiglas barrier I see him staring at me, his single good eye fixed upon me in wonderment. Her? My daughter? My Generva? Long a connoisseur of female beauty, now Max Meade is connected to the world only by a decidedly unbeautiful woman.

On these trips to upstate New York where no one is likely to know me, I wear nondescript clothes: flannel shirts, T-shirts, pullover sweaters, denim, khaki. I wear zip-up jackets, sun-visor caps. I'm a woman not-young yet still youthful you'd see in the parking lot of a downscale shopping center or in visitors' parking at Follette prison for men, a woman who hides her discomfort by smiling. Where I'm known as "Generva Hewett-Meade"—"Dr. Hewett-Meade"—I dress more conventionally of course. I wear conservative, usually dark, tailored and moderately expensive clothes of the kind I'd once scorned, in the Pierpont Avenue shops for instance. I wear trouser suits, never dresses or skirts. With my close-cropped hair and my stolid body I've given up all pretense of the "feminine" as I've given up hypocrisy in my determination to lead a purely ethical life.

My sickness was a moral weakness, I know now. I came close to dying of it.

After I recovered, after the public humiliation of my idealist father Maximilian Meade pleading guilty in federal court where for months so very adamantly he'd been proclaiming his innocence, I went away to

Europe. I traveled alone, I needed to be where no one knew the name "Meade." (I avoided Germany, where Max had supporters and political contacts in radical left-wing circles.) For a while I lived in Amsterdam, and in Paris, and in London where I took courses at University College. In 1978 I returned to the United States but not to the house at Chadds Ford, which had been sold to pay for my father's legal costs. By this time, Veronica had remarried (a Wilmington business man, a widower with grown children). I enrolled at the University of Pennsylvania as an older first-year student now officially "Generva Hewett-Meade," I received an accelerated B.A. in 1981 and a Ph.D. in 1986. My doctoral dissertation, which would cause something of a stir in academic circles, was a six-volume annotated edition of *The Works of Generva Meade* with a 100-page introduction and seventy pages of footnotes, bibliography, index.

Through my family connections, I had access to restricted materials in the Schuyler College Special Collections off-limits to other historians. Later, I would succeed in breaking the restrictive clause in the Generva Meade archive, so that others can have access to it.

Still, I benefited from this restriction. I am not proud of my family connections nor ashamed of them but I will acknowledge them.

I suppose I worked hard enough on the edition: four years. During this time I commuted to Schuylersville from Philadelphia daily because I could not bear to remain in Schuylersville overnight. (Dana Johnson was no longer on the Schuyler faculty. She had either resigned or been asked to leave at the end of the terrible spring 1975 term and had disappeared "no one knows" where.) When the massive dissertation was finally completed, and published by the University of Pennsylvania Press in 1988, it was widely acclaimed, and won several awards. By the age of thirty-two, I'd received numerous teaching and research offers. My choice, disappointing to my department, was unexpected: not an Ivy League university nor even a prestigious liberal arts college (Schuyler had made me an offer even before I'd completed my Ph.D.) but the Newark campus of Rutgers State University where the student population is anything but elite, including a large "minority" population.

Here, I'm "Dr. Hewett-Meade." Though a new faculty member, already I've become involved in university-level committees. I am an adjunct in the Women's Studies Program and an assistant to the Affirmative Action director. I am a strong-willed woman, not always an easy colleague. The tenured professors in my department, all men, mostly Caucasian, regard me with unease but are respectful of me. The administration sees in me a potential department chair, a dean of the faculty: one unafraid to trim budgets, terminate contracts and entire programs in the effort to shift funds about and revitalize a moribund university structure.

I'm not dependent upon an academic salary, in fact. Like my brother, I've inherited investments from my Meade grandparents, held in trust until I was twenty-one. I give away most of the interest from this money, approximately $100,000 yearly, since it's money I have not earned. I have channeled funds anonymously to the family of the black security guard who'd been killed in Niagara Falls, and to Reverend Swift's Temple Vale of the World Tabernacle of Jesus Christ. If I could find a discreet way, I would give some money to Minette's sister Jewel who, when I'd last heard of her, was a graduate student at George Mason University studying biochemistry. But I don't know any way that wouldn't arouse suspicion.

These long drives into upstate New York, I think of such things. My complicated and very busy life at Rutgers Newark seems to fall away, "Dr. Hewett-Meade" and her authority vanishes. I hate my weakness, my loneliness. In my car I play Johnny Cash cassettes. *At Folsom Prison* and *Love, God, Murder.* (If I have passengers with me on the return trip, to drop off downstate, Johnny Cash is likely to be a favorite of theirs, too.) I play classical music, I play gospel hymns. These past several months, composing my text without a title, I have felt Minette Swift's presence often, but it's Jewel to whom I must appeal. I wonder if I would have the courage to confide in Jewel, how I'd failed to save her sister. So fiercely Minette believed that Jesus Christ was her savior, yet her savior was meant to be merely her roommate, an eighteen-year-old white girl not strong enough for the task. For I'd seen those lighted candles dangerously close to the curtains, I had not moved them or suggested that Minette move them for I was fearful of incurring Minette's wrath. I'd been cowardly, not wanting my ex-roommate to "dislike" me. So weak, I'd lied to protect Minette from exposure and in that circuitous way I had caused her death.

Now I am an adult, and in control of my behavior. I will never make such mistakes again.

Between happiness and duty, I choose duty.

"Hey sure. I'd appreciate it. All the way from Yonkers on that damn bus, my ass is about worn*out*."

She has a rueful laugh. She removes her cat's-eye sunglasses, white plastic frames and dark green lenses, to squint at me.

Her name is Colombe, we've seen each other here before. Queueing up for AUTHORIZED VISITORS. Showing I.D. to the uniformed guards who stare at us rudely, spreading out the contents of our bags to be inspected, passing through the malfunctioning metal detector into the chill fluorescent air of the visiting area already befouled by cigarette smoke.

We've seen each other before on Saturday afternoons at Follette but Colombe won't remember me. In my rumpled car-clothes, sweatshirt, chino trousers, sun-visor cap on my head, I could be anyone. Colombe wouldn't readily identify me as one of her sisters in this place.

It's commonly known that when a man begins a prison sentence, especially a lengthy one, after a year or two only women make the journey to visit him. Mothers, wives. Especially mothers.

Adult daughters don't seem to be figured in. But we're here.

Like most of the younger women, Colombe is visiting her husband. She's a light-skinned black/Hispanic with a sulky-pretty face, early thirties, full-hipped in purple velour slacks and a matching top that strains at her large breasts. She wears glittering gold earrings, rings on several of her fingers, around her neck a gold cross encrusted with glassy jewels. Though she has been traveling by bus, she is wearing high-heeled open-backed sandals without stockings. Her eyebrows are fine-plucked, her eyelids are smeared with silver. In the queue outside I'd heard her talking animatedly in both English and Spanish with other women who'd come by bus from the New York City/Yonkers area. Her laughter was high-pitched and tremulous, like a fit of coughing. Abruptly she detached herself from the others, as if she'd had enough of them. As we shuffle in line to be I.D.'d she removes a compact from her shoulder bag, frowns savagely into it and makes a wet smacking sound with her crimson lips. She has been a beautiful woman only recently, now her face is dented beneath the eyes, there's a fleshy pouch beneath her chin. Her most glamorous feature is her long curved fingernails, which match her crimson mouth. I never fail to be amazed at such nails, and tell her so.

It's prison protocol, never ask why an inmate is here. Not why, not how long, not even when up for parole. I like it that no one, certainly not this woman, has the slightest idea whose daughter I am. If she heard the name "Maximilian Meade" it would mean nothing to her. My I.D. is "Generva Hewett-Meade." I show the beefy guard with a hairline mustache and suspicious eyes my Rutgers Newark faculty I.D. as well as my passport. Everything I am bringing to leave with Max Meade in my duffel bag. Though I have passed through this security checkpoint approximately 120 times (!) still the procedure fills me with anxiety, and when I feel anxious I want to make my enemy laugh. I tell the guard who's frowning at my miniature face in his hand, and at my living face above: "Excuse me! I was younger then, officer. In 1976 when that passport picture was taken."

The guard laughs. A grudging laugh but it's a laugh. A man can relate to a woman like me through laughter, banter. I want to neutralize the sexual contempt in his eyes.

Allowing him to know, too, and Colombe who's just behind me fretting and fussing, that I am not intimidated by him. Uniformed guy with a badge, a handgun at his hip. In the pay of the state.

Seeing Colombe, the guard leans forward on his elbows with an insolent smile. Makes a show of gazing down the length of her fleshy body, staring at her feet in high-heeled shoes: "Mmmm them could be weapons, ma'am. 'Contraband.' "

Colombe laughs nervously, isn't sure this is a joke. The guard motions her through with an impatient gesture and I know beforehand that Colombe will murmur in my ear, breathy and incensed, "Asshole."

Inside the visiting room, Colombe and I find ourselves seated together to wait for her husband and my father to be escorted in. Saturday afternoon at Follette is always the busiest time of the week, you can feel the strain, the pent-up emotion. Inmates can become emotional, violent. Visiting hours began at 9 A.M. and will end at 4 P.M. It's 2:15 P.M. now, Colombe and I will be allowed to remain for forty minutes if we don't disobey any rules. The place is a hive of noise rebounding from the cinder block walls, the ludicrously high ceiling and the sticky tile floor. (Why is the ceiling so high? My eyes ache glancing upward at rows of fluorescent tubing. Some of the tubes are glaring-bright, others flicker and buzz like dying wasps. Still others have burnt out.)

"Who you comin to see? Husband?"

Colombe's query is startling, for I thought I had already told her. Maybe that was last time? Six weeks ago, in August?

I hear myself laugh, I'm flattered. Colombe imagines me married. Imagines any man could love me. I tell her no, my father.

"Father. Ohhh."

Meaning: this is unexpected. The father will be an old man.

I smile at Colombe to reassure her. I'm accustomed to this, I take it in stride. Though I am possibly no older than Colombe, and might even be younger, I behave with her as I behave with my students at Newark: encouraging smile, intelligent and affable demeanor. I am an adult, you can trust me.

Colombe needs to talk, she's edgy, apprehensive. I hope that my first sight of her husband won't be a shock but often, in these circumstances, when I see the inmates some of the women are visiting, I feel a wave of despair. Colombe is showing me snapshots she's brought for her husband, family pictures, two young children, Chrissie and Felix. Seven, four. So her husband can't have been in Follette very long. Maybe she still feels emotion for him and I know, I can remember, I think I can remember, how emotion can hurt.

Colombe asks me about my family?

I hear myself tell her that my mother has remarried, my stepfather is an older man with whom I'm not very close. "He doesn't approve of me, I think. I make him uneasy." Since I smile at this remark, Colombe smiles, too. Making a man uneasy! Sounds good.

Colombe asks about brothers, sisters. The essential questions women put to one another, women who are strangers to one another, as if groping for a common language, a kind of Braille. I hear myself tell her that I have a brother five years older than I am, a "pretty successful businessman," but we're not very close. I had a sister, but she died when she was nineteen.

"Ohhh hey. I'm sorry."

For a while then we don't speak. The strain of waiting can be as exhausting as the strain of visiting. Beforehand, you can be so fatigued you want to lay your head down on the sticky Formica-topped counter, shut your eyes and sleep amid the raised voices, shouted manic laughter out of the ceiling.

Colombe nervously asks am I all right, I tell her yes of course I am all right, I speak quietly, I am not like some of the other female visitors whose voices sound like nails scratching. Maybe I wish that Colombe would fall silent but it's clear that silence makes her uneasy. She asks what have I brought for my father and I show her, only just printed material, photocopies of pages from law books Max requested, recent issues of the *Nation*, the *New York Review of Books*, the *Journal of American Historical Studies* containing an article by G. Hewett-Meade on the friendship between Victoria Woodhull and Generva Meade in the 1880s. And a photocopied manuscript of my handwritten text without a title.

I've brought the manuscript with me though I have not yet decided whether to leave it with my father. Our last visit, Max had been in a subdued state, somber but rational, not Mad Max. In such a state Max might read my text without a title.

Mad Max would probably destroy it.

Either way, my father would know at last who had betrayed him, before his young comrades had a chance to betray him.

Colombe is impressed! All those pages, all that handwriting, is it some kind of letter? diary? what is it called?

"It has no title, Colombe." Then, I realize: "I'm bringing it to my father, to supply the title."

"Oh hey. What's it about?"

"Our lives."

Colombe shakes her head as if suddenly she's seeing me as very different from her, I'm sorry for this.

On the drive back to Yonkers, we'll be more relaxed. Colombe can tell me about Chrissie and Felix. We'll play Johnny Cash. We'll sing with Johnny Cash. I never hear certain songs of Cash's, no matter how sentimental, with what predictable rhymes, that tears don't flood into my eyes.

I have blues cassettes, too. Billie Holiday, Bessie Smith. If we're in the mood. If Colombe isn't too shaken by her visit with her husband.

This interlude, before our names are called: almost, I don't want it to end. I am in dread of my first sighting of my father, who looked so aged the last time I saw him. Limping on his cane, shrinking into his body, the guard beside him young enough to be a grandson. I remember how, when Max and I spoke together, or tried to speak together, the young guard's gaze passed over us from time to time in utter indifference, over me, my strained face, without seeming to see me, oblivious of me and Max Meade both. Only if one of us had made a sudden move, attempted something forbidden, would the guard, and others stationed in the cavernous room, take note of us.

This time the door on the far side of the partition opens to admit inmates, I see my father among them. I hear the name: " 'Meade.' " I lift my hand to signal to him, half-rise to greet him, my poor doomed father the former Maximilian Meade in rumpled green prison uniform who has no one else in his shrunken world but me as, I suppose, if I am to be truthful, I have no one but him.